FLY THE NEST

A MARE'S NEST SERIES BOOK TWO

B. G. THOMAS

Cover design by B. G. Thomas
Editing by B. G. Thomas
Cover Photograph by Stryjek via Adobe Stock
Beta readers: Casey Britton, Carrie West, & Kim McLaurine

 Created with Vellum

To my Papa, the William to my Daphne, who has always taught me the beauty of writing, reading, and being at peace within myself. Thank you for everything, but especially for always supporting my dreams, no matter how many times they've changed over the years. I love you.

CONTENTS

DISEMBARK

As if the lights weren't dark enough already, they cut out completely when the shuttle jerked forward abruptly and made its way out of its dock and into the vast universe before us. It was like we were stuck in a free fall—like experiencing rough turbulence in an airplane and having that brief hint of doubt overcome you, even though the pilot assured everyone it was fine.

I cursed Ian in my head before I could think better of it, because the adrenaline coursing through me was too much to bear and I needed someone to blame.

Finally, after a few moments that felt like eons, the shuttle evened out and we all settled back into our seats a little more. I forced myself to unclench my jaw. To ease my shoulders back.

"Sorry about that drop, everyone," Ian said in my helmet.

"If I'd been driving us, it wouldn't have been any better than that," Harper chuckled after him.

I don't think I had taken a proper breath all morning, and the anxiety medication had only taken the edge off. I could feel my pulse in my temples and at the back of my throat like bile working its way up. As soon as the shuttle felt a little less doomsday and a little more normal, I inhaled and exhaled as deeply as I could, willing a sense of calm into existence.

And then I noticed that I was gripping Darrien's hand. *Hard.* So much for breathing.

His long, warm fingers were intertwined with mine, and I had a feeling from my grip alone that I had probably come close to cutting off his circulation. I eased my finger and began to slip my palm out from the safety of his hand. When I looked up, I saw that his helmet was turned toward mine, but I couldn't see his face in the dim lights and with the glare. All he could do was shake his head, and he returned my hand to his. Even through the gloves that we had on as part of our space suits, I could feel his warmth, and though I instinctively wanted to pull back and fall out of the emergency door and into space with crippling embarrassment, I kept my hand planted in his.

After a long moment of staring into his helmet and trying to guess where his eyes were, he turned his head away to look forward, but kept my hand safely inside of his own. I squeezed it slightly as a thank you, and he squeezed mine back. After sitting like that for a bit, and listening to the calming music that still played low inside my helmet, he began to trace circles on the inside of my palm with his thumb.

And for some reason, that small and simple act set fire to every inch of my skin.

Everyone else on the shuttle had disappeared and had been replaced with just Darrien and I during the chaotic liftoff and all that followed. Granted, it was hard to even *see* anyone other than Darrien and Jules. And it wasn't like we could talk to keep each other company.

I was somewhat happy to have no one talking inside of my helmet, to have only the low music as the background to my thoughts. If we had all been able to communicate during the ride, I had a feeling we would all hear screams we didn't want to hear and a lot of cursing and snide remarks.

It was hard not to overthink, but obsessing over the two attractive men next to me was better than worrying about whether I'd ever make it back up to the *Hippogriff* and see Jax and Dad again—or what awaited us down on planet Virginia. Not that I was thinking about Todd all that much, but I swore I could feel him look my way now and then.

My sense of time was stunted. I had no clue if it had been ten minutes or ten seconds. I remembered, then, that the information I could see on my helmet's shield probably also told me the time. I had been ignoring it for the most part, because keeping my eyes closed made me feel a little less nervous.

I opened my eyes and looked at the time. It was a shame that I couldn't remember when we'd actually left. For a scientist, I wasn't very observant lately. I made a note of the time and closed my eyes again.

Instead of focusing on the time, I tried to take my mind off of it by imagining that I was somewhere—anywhere—other than the shuttle. At first, I relived my very favorite trip that I had taken with Magda as a young, newly graduated, wildlife biologist. We had gone to the Northern Great Plains to help supervise the habitat's very overdue restoration and had been given the chance to reintroduce a handful of species that had been taken away while farmers and conservationists worked on the land.

It was one of the best trips I'd ever gone on, and it was even better that it was just me and Magda. I'd seen bison for the first time. We introduced black-footed ferrets that we bred at the conservatory back to their natural habitat back in the world, and we had spent hours with kind people and greater animals. Life was good back then.

But then my mind jumped around—to Jax, to Dad—to

how those beautiful black-footed ferrets and bison were more than likely long gone. I shook my head and squeezed my eyes shut, trying to search for anything in my brain that wasn't *that.*

Which led to thoughts of warm hands trailing my bare thighs, and beautifully carved lips moving up and down my jawline, gasping as I held his head closer into me. And his face came into view, and it wasn't Todd. It wasn't Matthew.

Darrien's light brown eyes were molten milk chocolate as he pulled away from my grasp and smirked at me before meeting my lips. In my mind, he tasted like subtle mint and sunshine, similar to how he always smelled, and my lips met his greedily.

The shuttle hit some turbulence, and I gasped. But Darrien's hand was there to steady me, and I couldn't help but squeeze my thighs together in need. His hand didn't leave mine, and I cursed the spacesuits, the shuttle, the rest of the crew, because I wanted his touch more than I wanted anything. My body was tight and hot. I gasped again, but not from the turbulence.

The images in my mind came back, and now Darrien had me in his lap. His bare, muscular chest that still had a warm glow from working outside, brushed up against my skin as he tugged at my bottom lip with his teeth, and his hands tangled in my hair, pulling me in closer, tighter, harder, because it was not enough. His breath was heavy, and my hips rolled over him in wild anticipation.

"Alright, everyone! Prepare to land in about ten minutes." Ian's voice in my ear brought me back to reality.

My fantasy had been so much more fun. I sighed and opened my eyes.

"The shuttle will slow down, and then it will hover for a couple of minutes before we land," Harper said. "Your safety harnesses will release on their own accord once we have landed once we are in the clear."

I had to force my body to cool off. I didn't even feel the safety belts around me anymore; my body was consumed with a need that reminded me of my teenage years, and my stomach and thighs were tight and knotted.

All of this from holding hands and trying to distract myself. Something was wrong with me. I'd never even been that hot over Matthew, though we had a decent amount of chemistry. And I certainly wasn't *that* hot for Todd. The familiar feeling of guilt washed over my neck and cheeks. I forced a deep breath.

You didn't do anything wrong. You are fine. Matthew is dead. Todd is irrelevant.

After many deep breaths and thinking of all the nasty things in the world, like tortoise shit and oozing cysts, my body finally relaxed enough for me to unclench my thighs.

I watched my stats and the time on my screen, and slowly but surely, my heart rate went down. I hoped that if I was still as flushed as I felt when we landed and the lights came back on, the helmet would hide it.

The shuttle halted a bit and slowed down as steadily as it could. There was the occasional jerk, but it wasn't nearly as bad as the liftoff had been.

"Prepare to hover," Ian said.

"And prepare to feel a slight drop before landing," Jules added.

Harper chuckled into the mic. "It sure looks like a beautiful planet from where we are."

Well, that was good. I hoped.

The shuttle stayed hovering in the air, and finally, the drop came. The drop felt a lot worse than what they made it out to be. It felt like my skeleton had been left up above us for a moment. And then, we hit the ground. The shuttle was still moving, and it was rocky as Ian prepared to park, I figured. My shoulder pressed firmly into Darrien's as we all tilted to the side.

And then we stopped, and we all jerked back to our regular positions. The music in the helmet was cut off, and all I could hear was my own ragged breathing.

"Welcome to planet Virginia, everyone!" Ian said cheerfully into the mic. I took his tone as a good sign. I had no idea what entailed flying a spaceship or shuttle, but I knew it couldn't be easy.

Without a warning, the safety harness that locked me to the shuttle eased and retracted back into the seat. I leaned forward and stretched out my back and shoulders. I hadn't realized how tense they had gotten during the trip. Darrien slid his hand from mine and stretched both of his arms over his head. Even Jules moved her neck from side to side.

"The lights are about to come on," Jules said. "And then we will get the oxygen set up while Harper goes out and makes sure everything looks safe to exit. After your oxygen is good to go, we will turn on your individual mics." Jules stood up and the lights slowly turned on. "If you all could give me a thumbs up if you are feeling okay, that would be great."

I raised my hand and gave her a thumbs up, though my hand was unstable. I looked around me and saw everyone had their thumbs up, though some hands were a bit shakier than others.

"Great!" Jules clapped.

The door to the flight deck opened, and Ian came through. I could still only see a little of his face through his gear, but his stance was much more relaxed now. If anything, he stood taller and more confident. My heart swelled for him. I made a mental note to celebrate his great accomplishment if we survived whatever was ahead of us.

Jules and Ian opened a floor hatch and together lifted a large, yellow box out from the floor. How many secret storage compartments did this shuttle have underneath it? I couldn't help but wonder.

Jules met her partners by the box and unlatched it, then opened up the massive lid. Ian started taking out small, rectangular boxes the size of books, and stacking them up neatly beside where he crouched. Jules took out long, stringy wires and placed them delicately beside the boxes.

The lights in the shuttle were much brighter now; almost like a regular room back on the *Hippogriff*. Everyone became more visible as my eyes adjusted to the overhead lights. Lata and Aleksy were pressed together, his hand on her thigh, and her shrouded head on his large shoulder. Saba tapped her foot nervously. Raymond sat like a statue, unmoving and stoic. Todd had his arms crossed, but he was close enough that I could see his face, which had an underlying green hue. I hoped that he wouldn't spew hit guts all over his helmet.

Darrien's hand rested calmly on his knee. He didn't fidget or seem uneasy. He hadn't seemed that way the entire ride—at least from what little I could tell. I stared at the gloved hand that had been holding mine minutes prior, and I noticed how large and comfortable it looked. I wanted to slip back into his grip but decided I'd better not.

Darrien caught me looking at him. Ian and Jules were hooking up the little boxes to the cords, and everyone else faded away. I peered into his eyes and thought that they burned a little brighter than the last time I'd done so. Then again, I could have been making things up. His face was shaded by the helmet, but I couldn't see his stats or anything else on his or anyone else's. Shadows overtook the bow of his lips and one side of his face, but even so, I could see that one side was tilted up in a small smile.

I looked away. Jules and Ian stood, and Jules came at me with a box and cord first, while Ian went over to Todd.

"This," she said as she held up the box, "is your oxygen. Just like the astronauts a century before us, we use Primary Life Support Subsystems—but they're obviously updated nowadays." She smiled down at the box in her hands. "The substack will provide you with the oxygen you need while taking out any carbon dioxide you exhale." Jules began connecting the box to the belt I wore across my waist. "Back in the day, they had to wear these really clunky suits, and underneath the suits, they wore garments to cool and ventilate their bodies. Now, all of that is built into your suit. We're really quite lucky."

Jules latched the box onto my hip and then ran the cord up my back. I felt her tug and yank at something at the back of my helmet, and then a high-pitched hiss sounded in my ears as the oxygen started flowing.

"This little guy gives you one hundred percent oxygen, whereas on Earth we only had about twenty percent." Jules looked at a few things on my helmet and did a little more tugging before grabbing another box and moving over to secure Darrien's substack. "That way, you can go to higher altitudes if needed."

I desperately wanted to know how many hours of oxygen the little box at my hip would give me. What if we ran out? I didn't like not knowing, even though I was almost sure my helmet would alert me if the oxygen levels dropped. As soon as Jules set up my oxygen, a little percentage symbol showed up on my screen that read O2 levels: 100%.

The airlock door opened once more, and Harper, fully equipped with her substack and her backpack holding her special supplies, came in full force like a commanding officer about to lead their troops into battle.

"How is it out there?" Ian asked.

"Woo!" Harper chimed into the mic. "It is nice. I tested the gravity, and the levels are about half that of Earth, so be prepared to have a little fun when you jump." I couldn't see Harper's face, but I could tell from the pitch in her voice that she was ecstatic.

"How's the atmosphere?" Jules asked. She had moved on from Darrien to work on Saba.

"Not quite safe enough for no helmets, but closer to the atmosphere of Earth than a lot of the planets we've encountered in the past. I think it was a good idea to make this stop. There's actually a little *too* much oxygen on this planet for us. But who's to say we can't thrive here like those on Mars did? Or do." She shrugged. Because Earth had lost contact with Mars years ago, no one knew about their well-being.

It all sounded horrible to me. I didn't want to live inside a building for the rest of my life. Then again, we might not have a choice when all's said and done. Harper was right about those on Mars—they had successfully lived on the planet while remaining inside their indoor housing. And they also didn't want anyone else coming to their planet and tampering with it. Now, with the Fester, I couldn't honestly blame them. But they were still assholes.

"And everything looked... okay?" Ian pressed.

Harper nodded. "I only hopped around for a little while, and there's quite a bit of water. *Beautiful*, clear water. And a shit ton of sand. I think I spotted some caves farther away. But no signs of life that I could tell."

No signs of life. Could that be possible? Perhaps I would find some microbes within the water or some microorganisms in the caves. Maybe what we stumbled upon wouldn't be micro at all. With the amount of water in Virginia, it seemed logical that *some* form of life lived here.

Ian and Jules finished hooking up everyone's oxygen, and finally, all of our mics were turned on.

"To talk to someone in particular," Harper said, "you can look at them and hover over their name which should show up on their helmet. To project to the group, just talk normally."

I wanted to try it, but I was scared I'd mess it up. I wasn't particularly known for getting things right on the first try. Instead, I was more likely to be the only one to fuck up on the first try.

"Are you all right?"

Darrien's voice flooded my helmet; low and velvety, and better in real-time than it was in my imagination. And his message was directed to me. We all stood up and prepared to exit the shuttle. Harper was in the process of opening the latch and letting down the ramp. Ian assisted, and Jules monitored them both, as was protocol, I assumed.

I looked around to see if anyone else had heard the message directed to me, but the spouses were all talking to each other, Todd was staring at the door, and no one even spared us a glance.

So, I looked into Darrien's helmet. Sure enough, his name hovered at the top in bright letters.

Before doubt could creep in, I replied. "Yes. Thank you... are you? Okay?"

He nodded and stepped in closer to me. "You seemed scared there for a while."

I laughed nervously. "Were you not?"

"Dat was one wild ride, eh?" Aleksy's gruff voice sounded in my ear, and I knew it was directed at all of us. "I hope de ride back is better." He chuckled, and Lata elbowed him playfully.

Darrien didn't get a chance to answer my question, as the

latch to the shuttle opened. The ramp came out from hiding and snaked its way down to the sandy land below.

The group stared at the ramp in silence and watched as Harper and Ian disappeared into a completely foreign world, out of sight.

SILICON DIOXIDE

As the crew-mates ahead of me walked down the ramp, I inched my way closer and closer to the land below. Soon enough, a sea of shimmering, blinding sand was all I could see. Though it was the color of most beaches back at home, it looked coarser, the granules larger—but there was something else in it, too. Something that made it glimmer.

"Any day now, Blake," Todd's voice taunted from behind me.

I rolled my eyes, but moved down the ramp, slowly, placing one careful step in front of the other. It was so normal, like exiting a plane or a car. I had expected it to be an earth shattering experience—to step foot on a planet where no other human had been before. Somehow, it felt anticlimactic after the shuttle ride, after all the adrenaline I'd experienced during lift-off.

Finally, my boots hit the sandy ground, and I walked over toward the others who had exited off to one side. The sand felt squishy under my large boots, and my body felt lighter, like I was floating. Like my limbs were put together with Chickadee feathers. The pack I wore on my back was weightless. I wanted to hop around and test out the gravity, but I didn't want anyone to tease me, either.

Todd and the others exited the shuttle in single file. After everyone made it safely to the ground, we all looked around at the planet with wide eyes. Harper and Ian employed the ramp to go back into the shuttle once more and then closed the latch.

The sky above us was lavender; like the part of an amethyst right before purple merges into clear crystal. In the distance, the largest planet, Arizona, was visible, and in the other direction, the star in the center of the stellar system was beaming down from above, hanging high up in the sky. It was smaller than the sun that we could see back on Earth, but the light it omitted was much more powerful.

Crisp turquoise water surrounded us on three sides, and I noticed the faint sound of waves rustling. It reminded me of the gorgeous water in the Maldives. There were no birds chirping, nor were any insects buzzing nearby. Despite the helmet, my hearing was still good, maybe even better than usual, and I could hear the waves and the unsteady breaths coming from my mouth, like they were blaring through a loudspeaker.

Raymond crouched down and inspected the ground right next to Darrien, who sifted through the sparkling sand through his gloved fingers. They cupped the shimmery matter in their gloved hands and studied it. Side by side, they almost looked related, and it had nothing to do with their similar Asian features. No, it was how they both arched their brows and frowned when they were deep in thought. It was the way that they both had their heads cocked to one side; how they both kneeled on their right knees instead of their left.

Todd came to stand by me. I stood there, unmoving, while I gazed at the water only several yards away from us. I wanted to touch it, to dip my feet in. I wanted to swim laps and only stop when my body forced me to from exhaustion. There was something about beautiful bodies of water that made my skin itch with desire.

"Not talking to me anymore?" Todd purred, his voice filling my helmet with velvety desire.

I rolled my eyes and shook my head. His lips turned down. I had a feeling that the famous, wealthy Todd Darcy was not used to being rejected by women whom he'd just slept with.

"But last night was so fun."

"Yes," I sighed. "It was. Fun that will not be happening again." My eyes met his, and though Todd was a cocky asshole, I knew there was more to him than that. I didn't want to fuck around with him anymore, but I didn't want to hurt his feelings, either. "Not that I didn't enjoy it." He cocked a brow. "I did. But–"

"But, you have your eyes on someone else." Todd feigned a glance at Darrien, who was still kneeling down in the sand by Dr. Ishida.

I shrugged, not wanting to be obvious, though apparently it was obvious enough. I was so terrible at hiding my emotions. Even if I *did* like Darrien like that, it could end up just being a dumb crush in the long run. Maybe one that wasn't reciprocated.

But, as much fun as last night had been, I craved a connection, unlike Todd. I didn't know Todd's mother's name, and I didn't know what he was like aside from what I had noticed in the media for years. And I had a feeling that what I had learned from last night and what I'd noticed in the media were the same. Which was typically false, anyway, except for the factual progression of his company and the technologies he manufactured. I couldn't help but need to know more and want some sort of intimate connection with him—and Todd Darcy wasn't the kind of man to give me that.

I guess I wasn't the kind to sleep around. I'd never really had that experience, but I'd also never wanted to. And for the love of all that was holy, I did not want to be talking about this while we were on a new fucking planet. We had work to do.

"It's not necessarily that," I said. I shot my eyes back to him. "I also don't want to talk about this while we're here. Can we talk about this later?"

He wiggled his eyebrows. "I'm always willing to *talk* with you, Dr. Blake." I didn't like his tone or what it insinuated, but before I could snap back at him, he was sauntering over to Harper. Good. Maybe he could fuck with her instead.

After several minutes of gazing around at our surroundings, Harper barked, "Alright, crew! Time to separate into our two groups and do what we came here for. Remember to sample as much as you can. Keep together. If you separate, always go in groups of at least two." Her instructions made me feel like I was back on a field trip in middle school, after Dad had stopped homeschooling me and put me into public school. "It's about noon now, which means it's already late afternoon back on the Mothership. Let's plan to meet back around three." Harper looked at Jules to make sure that the time was good for her, and she nodded curtly. "We'll meet back at three, have some late lunch if we can, and then, if need be, we'll go out and explore some more. If we're finished, then we'll head back."

We all nodded in mutual understanding. I found myself restless, ready to explore as I gazed out at the pristine water and glittery sand. It had been a long time since I'd been out in the field for research, and doing so on an unknown planet already had me curious and ready to go. Most people seemed to feel the same: Saba tapped her foot impatiently, Ian drummed his fingers on his biceps, his arms crossed, and I was rocking in my boots, ready to go as I took in the sparkling planet before me.

Darrien and Raymond stood up and walked over to join me and Lata, who had walked over to me seconds after squeezing Aleksy's hand and telling him something that only he could hear. Harper walked over to our group as the others formed theirs. Jules leaned casually against the side of the shuttle.

"I think that your group," Jules said, nodding over to where we were standing, "should go east, near those hills in the distance, and our group will go west, where the land is more flat."

Harper and Ian nodded. "If you all change directions, let us know." Harper tapped her helmet. Jules and Ian nodded, accepting their instructions. "And if we go elsewhere, I'll do the same."

We all stood there, separated into our groups, staring at one another like, *Is this even real?*

Harper gave Ian and Jules a thumbs up and said, "Be safe." She turned to our small group and asked, "Ready?"

I mean, it wasn't like we really had a choice, but yes. Physically, we were ready.

WALKING through the sand in the heavy space boots made my severely unfit calves ache and scream. Though the gravity helped make me feel a little lighter, it was still a bit of a struggle.

I was more out of shape than I thought. Maybe I'd actually utilize the fancy gym on the *Hippogriff* if we returned.

Water was on one side of us, but we eventually walked higher and higher above it. It glistened in the sun, and the purplish sky made it look like a watercolor painting had come to life. Sadly, after several minutes of walking up the incline, the water disappeared, but I could still hear it. On the other side of us was sand. Sand, sand, and *more* sand. No trees or shrubs. Just a beautiful desert stretched out before us.

The land remained flat for what seemed the longest time, but I knew it had to be inclining because I had to take more breaks, and the terrain, which started out as a smooth walk, gradually became steeper and harder to walk on. My breath was ragged, and I fell a little behind the rest of the group, next to Lata, who looked to be struggling, too.

"This is what we get for not using our muscles enough after that damn hyper-sleep," Lata muttered purposely. I couldn't help my grin.

Harper led the way, of course, with Raymond and Darrien trailing behind. Lata and I kept up with them as best we could, though we occasionally had to stop and catch our breath, and then jump, thankfully with gravity's help, to meet up with them again. The jumping part was fun, at least. Whenever we jumped, I felt like a bird for a couple of seconds, and my heart thumped hard in my chest as we soared higher than we ever could on Earth.

Every time we jumped, I couldn't help but notice that Darrien turned his head around to take a look. I couldn't tell if it was just to check on our well-being, or if he did it because we looked completely idiotic.

It was fun, either way.

The clock on my screen read that we had walked for a little

over thirty minutes. I kept a mental note of how long it took us in case we needed to rush back, or if we fell behind on time.

Finally, we came upon a very large hill. It wasn't big enough to count as a mountain, but it was still steep. Ahead of it were larger caves and more unknown, soaring terrain that grew larger with each step we took.

Once we were on top of the smallest hill, we stopped at the edge and looked down. No one spoke as we gazed down. The small hill had an opening down below, and the shallow water crept into it. A little cave.

"Wow," Raymond sighed. As a person who breathed and lived on geography, I was sure he was thrilled about the little cave we'd stumbled upon.

I turned my head to the larger hills near the one we stood on and wondered what lay beyond.

"How do we proceed from here?" I asked.

Harper was entranced by the water below, but she lifted her head and turned to us after a moment of silence.

"I'm interested in exploring that." She cocked her head downward, hinting at the cave below our feet. "What about you all? We have time. We could get into smaller groups, too."

Raymond definitely wanted to explore the cave with Harper. He didn't have to say anything for that to be clear. He had already taken out several sample containers from his backpack, and I think I actually saw a hint of a smile on his lips.

"I think I'd like to walk a little further," Darrien said. "See what's over those hills. There could be a lot over there."

I waited for Lata to say something, but she didn't.

"I'll go with Dr. Park," I peeped.

Lata looked at me. And then she looked at Darrien. "I'll stay with Harper and Ray. I think I'd like to explore the cave, too. I'm bloody sick of walking." She glanced at me and did nothing to hide the smug smile spread across her lips. "But please be careful, and if you need medical attention, alert us and we'll come running, yeah?"

I nodded at Harper and Lata, and Darrien... moved closer to my side.

"We promise to be safe. Extra safe. Should we meet you all back here in a bit?" Darrien asked.

"Sure. An hour?" Harper suggested.

"Sounds good," Darrien and I said at the same time.

He looked at me and grinned. "Jinx."

The other three in our group had already started descending down the hill. We began our trek in the opposite direction, side by side.

"What do I owe you?"

Darrien looked at me pensively. Wind must have been heavy, because the sand that surrounded us shifted. I wished we didn't have to wear these helmets so that I could feel the wind run through my hair and graze my cheeks. It's funny the small things that I used to take for granted before the Fester. Never in my life did I think I'd feel the wind move through my hair and hit my skin for the last time.

"Hmm. Perhaps you can join me for a *very* strong drink once we're back on the Mothership." He looked at me with a feline smile. One that reached his eyes and made his dimples appear on either side of his mouth. "Or you can take Aster for a few laps around the track. That dog loves you."

"There could be worse tasks."

"So, you'll have a drink with me, then?" He asked.

We trod carefully down the hill and then worked our way up another one. There was still nothing but sand and water below us.

"I will have a drink with you," I agreed playfully. "If I can *also* take Aster for a run in the mornings. Walking up and down all these slopes is a painful reminder that I need to start working out again."

Darrien stopped abruptly and faced me. My breath caught at the back of my throat as I peered up into his eyes. He was much taller than I was, towering over me, shading me from the star's light above. The spacesuit defined every hard muscle in his arms and across his broad chest, and I dared not look lower. I was already ogling without an ounce of discretion. My cheeks burned.

He held a large hand out to me. "Deal."

I took his hand in mine, and we shook on it. A drink with Darrien when we got back, and time with Aster in the mornings. The thought of that—especially the first part of the deal —was more thrilling than exploring planet Virginia, living on an actual spaceship, and pretty much anything else. I felt stupid for feeling so giddy, but I wanted to talk with Darrien—wanted to get to know him besides the nightly dinners and the small bump-ins we had with each other in the lab. More than that, I wanted a do-over of our time in the hot tub. And I was totally getting carried away, because one strong drink with Darrien Park didn't mean all that much in the grand scheme of things.

Eventually, we reached the top of a very steep hill after barely talking while we climbed. We had been too busy observing, keeping our eyes out for plants, for organisms, for anything that could be a sign of life. The beauty of the planet was overwhelming. There was no pollution. No houses or condos which made it hard to see the skyline. No roads to herd us where we wanted to go. It was beautiful because there was nothing. I prayed up to something because I'd given up on a God a very long time ago, that wherever we ended up we wouldn't kill it. Again.

We halted at the top. Stretched out before us was a valley that must have spanned miles and miles. The hills and mountains were all covered in the same sand, but there was a small river running in the middle of the valley, the same color as the turquoise ocean.

"Should we go down there?" I asked. "The river could be promising."

We could go down and explore the valley a bit before meeting up with the rest of our group. I glanced at the clock. We had about forty-five minutes left before we needed to meet up with the others.

Darrien nodded and held out his hand to me. I stared at it for a second too long, then placed my hand in his.

"It's going to be an abrupt drop to get down there," he said. "I think we should... slide down."

I stared at him with alarmed eyes. "Slide?"

He nodded, as though this was perfectly reasonable. "It's steep, and we might actually injure ourselves if we try to walk or jump down."

"Well, I'm certainly not jumping off of a hill."

My voice was higher than normal, and my heart rate began escalating higher at his suggestion. Darrien led me closer to the edge. I glanced down and became dizzy. It was very steep, but not *impossible* to walk down, though it would take us much longer. If we slid down, we could plausibly land in the river. But what if the river was acidic and destroyed our suits and ended up killing us? What if there was a sand monster living underneath this hill, waiting to snatch us up and have us for lunch?

"You look like you are having irrational thoughts," Darrien pointed out with a raised brow. I was, and I was embarrassed he had noticed. "I think it's the best way."

"How will we get back up here later?" I asked.

He shrugged his shoulders. "If we're down by the river, we

should be able to walk back to the cave where the others are by the shoreline."

That made sense, whether I wanted to admit it or not. I definitely wouldn't tell him that out loud, because I was still scared shitless.

"Should we take some samples for Raymond as well?" I asked, trying to change the subject.

Darrien nodded, then gripped my waist and pulled me down to sit beside him on the top of the hill. My ass slammed down next to him but bounced a bit because of the gravity. I clutched onto Darrien's arm to keep myself from slipping. Darrien chuckled in amusement as he rubbed my back. It was an oddly intimate gesture of comfort, one that made my heart squeeze.

I didn't want to look down at the river or observe how far of a drop it was. The hill we were on was significantly larger than the other cave we had encountered, and though it wasn't miles and miles down, or a straight drop, I still did not want to slide down it.

"It'll be fine. I promise." Darrien smirked. "Pretend we're in grade school, and we're just sliding down a small hill. We're going to race down to the bottom. Make it a fun experience instead of a scary one."

Make it fun. I wasn't entirely sure I could do that. The excited glimmer in his eyes told me that he actually *wanted* to slide down this fucking hill. He didn't peg me as an adrenaline junkie, but then again, what did I know?

"Tell me something to take my mind off of..." I trailed off and waved my hand at the river. "This."

"Okay," he said. He moved his head from side to side, deep in thought for a moment before going on. "Tell me more about Jaxon. He's a very cute, extremely bright kid. But I don't know a lot about him yet."

I felt my lips tug upward as images of my beautiful boy flashed before me in my mind. The day he was born, with a full head of platinum blond curls, and how he would cry if he was away from my chest for more than a minute. I remembered when he sat up and rolled over for the first time, way ahead of the age he should have been before doing so. How he walked before he was even a year old. My precious boy, who always brought so much life and light to my days.

"He has always done things early." I laughed and blinked away the tears at the corners of my eyes. "Even without his father growing up, he's always been the happiest, most curious kid. When Matthew died, I thought..." I swallowed down the knot that had grown in my throat. "I thought maybe he wouldn't be the same anymore."

"How old was he when your husband passed?" Darrien asked softly.

Tears fell down my cheeks, leaving my lips and chin wet. "A year and a half."

Darrien reached for the hands in my lap and held both of them in his. He squeezed and let me take my time.

With a sniffle, I moved on to happier things. "When Matthew died, I couldn't function for a while. I guess most people wouldn't be able to." I shrugged. "Dad moved in with us the same day I got the news. I don't think I would have survived without him. Once I was finally back on my feet, I kind of threw myself into my work. I didn't want to pause, even for a second, because all of those emotions would come back. I couldn't sleep, and could barely eat. But Dad stayed home with Jaxon every day. The M.E.I. and the higher-ups at the Dome let him work from home so I could come in every day. When Jax got older, Dad started homeschooling him, just like he'd done with me. I think a lot of grandparents would be tired after being with a young kid day in and day out—but not my father. He loved it. Every minute of it."

I choked as more tears sprung to life.

"Your father seems like a wonderful man. And from what I've seen, he's also got one hell of a personality on him," Darrien said with a laugh.

I nodded and wished I could wipe the tears away from my face. Damn helmet.

"What about you?" I asked after collecting myself. "Any kids? Partners of the past?"

Darrien grew rigid beside me. He looked down at our hands in my lap. "No children. I did have a fiancé. Once." He inhaled deeply, his shoulders rising and falling. "We met in undergrad. After we graduated, though... I took a position at Oregon State where I taught botany and horticulture. Anyway, Camille got her degree in English lit. She struggled to find a job after graduate school, but finally landed a position at Oxford." He shook his head. "We tried to make long-distance work for a while. We were engaged by then. I was trying to land a job at Oxford, too, to make it easier. But she ended up falling in love with some guy over there. Another English professor." He snorted. "Not that there's anything wrong with teaching English, but it was just so cliche."

"Fuck. That had to hurt. I'm sorry that happened to you." I squeezed one of his hands. "Did you see anyone else after?"

He snorted. "Here and there. It never worked out with anyone."

I wanted to ask why but refrained. It was obviously a sensitive subject.

"Well, I don't understand why, but I don't want to pry." I turned my head to face him so he could see my smile. "But I think I'm ready to slide down now. If you are."

Darrien beamed at me. "Let's do it."

I wasn't ready, but we'd stalled long enough. Every minute wasted was one we could be using to explore and take samples. With a tiny squeeze of his hand, I huffed out a breath. I didn't dare close my eyes for fear of making my anxiety worse.

"Alright. Here goes fucking nothing, I guess."

Darrien winked at me, then pulled me along as he scooted up right to the very edge of the hill. Only centimeters separated us from the ride down. With a tug on my hand, he sent us gliding down the steep, dusty slope. I tried my hardest not to look down because the one time I'd done so had made me nauseous. It felt like we were on a rollercoaster with no safety precautions—or like we were about to take off for a literal flight. The lesser gravity made us bounce every so often, as the decline grew steeper and steeper. I stopped breathing altogether, and I was simply *not* having a wonderful time, but when I spared a glance over at Darrien, he was having the time of his life. Even through the harsh glare on his helmet, I could tell that his features were excited and warm. That there was a giant, exhilarated grin spread across his face. Meanwhile, I couldn't wait to be steady on the ground again.

Our bodies hastened to a dangerous speed as we neared where the sand met the river. As soon as we reached the end, our bodies cascaded down and then rocketed up, straight into the freaking river. Because, *of course*.

THE DEPTHS

E ven through the protective suit, the icy water pierced through it and chilled my body to its core. Our hands were ripped from each other as soon as we crashed into the current, and I thrashed around in utter shock and fear of losing sight of him. Underneath the depths, the river was darker and murkier than it had appeared from atop the hill. It was hard to see much of anything—I definitely couldn't tell where the bottom was. My childhood phobias of being vulnerable in the middle of a vast ocean, and not knowing what lurked down below, perhaps only inches from my toes and ankles, inched up my spine. I swam up, up, up, desperate for the surface, the light, and the safety of the ground.

I held my breath because emergency signals were blaring on my helmet's visor. I didn't know if my oxygen was still good or not. As I kicked my way to the surface, I spiraled around underneath the water for Darrien. Nothing but deep cerulean water surrounded me on all sides. Something curled itself around my ankle. Bile shot up the back of my throat, leaving my mouth tasting bitter. I was so close to breaking through the surface, so I didn't stop kicking. I just prayed I didn't puke on the way up.

Luckily, whatever was wrapped around my ankle let go. It brushed against me and didn't latch onto me again or pull me down. I didn't dare look down.

Finally, my helmet broke above the river. There was a steady current, but it wasn't anything too strong for me to escape. As I swam to the nearest shore, I skimmed the surrounding surface and the land for Darrien, and was met with nothing but more sand and more water.

I practically rolled onto a dusty bank once it was shallow enough. My knees were too weak to stand. My lungs were tight and burned in my chest, almost as though I had drowned, when in reality, I had just held my breath for a little while—something I'd done hundreds of times in my life.

"Darrien?" I screamed into my helmet. I wasn't sure if the others would hear me in their helmets from the distance we had traveled or not. It was stupid not to have asked before we parted ways.

I laid there on the bank, chest heaving, mind racing. After a moment, I forced myself on to my forearms to get a better look. Nothing green, that was for sure. Just blue and beige. I blinked all around me. Had something taken him? Had his suit failed? Was he currently struggling for his life somewhere at the bottom of the river? Why the hell was I doing *nothing*?

"Can anyone hear me?" I trembled.

Thankfully, Harper answered almost immediately. "Dr. Blake? Are you okay?"

Right as I was about to explain that no, I was absolutely not fucking okay, I spotted something further down the riverbank, closer to the coast.

Though my legs still felt like Jell-O, I fought to stand. I walked until I was sturdy, then broke into a sprint. Harper's voice continued barking at me inside my helmet. It took me a few minutes before I remembered I could stare at what *looked* like a helmet in the distance, and hope it was Darrien before trying to communicate. It seemed like it could be a helmet, but the distance was still too great to know for sure.

"Harper, please wait," I said, breathless, as I continued running.

Please be Darrien. Please don't be dead or seriously injured. That's all I could think of as I pushed my legs farther and farther.

"Darrien?" I asked, staring into what I prayed was the helmet. If it was Darrien ahead of me, if he could hear me, he probably heard a lot of unflattering cursing and my hitched breathing reminiscent of a person in their eighties rather than a woman in her early thirties. I hoped he heard it, anyway.

"There you are."

His voice was calm, because of course he'd still be calm in a situation like this one. I sighed, and though my knees grew shakier, I continued on.

Harper let out a breath. "Let us know if you need Lata."

Now that I had run what felt like miles but was more than likely about half of one, I could see that Darrien was hugging a small boulder in the river, with only his helmet and a small part of his shoulders visible. I couldn't tell why he hadn't made his way to shore, but I was happy that he was talking. Alive, and not dead or injured.

"What the hell?" I cried. "How–did you get–all the way–" Talking and running was hard. "–down here?"

As I closed the distance between us, my pace slowed.

"I can't feel my goddamned legs!" He said. His calm voice had been replaced with a tone that sounded impatient and anxiety-ridden, and now that I was only a couple of yards from him, I could finally see why.

Darrien was several feet from the shoreline. The large body

of water we had walked next to on the way up the hills sparkled in the distance.

The last thing on Earth (or, well, on planet Virginia) that I wanted to do, was to get back into the water, but as I took in Darrien's situation, I knew I'd have to.

"Can you feel your legs at all?" I asked.

I took off my backpack and set it down a foot from the water's edge. Despite being in the river myself only a few minutes prior, the magical Todd Darcy spacesuit and backpack were already almost close to dry.

"They just feel–" he broke off, "–constricted. But I think something is cutting off the circulation."

I could still feel the slithery tendril that had wrapped around me when I was underneath the water. Shit. Could that be the same thing holding Darrien in the water? Going back into the river with weird organisms and murky water didn't sound particularly great, but it wasn't like I had any better idea. So I rolled my shoulders back, took a deep breath in, and made my way back in.

WHEN I WAS VERY YOUNG, the water terrified me.

Dad had let me watch *Jaws* with him one night when I was barely six and he found himself regretting that decision a couple of months after he enrolled me in swimming classes. Of course, we hadn't seen the original *Jaws* from whatever year it had been made in the twentieth century. The franchise had been rebooted twice since then, and he had allowed me to watch the latest version, which included Virtual Reality.

Not only was I scared shitless of all bodies of water after that, I also didn't sleep for weeks. Many nights, I hopped into Dad's giant bed and curled up next to him while he snored. In the morning, when he realized I'd taken over his bed, he would roll his eyes at me. *It was just a movie, kid.* Yeah, it had been just a movie, but sharks were real. Sharks killing people was a thing that happened. Not a lot, but still.

The river water sloshed around my thighs while I inched closer to Darrien, and I couldn't help that visions of giant great white sharks—or megalodons, or giant squids, or any form of something that lived in the water with teeth, quite frankly— stopped me in my steps.

Darrien's eyes were focused on me. I wondered what he was thinking; *Is this woman going to leave me here? Is she having an attack of some sort? Are we both going to die because she won't get in closer than three feet?* I shook my head and started moving again. The bite of the water reached my groin, and I couldn't help the gasp that escaped my lips.

"Are you okay?" Darrien asked.

"I'm the one who's supposed to ask you if *you* are okay. You're the one hugging a rock in the middle of a weird river. Not me."

Darrien shrugged as well as he could. "I don't love the situation I'm in, but that's beside the point." I could tell by his tone that he was smiling, but I couldn't see it. I was too focused on putting one gentle and calculated step in front of the other. The water was up to my belly button.

I had to look up in order to ask, "Are you in pain?" I wanted to ask if something was nibbling on him or trying to jerk him down, but that didn't seem appropriate.

"No," he huffed. I could tell his arms, though strong, were straining to hold on. I tried to pick up the pace. "It feels...like something has wrapped around me. Tight. I still have sensation in my legs. I'm sorry I was a bit dramatic earlier when I finally spotted you—but whatever it is, it's wrapped around me pretty tightly."

"Can you see what it is?" I gulped.

I didn't want to blindly walk over to Darrien and then get caught up in whatever had him trapped. But I surely couldn't leave him there, either. This should be nothing. But there was a vast difference between swimming under the dome, or in a well-known ocean, and willingly stepping into a foreign river. A shiver made its way up my spine and down the back of my neck. I rolled back my shoulders and shook it off as best I could.

"I couldn't get a good look at it." Darrien's voice was higher than normal, his cool facade was starting to fade.

A thought hit me. Seeing as I was scuba certified, and I was an experienced diver, I wondered if the spacesuit would allow me to go down. Earlier, after I had finally made it to the surface of the river, I noticed that the helmet acted as a type of buoy and sped up my ascent. It would have taken me a lot longer to break the surface without it on. Now, I was worried that if I went under, the helmet would keep me from reaching wherever Darrien's legs were trapped.

"Harper?" I called. I was fully in the water now, with only my helmet out in the open, above the current. "Is there a way to, um, dive in this suit? I need to get Darrien out of the water. Something is holding his legs down."

There was a beat before she responded. "Let me get in touch with Todd and get back to you. I'm pretty sure you can change it, but I've never done it."

Well, that was comforting. Darrien and I stared at one

another. I was about a yard away from him now, and my feet didn't even touch the bottom. What I thought had been a small, shallow body of water from up above was clearly larger than we'd imagined. I waded and tried to even out my breathing as I mulled over the best course of action.

After a few moments of very awkward silence, I remembered, "I have a knife!"

I didn't mean to exclaim my thoughts out loud, but unfortunately, my message didn't just go to Darrien—it went to the whole group. I knew I would fuck that up at some point.

"You go, girl!" Lata laughed.

"Do you want a medal or something?" Harper snipped.

I rolled my eyes. At least Raymond, as per usual, was quiet.

In the water, I felt for my belt and found my knife sitting snug in its holster. Carefully, I opened the holster and took out the small blade. Knowing me, there was always a chance I would drop it or that it would get washed away in the current, so I made sure to really hold on to it as I raised my arm and took it out of the water.

"You're going to cut the..." Darrien looked for the right word, but there really wasn't one. "Whatever has me trapped?"

I nodded.

"But we don't know what it will do," he pointed out. His voice was shaky now, instead of the usual cool as a cucumber, level-toned one that I was used to hearing. "They could–I don't know. Whatever it is, could drag me down or—"

Darrien was starting to remind me of myself.

"Any other ideas?" I cocked a brow.

Just then, Harper said, "Todd just got back to me. The suits really weren't designed to dive or swim, but more made to keep you alive *if* you happen to be in the water." She sighed. "Because the oxygen is one hundred percent in your helmet, even going under temporarily might harm you."

Well, fuck.

"Um, what if, you know, we just turned the oxygen off in my tank for a couple of minutes?"

Even with the helmet as a floatation device, I should be able to get down deep enough to free Darrien if I scaled along the boulder he was latched onto.

"Are you crazy?" Harper shot back.

I shook my head. "No." I glanced at Darrien. "Well, maybe."

"That's insane, Daphne," Darrien murmured. "And that's a long time without oxygen, too."

"Not really." It seemed my middle and high school hobby might pay off, after all. "I'm a really good swimmer. I'm a certified diver. I can hold my breath for a little over three minutes." I gulped and squeezed onto the hilt of the blade in my hand. "And there doesn't seem to be any other way."

"We're coming to you," Harper said.

"No, no. Just—wait." It felt weird to be the one ordering Harper around, but it had to be done sometimes, I supposed. "Just let me try."

No one spoke. Darrien and I stood as still in the water as we could with the current rocking our bodies to and fro.

"How do you turn off the oxygen?" I asked quietly. I knew they could hear me.

Harper let out a long sigh. "You can't. Jules and I are the only ones who have the power to override the system. And I still don't like this idea. At all."

"I'm not saying that I particularly like the idea," I said weakly. "But I think it's our best shot."

More than anything, at that moment, I was just happy that Darrien and I were still alive.

"We don't even know if turning the oxygen off will make a difference," Lata pointed out. Worry laced her voice.

"Exactly," Darrien said. His eyes were suddenly fire and doubt. "This is ridiculous. You could die."

"So could you," I pointed out.

Though adrenaline was probably the only reason I was so adamant on the quest, I also realized that there really wasn't any other way. Even if the others came to help us, what help could they truly offer us? I was the best swimmer. Darrien was tangled up. Common sense. I'd be quick, I'd be thorough, and I'd be done in no time. So long as I kept acting like I would.

Right before Harper turned my oxygen off, I would take a breath in. A steady and deep one. And then I would use everything in my power to push my way down, hopefully near Darrien's knees or thighs. My knife would be ready to swipe, and I would get him out of there.

"Okay, Harper. Give me a countdown."

Darrien shook his head, and Lata said, "Oh my God," in my ear. Raymond even spoke up long enough to ask me to be careful.

"You're one crazy bitch," Harper huffed. "But fine. I guess this is the best way." I smiled a little, knowing that it probably took a lot of willpower for Harper to admit that out loud. "I'll give you ten seconds."

My heart skipped a beat. Darrien's eyes bore into mine, and a deep frown was etched on his face, making a vertical line appear in between his brows. I had seen him broody, but this was different. This was fear.

"Okay," I confirmed. Darrien shook his head.

If I didn't get it over with, though, I'd give up. I knew that much.

"Ten, nine, eight..."

I allowed myself several last breaths before taking in my long one.

"Seven, six, five, four..."

"Jesus, Daphne." Darrien looked like he was on the verge of tears.

"Three..."

My steady inhale expanded my lungs. I let the oxygen fill me up, and I told myself it would be fine. Even if it was just a lie.

"Two, one..." Harper stopped.

Red lights blazed all over the screen in my helmet, and I stopped my inhale. My fight took over my flight; without hesitation, I slammed my body down, demanding that my body and gear would go as deep as I needed them to.

My hip brushed against Darrien's thighs as I made my way deeper. The helmet made it incredibly difficult to stay down, as I assumed it would. I wished that this was a free dive back on Earth—then this would be a piece of cake. My ears popped and a sharp pain shot through my eardrums as I managed to sink deeper with the assistance of the large rock. I used its crevices and fissures to sink my fingers into, forcing my body down against it.

The water was foggy and close to pitch black, despite the light from the star above the water. Deeply cast shadows loomed to the point that Darrien's knees were barely visible.

Thin, sparkling indigo threads that resembled small spider webs branched together and off of one another, and spread up and down Darrien's kneecaps, calves, and presumably his feet.

How could something that looked so breakable hold him down so tightly?

I would have to force my body down even farther; I wondered how much time had gone by already. My lungs were okay but started to tighten a bit.

My palms forced my body down again, sliding down the rough rock. I was careful not to touch the weird, silky substance that had claimed Darrien, but it was incredibly difficult to see where it was coming from and to see whether there was more of it near my feet.

As my lungs tensed inside of me again, panic washed over me just like the chilly water had seconds beforehand. I wished I could take a breath, or distract myself, but no. I was there, in that moment; no going back, no regrets now. I hoped there would be time for regrets later.

I couldn't see shit. In hindsight, I found myself cursing in my head that I hadn't asked Harper before I'd gone under whether or not the state-of-the-art, fucking high-tech helmets had a light on them.

The minuscule strands jerked a bit as I neared Darrien's feet.

Were they capable of jumping off of him and wrapping around me?

Harper was right. I'm an idiot, and I will die an idiot.

I could barely make out the knife I held in front of me as I desperately inched down more. One inch, two...

The webbing stopped jerking, and it felt like my heart stopped beating the second that they did.

Now was the time to swipe my blade across the thin webbing.

Now was the time.

But, being the trained and disciplined scientist that I was, I couldn't help but ponder the hypothesis I would conjure up given just what I knew then, had I been in a safe lab and *not* about to suffocate: a strange, unexplored planet, a deceivingly weak-looking organism that held impeccable strength that seemed to be bursting out from something *else* that was not visible. Was it a defense mechanism? Would whatever it was do something horrible to us the second I made my attempt to break Darrien free? Was it actually a friendly creature, just saying hello? The possibilities were endless.

By the burning in my lungs, I knew my time was close to up. I hastily decided that I had better just swipe at the thing, and hope for the best. I planned to cut at the portion that constricted Darrien's calves, and then rip upwards towards his thighs from there. Maybe that would give him enough wiggle room.

Maybe.

There wasn't enough time to think, to calculate, to reason with myself—so, I wrapped my arms around Darrien's torso in the water. My legs bobbed horizontally and danced with the gentle current. I was careful not to touch the navy blue strings as I glided the knife best I could across the delicate structures. I ducked down and cut across his calves in a jagged motion. The hold they had on him was incredibly tight, and I was no longer surprised that he could no longer feel his legs.

To my surprise, nothing happened. And that was good because my lungs and chest and throat were on fire, and claustrophobia was taking me down a nauseating path. I moved up several inches and sliced across the back of Darrien's tight hamstrings as quickly as possible while remaining steady and precise. The very last thing I wanted to do was cut him.

My lungs could take no more, and lightheadedness filled my head and made it heavy. I strained myself and braced to shoot to the surface. I pressed the emergency button underneath my chin right as I lurched up and sent a silent prayer that Harper would understand my plea to turn my oxygen back on.

I shot up and out of the river, and didn't stop moving as I made my way into the shallow end of the riverbank, my flight or fight response going into overdrive. I continued to hold my breath while the red warning lights continued to blare. I could barely make out the words: ***BLAKE, D., NO OXYGEN, ALERT, ALERT!***

Suddenly, my vision blurred on the sides and started to

fade, like the end of a movie before the credits rolled. I collapsed back into the small current, right before making it fully to shore, unable to stay propped up on my elbows or keep moving. The river sloshed on either side of my helmet, and that was the last thing I heard before everything went pitch black.

4

ANIMAL INSTINCT

Someone was whacking me over the head with a cement block. There was no other possibility.

An excruciating pain deep behind my eyeballs reminded me that I was alive. It was close to unbearable, and a groan erupted from within my chest. The pain was simultaneously achy, dull, and sharp, and I wished whoever was fucking me up would just end it for me already. Put me out of this treacherous feeling and serve me some well-deserved mercy.

"Daphne?" a voice called. It sounded like it was far away.

All I could do was let out another hoarse groan in response. A deep breath filled my lungs, and I hastily fluttered my eyes open. Everything hurt, but I was breathing. Which meant I was alive. No longer under the water. And that voice—

"Darrien?" I croaked.

My mouth was incredibly dry and scratchy like I'd consumed scratch paper and cotton as my last meal. I swallowed hard, which didn't do much to help. The pulsing in my temples and behind my eyeballs shrieked for me to remain still, but I fought it. I struggled onto my side and propped myself up as much as I could.

Darrien squatted directly in front of me, hard muscles

stretching underneath that damned spacesuit. In my haze, I caught myself looking at his crotch in mere seconds. That suit —it didn't hide *anything*. And his...*thing*, well. I didn't have any appropriate words in my head to describe it and figured it would be best to tear my eyes away before I became more lucid. Darrien dropped all the way to his knees, and I realized I had been successful. He had escaped from the boulder, the river, the weird un-spider webs, whatever they were.

"What?" I croaked again.

"Shh, shh," he said.

He pulled me across the sandy bank where my boots still met the water, up into his arms. He sat back on his heels and placed me gently in his lap as if I were a fragile piece of glass.

"You got out." It was a statement, not a question.

Darrien nodded, those deep ochre eyes boring into mine. He supported my back with one arm, the other one was draped lazily across the tops of my thighs. One of my hands rested delicately atop his taut chest, and I could feel his every breath, his steady, sturdy heartbeat. My other hand looped around his neck lazily.

My head and body screamed at me, and yet, I think I would have jumped him had it not been for the helmets and the post-suffocation haze. That, and the thought that the rest of our group could stumble upon us. Yet, my mind went to the dirtiest of places.

Darrien cleared his throat and tore his gaze away. He stared out at the twinkling river, whose current had grown rough and wild. "After you cut those things off of me," he started, "I did my best to get out of the water. You were already passed out. When I saw you collapse, I panicked and somehow managed to wiggle out. But—whatever it was, whatever it was latched onto near the bottom—it came for me."

My jaw tightened, and I was hyper-aware of the sound of

my teeth grinding against each other. I forced a breath, and my lungs burned in response.

Darrien continued on, "It's safe to say we aren't on Earth anymore." He let out a dark chuckle. "The ugliest, most bloated-looking creature came up from the breaths and tried to attack me. The webs came from it, somehow. I don't know how they were attached because it was hard to get a look. Honestly, I didn't want to get a good look. It grew more of those things, those webs, and they shot out fast and struck me." Darrien pointed down to his ribcage with his gaze, and I noticed a dark splotch underneath the silver of his suit. "Don't worry. The suit was stitched up immediately, and I don't think it's too deep. For looking like little pieces of thread, it hurt like hell."

"But it could be–" I broke off and shook my head.

"Poisonous, venomous, and the like."

"Right." I sighed roughly. "We need to get back to the group, I suppose." Though, I did *not* want to leave his arms quite yet. "What happened to the weird creature?" I looked around us, scouring the water's edge for some monster forged by Darrien's words and my overactive imagination.

Darrien held up my knife and handed it to me. "You let go of this before you got out. Lucky for me, too, because my only weapon, a smaller knife, is still in my pack. Because I'm a moron and suggested we slide down the hill and didn't even consider what kind of danger could be in the water." He rolled his eyes. I grasped the butt of the knife and secured it back on its spot near my hip.

"How long was I out?"

He shrugged. "Not long at all, actually."

"And why is my skull threatening to split in two?" I asked.

He smirked a little, with one corner of his lips tugging upward, sporting one of his cute dimples. "Well, lack of oxygen, falling back out of the water, and..." he trailed off, "I may have landed on you a bit when I finally stabbed at and escaped the weird blob fish thing."

I stared at him, and it was apparent that he was *not* joking, and that he felt bad about it. However, the smug look on his beautiful face told me he also found it humorous beyond measure.

"You landed on me."

He nodded. "But not on your head. Just your, um, other parts."

"Other parts?" I repeated with a cocked brow, my voice rising.

As much as he tried, Darrien couldn't keep his wide gaze from traveling down to my breasts. My nipples were suddenly hard and made their presence known, and I then realized how cold I was, despite my core being so fucking hot and tight.

"You landed on my tits?" I guessed, trying my damnedest not to gasp or run away at the thought. My cheeks heated uncomfortably.

"I may have face-planted. A bit."

"A bit?" I shot back.

Christ. I was going to die from embarrassment, and this man had the audacity to look smug. He bit his bottom lip, and if we hadn't been in the helmets, I would have attacked him like a starved, rabid animal. The way his teeth grazed his plump bottom lip was sure to consume me. His eyes dipped lower and stared sheepishly at my chest, and that fucking gorgeous blush that crept up and took over his lightly freckled cheeks had me ravenous. A blush spread across my own cheeks, and we sat there for a moment, just staring. He released his bottom lip, leaving it glistening and wet and perfect for tasting. Darrien inhaled sharply and stood up, hauling me with him. Stupid planet. Stupid spacesuits. Stupid helmet. Stupid, *stupid, stupid.*

Darrien planted me down softly on the sand. To my credit, I only swayed slightly after everything we'd just gone through.

He steadied me a bit before he said, "I think it's best we make our way to the coast." He let out a long sigh like he was pained. I wondered if his ribs hurt more than he let on. "We were going to do that anyway, but maybe we can get samples on our way back before we meet up with the group. I already told the others we'd be heading that way after you passed out."

I let out a loose, shaky breath. We fell into staggered steps side-by-side. Darrien was holding back his usual pace for me. I could tell. Given his height, I knew he could walk much faster. Yet he walked beside me without an ounce of impatience. I struggled to stand, and walking was treacherous. I was grateful that he wasn't trying to hurry us along.

"I hope Lata has some good pain meds," I muttered, stepping around a rock in the sand.

Darrien chuckled and looked at me. "I am sure she'll be able to take care of both of us later back on the shuttle."

"Are you okay?" I asked.

He nodded and threw me an aloof expression, as though almost being some alien's late lunch was nothing to come back from. We continued on. Large hills and mountains decorated the terrain on either side of us. The steep hill we slid down not even an hour earlier taunted us to the right.

"At least we can report back that there is life on this planet," I said.

Darrien huffed a laugh. We walked on for a while before another intrusive thought surfaced.

"How the hell did you end up so far along the river?" I asked. "We went down together. Our hands were even gripping each other. It doesn't make sense. I thought–"

Darrien looked down at his boots. A stray strand of dark hair fell over his brow, and I wished I could reach up and push it away from his eyes. "I honestly have no clue. As soon as we hit the water, I swear something grabbed me and took me away from you."

"Was it the weird blob-fish-alien-creature-thing?"

He looked at me. "I don't think so. This thing felt... bigger. And then, the next thing I know, I'm trying to swim to the surface, and I feel something wrap around me. It felt like nothing at first. I thought I might be making things up, but then whatever it was tightened around my leg and I freaked out. I feel fortunate I even made it to that freaking rock in time to stay above the water."

"So it wasn't the fish thing... so, what was it?" I asked, already knowing he wouldn't know. How could he? Still, I couldn't help asking, "Did you see it at all?"

"Such a scientist, Dr. Blaine," he mocked as he playfully nudged my shoulder with his. "No. I was a little busy trying not to shit myself."

I laughed, and the apples of my cheeks warmed.

"I *did* manage to get us a sample of whatever was around my legs. There were a few stands still stuck to my calves when I reached land." He tapped the backpack strapped to his back. "It's in my pack."

The fact that Darrien had gotten me a sample, and to even think to do so, after everything that happened while I was unconscious and he was injured, right after fighting for his life, awed me.

"I think that might be the nicest thing anyone has ever done for me." I grinned and placed a hand over my rapidly-beating heart. The funny thing was, I wasn't even kidding.

We stopped in our heavy tracks as the river grew wider. There was only a small passage of sand that remained stretched before us, and we would have to walk one in front of the other to cross. I hoped the ground was sturdy; that one or both of us didn't fall in. The river roared next to us as we stood there, unmoving, both of us equally terrified to keep going.

Finally, Darrien broke the silence. "Me or you first?"

I was smaller, so I could test the weight out. I was worried that the sand would give way and send us back into the depths, and that was definitely not preferable. But it was sand, after all, not a rickety bridge or thin ice. We should be okay.

"Me first, but I–I'm worried we'll get separated again," I admitted. I didn't want to lose him again. I didn't want to end up alone again, either. I was sure he felt the same. As soon as I'd noticed Darrien was nowhere near me in the river, it had taken a lot for me not to freak out or have a full-blown panic attack. I was sure those emotions would hit me hard later.

Darrien held up a finger to me and took his backpack off. He set the pack by his feet and dug around before pulling out a rope and a couple of carabiners. What the fuck? My kit didn't come with that. I made a mental note to take that up with Todd or the Captain whenever I could. Was that some sexist bullshit, or what? And here I thought we'd come so far in the twenty-second century.

The rope he provided was long, so I handed my knife to Darrien so he could cut it. He cut it shorter than I thought he would, leaving only a couple of feet in between our bodies as he clipped on the hooks to our belts.

"Better?" he asked.

I nodded. The carabiners of the past had been easy to open, but I observed that the ones Darrien had in his pack were almost impossible to open unless you pressed a specific button on the side. Having a safety net in place eased my nerves, if only by a little.

"Ready?" Darrien breathed.

"Absolutely not." We shared a smile. "But we have to get back somehow."

I took a step toward the small strip of sand and felt Darrien's body follow close behind me. Every time I took a step, he did the same, in perfect synchronicity. I tried not to look at the water for fear of something resembling a bloated monster fish jumping out and attacking us. I kept my eyes in front of me and focused on my steps and my breaths, trying to ease away the ever-present pounding in my temples and sinuses.

There truly was nothing interesting to look at. Not a single thing that could be an organism or plant was anywhere in sight. The sand occasionally blew in the wind, making it glitter, but surprisingly enough, the magic of it that had entranced me when we first arrived was starting to fade away.

The hills on either side of us grew taller. Several caverns opened up on either side of us. I was about to turn around and ask Darrien if we should go into one to explore for a minute or two and gather some samples, when a rough wave crashed into a nearby boulder out of nowhere, knocking us over and into each other.

The wave hurled us into something sharp. Darrien fell on top of me, and the rough ground (at least I hoped we were on the ground somewhere) underneath felt slick and slimy, like the algae on river rocks back home. Water foamed over us as the river's current let in another wave until it calmly subsided and retreated. With the water gone, I moved to get up, then stopped.

Darrien's arms were on either side of me in a plank. His hips dug into mine, and I could feel every warm and hard part of him. His eyes were wider than I'd ever seen them—his lips were parted. He gently laid his helmet to rest on top of mine. *Fucking helmets.*

We both knew we needed to get our asses up and get our bearings. We both knew we needed to start moving back in the direction of the others. Our time was limited. But the way he looked at me was unreal. His heated gaze sent electricity down the length of my body. It wasn't like how Todd looked at me the night before. No. This was something deeper and more intimate, like he held the same amount of desire for me, if not more.

"You're fucking stunning, Daphne," he groaned. I prayed the mic wouldn't have a sudden malfunction and that the rest of our group couldn't hear, because I wanted him to keep saying things like that, and I wanted him to touch me, and I never wanted to leave this fucking cavern or wherever we'd been dragged into.

It was so quiet. I could hear Darrien's every shallow breath as he pressed himself into me, and took one hand from the ground to caress his fingers along my collarbones, then down lower, dangerously close to my breast.

It had to be nearly impossible to arch my head back in a helmet, but God, did I want to.

His fingers trailed down lower until his thumb circled around my nipple. He brought his index finger in to meet his thumb and squeezed lightly. His breathing hitched and his cock, pressed exactly in the right place, grew harder in seconds. Darrien moved his hand to my other breast and repeated the same motion. He was going to drive me mad, and I would surely suffocate to death trying to get him naked right here in the middle of nowhere.

"I am aware this is not what we should be doing," he pointed out in between hitched breaths. "But I would love to stay here for a couple of minutes longer. If you'll let me?"

His eyes were so famished, I knew he wanted much more than what we could take in the cavern. I couldn't breathe right, and I didn't want to. I nodded my consent, and he immediately rolled his hips into me, grinding himself on my pelvis. And though it wasn't sex, and there were several layers between us, it was the greatest pleasure I'd felt in years; eyes rolling back into my skull I couldn't get enough. I was fucking ravenous, high off the euphoria his movements gave me.

One of his hands still played with my breast. I took the opportunity to slide my hand in between us and fully grasp what I could of him. Thank God for the scantily clad space-suits. Or...should I thank Todd?

I rubbed him, delicately at first, and was delighted when he shivered. I stroked him rougher after his heated response, right before squeezing his tip a little.

"Oh, fucking *hell*," he gasped. His breaths were fast now. Darrien was practically gasping for air. His cheeks were red hot, and an ache formed inside of me that was so deep, I almost cried out. "Now be a good girl, and turn off your mic," he ordered.

I obeyed, turning my mic off with a flash of my eyes. Darrien got up and kneeled in front of me, then hastily grabbed my ass so that I was straddling him right there, in the middle of a random cavern covered in slippery water—and God knows what else—but my headache was fading, and my worries were, too. The last thing I was going to do was object to *this*.

While I sat straddling his waist, he lowered his hands from my chest down to my ribs. He trailed his fingers down the span of my abdomen, squeezing my curves with his starving fists. I couldn't help but think that I would willingly do the river fiasco all over again ten, or maybe twenty, times, if it meant he could fuck the ever-living shit out of me right here.

His right hand dug deep into the crevice of my hip while his left squeezed my ass. I moaned deep and loud and rolled my hips against his length. With two fingers, he trailed his way from the center of my stomach, down to where my clit throbbed and ached for attention. His fingers pressed in and rubbed against the suit, and I was dying for more because even through the fabric, he knew exactly where to find me and how hard to press.

"You know," he huffed, turning his mic on, just for me to hear him. "That drink you promised me when we get back can always be followed by a sleepover." He turned off his mic again as he grinned. I'd never seen this way before—all heat, need, and want. Completely lost in a frenzy. Like a lion licking its lips right before going to pounce on a galloping gazelle. He kept running his tongue over his lips, and I couldn't help but wish that his tongue was in other places.

We became wrapped up in one another, moving in sync. I wanted to kiss those lips so badly. They were all I could stare at as he gazed down at my body, totally blissed out and full of lust. And then, we were covered in another blanket of icy water, which is exactly what we needed to come back to our senses. We were acting like horny ass teenagers after prom. Even though I wanted to continue our groping more than anything, I knew we needed to press pause, and hope there would be a chance later on to press play. And possibly rewind and start again.

Darrien gazed at me through heavy lids, and squeezed my hips one more time, right before Harper's shrill filled our helmets and barked, "Are you two alive? Why are your mics off? I swear to God. We have your location and we're two minutes out. You'd better be alive when we get there, or I'm gonna be so pissed."

And so, we separated for those two minutes, because if we spared a single glance at each other, there's no telling what more trouble we would get into.

5

FAUX DAHLIA

I f we hadn't been on a foreign planet where we relied on the oxygen and carbon dioxide inside of our helmets to keep us breathing, Harper wouldn't have had to rush to our aid. And if we hadn't heard Harper in our helmets, there's no telling what they would have walked in on.

When they arrived, I did my best to look and act normal. Though, I couldn't have been normal, anyway, given the whole diving to save Darrien without oxygen, surviving, and then passing out fiasco. Still, I put my best efforts into maintaining a cool facade.

Darrien was taking samples of water in a shallow pool that rested deeper within the caverns—now that I was focused on my surroundings and not Darrien, I knew that's where we'd ended up. Meanwhile, I observed the stalactite-like spears that crowded above us, when suddenly Lata rushed in and hugged me. I had just managed to take a sample of one of the spears that hung down on the side of the walls. It had been a struggle to reach because of where I stood at my little below-average height.

Lata's helmet knocked against mine, which certainly didn't

help with the headache that lingered, but I was happy for her embrace.

"Oh my God," she all but screamed. "You had me worried *sick*."

Harper and Ray walked into the cavern like they were on a mission, all straight-spined and with alert eyes. As soon as they took in the cavern, Ray gasped after noticing all the stalagmites and stalactites. From his slack-jawed gaze and googly eyes, I could tell he was awestruck and nerding out. I considered that perhaps the structures had turned him on in some strange, geeky geographer way, and shivered, forcing my intrusive thoughts back into whatever hole they'd come from.

Harper stalked over to me and Lata and crossed her arms defensively, but there was a smile tugging at her thin lips. "You've got balls, lady. I'll give you that. I don't think even Carnell would have done what you did. Plus, he's terrified of large bodies of water, so." She shrugged while I snorted a relieved laugh.

Lata grazed my arms with delicate fingertips and observed me. "Are you okay, though? I don't like that you passed out." My friend Lata was quickly replaced by Dr. Dhawan in less than a breath.

Darrien assisted Raymond with a stalagmite sample a few yards away, but Darrien's helmet was pointed in my direction as he assisted. He held out a sample tube but looked right at me. My breath caught in my throat.

I'd never seen Raymond so excited. Could it be possible that he had a personality, after all? He darted all over the place, crouched down here and there, reaching up on his tiptoes and I swear I saw him hop excitedly at one point.

Darrien's eyes didn't waver from mine. They made me hot all over again, right when I thought I'd finally cooled off and gotten my head screwed back on straight.

"What were you saying?" I cleared my throat and turned to Lata.

Lata and Harper looked at me in a funny way, with their eyebrows raised and small smiles on their lips.

Lata cocked her head. "I want to check you for a concussion when we get back to the shuttle," she said.

I chuckled. "Sorry, my thoughts... I wasn't focusing." I cleared my throat again. "I'm fine, seriously. I have a bit of a headache. That's it." I motioned my head over to Darrien. "Dr. Park got into a brawl with a creature from the river, and whatever it was that was holding him down somehow injured his ribs."

Lata wagged a finger at me. "I am not done with you, and I *will* examine you when we get back and we can get that helmet off of you." She huffed, stomped over to Darrien in a flash, and immediately bent down to examine his ribs. She applied a little pressure, and from where Harper and I stood, I could see him wince.

Another large slosh of water made its way into the cavern and swirled around at our ankles. I gazed down at my boots and hoped I didn't see anything resembling spiderwebs. Or worse.

Harper kept her eyes on me. They were hard, and her lips were turned down. Whatever had amused her a moment beforehand was long gone.

"You must have one hell of a disappointed mom face if what you're giving me now is any implication," I said.

The little comment, which I'm sure reminded her of her two adult daughters living on Earth with their father, made her frown deepen. It had been hard on everyone who had left their families behind on Earth, but I couldn't imagine leaving behind two children on a plagued planet—adult or not. I knew she was thankful that she still received video mail, but those messages were weeks old by the time we got them, and it was nothing like being present with your kids.

"All I was going to say is that you're a complete and total ass with idiotic and reckless tendencies." She exhaled a very large breath, but her shoulders relaxed ever so slightly. "And I'm glad you're alive. And you're right," she smirked then, "I do have pretty wonderful mom faces."

I beamed at her. Whenever broody Harper turned into lighthearted, jokester Harper, something inside of me eased. Once she stopped being so serious, she could actually be fun and comforting to be around.

"Alright!" Harper clapped her hands together, making me jump in my boots, quite literally. "We're running late on our trek back. We have to get going."

She was right. We should have already started on the path back minutes ago. I felt pretty guilty, knowing we had stalled the group and our mission, but then I again... I felt perfectly good about it all as soon as Darrien worked his way closer to me, followed by the others.

"It's okay, though," Harper reassured as she led the way out of the damp cavern. I was happy to have some light back as I stepped outside and onto the very slim riverbank. "The other group is lagging behind a bit, too, from what Jules reported a few minutes ago."

I walked carefully behind Harper with Darrien trailing behind me, and the others following him, all single file, as though we were in kindergarten and being ushered to the lunchroom. We focused on our footing and fell silent. Now that I knew of one thing that lived within the depths of the ominous river, I was more scared to fall in. I didn't want to encounter any more foreign organisms today.

"Is their group okay?" I asked meekly while matching

Harper's boot marks in the sand ahead of me. Lighter gravity or not, I did not want to misstep or go tumbling.

"Yes," Harper replied tightly. "They just lost track of time."

I could tell she was trying to focus, and I was being a nuisance, so I shut my trap accordingly. As we walked more and more, the glistening, aquamarine sea finally came into view. The waves were so unlike that of the cloudy depths to our right. It was tempting to look at the river to see if I could peek at anything watching us under the blanket of water, but no. Nope. I didn't want to know. If I thought *Jaws* was bad, I couldn't wait to see what nightmares I got from our adventure in the river.

I wanted to look back at Darrien, too, but that was a worse idea, because I would likely just end up falling over my own two feet, all because I wanted to see if he was focusing as hard on the sand as I was. Or if he was looking at me instead. *Stupid.*

We finally reached the coastline after a fifteen-minute walk. The exhaustion hit me hard about halfway through, and as we continued back to the shuttle, my body ached, my eyes grew heavy, and I fantasized about my bed back on the *Hippogriff*. It didn't take long for me to fall to the back of our group as our small stretch of sand grew and eventually became a beach.

There was more space to walk now, and without fear—or without that *particular* fear. Lata and Harper led at the front and Raymond walked in the middle, stopping every so often to crouch down and inspect something he made up in the sand. Darrien walked with Ray for a while, but when he noticed that I had fallen behind the rest of our group, he slowed down until he was beside me.

"Are you okay?" he murmured.

I nodded. "Tired."

He chuckled and grazed the ribs that had been injured with his knuckles.

"Are *you* okay? Are your ribs okay?" I eyed his torso. "You're not going to grow a tail or anything, right?"

"Hopefully not," Darrien said. "Though I think worse things could happen."

We walked on. Up ahead, I could spot the shuttle, but it was so far from us it seemed to be the size of a puny pebble.

"Tell me something," he said.

I thought he was going to ask me a question, but he stopped. I looked up at him, though I couldn't see his face through the glare of the sun.

"What?"

"Tell me something. You know..." He shrugged. "Keep talking so that you wake up enough to make it back to the shuttle. Because, as much as I'd love to carry you back, I probably shouldn't given my ribs."

Darrien carrying me back while I lulled into a light sleep against his back sounded like heaven. I forced my legs to keep moving.

"What do you want me to tell you?" I asked.

"What do you want me to know?" His voice was low and velvety, and whatever words I had prepared in my head disappeared into thin air.

What did I want him to know? A lot of things—that I liked the spread of beige freckles that spanned across the bridge of his cheekbones; how I loved that he had carried Jaxon to bed on the first night we bonded over dinner back on the Mothership. That I craved to know his quirks, his passions, and his scars. But he was asking about me. What did I want him to know about *me?* He knew I was a mom. Knew my mother was dead, and I assumed by now that he had figured out there wasn't a partner in the picture. He knew I loved animals; what

I did for a living. Besides work, being a mother, and daughter, and occasionally sleeping, I was at a loss.

"I don't know," I admitted somewhat somberly. "You know my family already."

He hummed as if he disagreed. "I know your family, kind of. But I didn't ask about them. I asked about you."

Truthfully, I didn't like thinking about myself all that much. I guess it was easier to focus on other things. My son. My father. My career. And avoiding the grief that dug its claws into my flesh each time I was off my guard. Before the Fester came about, I tried to live day by day, sometimes minute by minute, and some days I had to focus on everyone *but* myself to survive.

"I like to swim."

It wasn't what I'd expected would come from my mouth, but it was true. Swimming was my outlet. It was what gave me joy and forced all the bad shit in my life to fade into the background. Unless I was swimming to save someone from a weird alien fish. In which case, *no,* I didn't like that kind of swimming. At all.

"How old were you when you learned how to swim?" he asked.

"Young," I said. Harper and the others had picked up their pace, probably eager to get back to the shuttle. I tried my best to keep up. "Dad forced me into swim lessons not long after he let me watch the VR version of *Jaws* for the first time."

Darrien threw his head back and laughed deeply, genuinely. "I don't know your father that well, but that seems like something he would do."

I nodded thoughtfully. "Yeah—so, as you would expect, I didn't want to get into the pool at all at first."

"What made that change?"

I halted my stride. It took Darrien a second to realize he

had left me behind. He turned back to me and jogged the yard of distance between us. I resumed walking after I let the memory flood through me. After I got used to its presence in my head again. It was a memory I thought of often. The Dome, Magda, the water, and the tortoises. But seeing her face flash across my memories never ceased to make my throat constrict.

"Magda."

"Magda?"

I exhaled roughly. "The swimming lessons really didn't do me any good. I could pretty much just float in the water. I didn't enjoy it, because I didn't really know how to swim yet. You know? I was in a constant state of terror every time my skin hit the water." I took a pause and looked out at the ocean before us. Darrien remained quiet. "A couple of years after that, Dad started volunteering at the M.E.I. Wildlife Conservatory, and he'd bring me with him." I smiled as I thought of the day I ditched Dad and took my chance at breaking into the habitat. "One day, I met Magda."

Softly, Darrien pried, "Magda... Dr. Magda Fuchs, right?"

Confused, I looked up at him.

"You know that horrible video they made us watch on the way here?" he asked. "Your bio mentioned Dr. Fuchs as your mentor. That you–you took over for her. Right?"

"Right." I'd forgotten about that video. "Magda wasn't the director yet when I met her. She took that on when I was in high school. When I met her for the first time as a kid, she was still the head of the Herpetology division. She really, *really* liked tortoises."

I squeezed my eyes shut and did my best to remember her snarky smile. How she always smelled like dirt but also honey-suckle, even after she showered. I tried to feel her hand in mine.

Those memories faded every day, and I wanted to clutch onto them for dear life.

"Anyway, when Magda was younger, she would swim in one of the conservatory habitats—the Galapagos Habitat. Which is ironic, because before she died, she got mad at me for swimming in there." An eye roll I couldn't control escaped. I blinked away a few tears before continuing. "One day, she offered to take me to the pool while Dad was working. By then, he worked there full-time." I took a breath through the exhaustion. Walking and talking while being mentally and physically exhausted was hard. "So, she took me to the pool in my neighborhood. It was small, but since it was the summer, it was packed. She watched me get in and... I just stood there. Totally terrified and overstimulated.

"I wasn't in there for more than a minute before she pulled me out. I'd barely gotten past the stairs to the shallow end. Magda didn't say a word as she ushered me back to the car. Before I could ask, I realized she was driving us back to the conservatory. So I figured she'd give me back to Dad, and I'd be in trouble or something." I shrugged. That thought seemed so silly now that I was grown. "Instead of taking me to Dad, she took me to the Galapagos Habitat, and for the rest of the afternoon, we played in the water. She didn't teach me anything. We just stood there and splashed each other. Occasionally, the penguins would come in and circle us." A repressed laugh roared from my lungs as I remembered that day. Magda had twirled us around in the water while the tortoises judged us from the bank and munched on leafy greens.

"She got you used to the water," Darrien said.

"Exactly. She made me fall in *love* with the water."

"So, she taught you as time went by, or?" he pressed.

"Mhm," I mumbled. "That summer, she taught me little by little. But only when I asked how to do things, and only if she did them right there with me. I got a junior diver's certification when I was eleven, and just," I shrugged, "went from there."

We stayed quiet for a while. Finally, Darrien broke the silence. "Daphne, I think that's probably one of the best stories I've heard in a long time." Darrien's gloved hand brushed my own. "She sounds like she was marvelous."

He had no idea just how right he was. My lips parted, and I was about to reply when I noticed Harper and Lata crouching down where the sea met the land. Raymond jogged to meet them and knelt down beside Lata.

"Dr. Park!" Raymond yelled, even though it was completely unnecessary in the helmets. He waved at us. "I think there's something here you would like to see."

Darrien grabbed my hand and pulled me alongside him as we sprinted as best we could over to them. I knew he probably would have run if it weren't for me.

"What is it?" Darrien asked.

The small sprint left me dizzy. I decided I would sit in the sand while they all fussed over whatever they had found. Screw crouching. It had been a long day.

Darrien arched his head above everyone else, leaning forward and bending to get a better look. "Whoa," he gasped.

His gasp almost gave me enough energy and curiosity to get back up. Almost, but not quite.

Darrien circled around whatever they were so mesmerized by. Harper and Lata backed away to give Darrien some space on one side, and Raymond whirled around and stepped behind everyone to get out of the way.

In the window that they had made with their bodies, I could see what all the fuss was about. It was a large purple flower. Similar to a dahlia. But it was massive, and even from where I sat several feet away, I could tell that the petals were thin and veiny. In the light from the star above us, and from the angle I was sitting, I gawked at the silvery veins that consumed the underside of each petal. It was probably the most gorgeous plant I'd ever seen.

The center part of the plant was not like any flower on Earth, though. Instead of a yellow or orange stigma, there were many small, black spikes that shined like dainty crystals. The plant came from the water. Its stem seemed almost too thin to support the large bloom. The spindly stem wasn't green. Instead, it was the same color as the sand. The perfect camouflage. I skimmed around the shore for more flowers of the same kind, but it was the only sign of plant life in sight.

"What are you all looking at?" Ian's voice sounded.

I swiveled my body as much as was comfortable and saw the second group approaching from several yards away.

"Some beautifully weird flower," I replied.

Darrien stared at it, fully enamored. Raymond fidgeted behind him, obviously jonesing to take a sample. Harper and Lata stood up and brushed the sand off the back of their thighs.

"I'm going to go meet Aleksy," Lata said to me as she passed. "And Harper, before you say anything about staying in pairs, I can literally see him waving to me now."

With that, Lata took off to meet her husband while Harper joined me in the sand.

It was entirely charming how Darrien moved his head this way, that way, all around, getting every single angle. I was sure he was taking pictures. It was lovely to see him in his element, and I greatly enjoyed watching his body bend and flex as he got the pictures he wanted. But I was desperate to get my ass safely on the shuttle—which was funny given I was so *not* happy to be on the shuttle only hours prior.

"Are you going to take a sample, Darr?" Raymond asked.

Darr? Like, Dare. But, Darr? I made a mental note to ask about how well *Darr* and Raymond knew each other later. Darrien didn't respond. He placed his hands on his knees and inched closer to the flower.

"I don't want to if I'm being honest," he said. "I know I probably should, given it's the only thing that resembles a plant on this sandy planet."

Raymond nodded. "I'll prepare a container for you. Scissors?"

"Sure. Thanks."

"I want to see dees strange flower," Aleksy said from behind me.

"Come on, Leks, they're going to bring it back to the shuttle, I'm sure," Lata said, almost whiney. She wanted back on that shuttle, too. "You can look at it in the lab."

The second group stood by the shuttle now, all together and close to the ramp that hadn't been let down yet. Ian and Jules were working on getting it down while they waited, and the others leaned against the shuttle or sat in the sand. Aleksy and Lata stood beside me so Aleksy could get a better look, despite Lata's pleas.

Raymond waited impatiently for Darrien to take the sample. Darrien stayed crouched near the stem, scissors in hand, unmoving. I could sense from his tense shoulders that he really didn't want to cut it. I knew what that felt like, because I, too, had taken various small organisms from their natural habitats and back to the lab on many occasions when I had been in school, and I'd felt bad about it every single time. It wasn't an easy thing to do. To sacrifice something untouched, something so pure and beautiful for the sake of research. Especially something that looked like *that*. I would bet that the rich would eat that flower up, try and formulate it and reproduce it, and sell it for boatloads of money. I kind of hoped Todd would never see it.

Darrien opened up the scissors and leaned in closer.

"Great. I'll be glad to get this show back on the road," Harper said as she stood.

She moved to walk back to the shuttle, but a loud, sharp sound erupted around us. It was like someone was sharpening a very dull blade. I peered up at Harper and saw her freeze in her tracks.

Darrien.

I snapped my head back to Darrien and Raymond. There was something long, sharp, and glistening sticking out of Darrien's shoulder. In horror, I gasped and reached out my weak arm in Darrien's direction. I willed my body to stand, but I sat there, frozen. The tiny crystals in the middle of the flower had grown into a thin spike. It must have struck when my head was turned, right when I had turned my attention to Harper.

"Darrien!" I screamed.

Raymond ran. I couldn't really blame him, either. Harper threw her backpack onto the sand in a rush and shuffled through the contents.

"Fuck!" Harper screamed "*Fuck!*"

It took me much longer to get my ass into gear amidst the chaos. The spike flung out of Darrien, and he groaned. He barely made it to a sitting position before the thing stabbed him again—but this time it hit him harder. Right through his chest. I was standing before I could think straight.

No. Not Darrien. Please.

6

HOLDING ON TO YOU

"**D**arrien!" I belted out.

My lungs felt like they had collapsed in on themselves, and my throat was raw. I didn't care. *Not Darrien.*

Jules was beside us now, shoulder to shoulder with Harper. She gripped a laser gun in her hand so hard that her gloves strained. She didn't move, though, and neither did Harper.

I shot past them, flailing in the sand on my weak legs to the point I almost bounced over in the gravity. Luckily, the atmosphere was on my side, and I made it to Darrien far faster than I would have back on Earth.

As soon as I was above the vile plant, I stomped on it with my boot, *hard*. My actions were wild. I knew I should have gone about the situation in a safer manner. Fuck that. There wasn't time for safety. The crunch of the crystals sounded underneath my foot, but I kept stomping, slamming one foot, then the other, over and over on top of the petals which had become embedded into the sand. Before I knew it, I was gripping my blade again, and with one swift motion, I severed the stem in half.

Darrien was keeled over a couple of feet away from the floral remains. He clutched at his chest and watched me destroy the plant he'd been so mesmerized by minutes prior. A garbled breath filled my helmet, and I knew it was his. Finally, I lifted my boot up carefully. Perhaps all of my efforts had been in vain.

Jules and Harper, and now Ian, looked at me with wide eyes and slack jaws. They had gotten closer to me during my rampage. Aleksy came up to me in a rush. Ian came closer to help, and the two of them hauled Darrien up as I looked at the wrecked plant I'd pounded into the ground.

"Come, come," Aleksy nagged at me.

I stared down. "Watch it for a minute, please?" I asked Harper and Jules, who had their guns at the ready. As though guns would help us now. Maybe it would have been better if they'd shot the stupid fucking flower after it struck Darrien for the first time.

"Um, yeah. Sure," Jules said.

Harper just stared at me. I ignored her as I slammed my bag to the ground and rummaged through until I found a container because cowardly Raymond ran off with the other one. Then, I scooped up the remnants of the flower, the little crystals now hardly bigger than a mustard seed, as well as the sand and stem it laid on, careful not to touch anything with my gloved hands. Without an ounce of grace, I dumped it all into the container, sealed it shut as quickly as possible, and then shoved the thing down to the bottom of my pack.

"Can we get the fuck out of here now?" I asked them as I stood.

"God, yes," Harper sighed.

Aleksy and Ian had successfully carried Darren closer to the shuttle. A familiar pain threaded throughout my chest: fear. How would his death affect me? I didn't want Darrien to be another tally on my list of lost loved ones. Even if he was new to me, my fragile heart couldn't take another beating like that.

Lata rushed over to Darrien. The ramp was down, and Lata, Aleksy, and Ian worked as a team to get him up the ramp and into safety. I allowed myself to breathe if only a little. I didn't want to feel relief—it was too soon, and couldn't let myself get my hopes up.

As I started to force my weak limbs toward the others, I noticed that Jules had stopped in her tracks and was staring at something. Harper apparently had no clue, because the gun in her hand dropped to her side. Jules, however, her gun was still up and pointed at the sand near my boots.

"What?"

A blood-curdling scream filled our helmets, and I winced. Without looking back, I ran as fast as I could toward the shuttle along with the others. It took me a minute to figure out that the scream was Todd's. He was farther away from the shuttle than the other crew members, and something had wrapped around his calves and boots. Todd's arms flailed, trying to keep his balance, but gravity messed with him, making him bounce the more he struggled.

Now, I noticed that something was moving underneath the sand, trying to catch up to us. Oh, no. Fuck no. It slithered in a snake-like side wind, shifting from side to side in a restless vibration. It was fast, and there was obviously not just the one following us. I had a very bad feeling there were many more underneath our feet, and if they weren't there yet, well, they were coming. And here I thought I'd had my fill of pesky alien life forms for the day.

Todd had not managed to get any closer to the shuttle. In fact, he'd almost made his way farther from it. Ian and Aleksy shooed everyone else onboard, then came back outside to help. Luckily, they had more guns with them when they returned. Ian ran to Todd's aid while Aleksy stood at the bottom of the ramp and shot at a few spots in the sand on either side of us.

The bright lights and sharp, high-pitched sound of the laser made me jump more and more each time they shot.

Ian shot wildly around Todd's body, at every spot he saw movement, all while Todd sobbed and moaned helplessly. It was nauseating to watch, but so more haunting to hear as the echoes of Todd's pleas for help echoed within our helmets.

One of the wretched things struck out at Harper, and the next thing I knew, she fell head-first in the sand. I didn't want to stop running, nor did Jules, I'm sure—but damn it all to hell. We had to. We couldn't just *leave* her, even if a small part of me wanted to for how she froze up when Darrien was attacked.

Despite my natural instinct to fly, fly away as fast and high as I could—Jules and I abruptly stopped in our tracks.

"Harper?" Jules asked, breathlessly.

We couldn't see her face, but her body squirmed and thrashed around in the sand—similar to the creatures that attacked her. Harper's feet kicked wildly. One of the creatures had made its way around her right ankle. Unfortunately, that meant I was finally face-to-face with the things causing so much mayhem, and I really wish I could have avoided it altogether.

It was an ugly leviathan of a creature. One that I knew would haunt my nightmares until I took my very last breath. I had come across, observed, and researched a wide variety of organisms in my career that weren't my favorite. In fact, a lot of them downright made my skin crawl. I'd encountered hundreds of Madagascar's famous hissing cockroaches, handled the world's largest leopard slugs in the Mediterranean, dissected not one, but two blob-fish in graduate school, had blood sprayed on my neck and chin from a rescued horned lizard at the conservatory, but the second I looked down at what held Harper down in the sand, I was disgusted to my core.

It was several feet in length and looked like what I'd imagine a centipede-worm hybrid would. It was the same color as the sand—the perfect camouflage, just like the stem of the murderous flower that stabbed through Darrien's chest. Now that it was out of its hiding place, we could see its severe, sharp antennae, hundreds of legs on either side of its thin body, a stinger that reminded me way too much of my knife, and *teeth*. Razor-sharp teeth. It did not have much of a protective shell on it, such as a centipede or millipede, leaving the creature able to wrap easily around its prey. However, the top of the monster had more spikes, which made it harder to hit.

Luckily for Harper, at least from what I could tell in the hysteria, the thing did not have anything horrible and pointy on its underside. Not so lucky for Harper... the rows of small, pointed teeth were chomping wildly as the alien lunged for one of her legs.

"Harper!" Jules shouted.

All around us, more of the sand worms slithered ominously underneath the sand, like sharks circling prey in the ocean at dusk. I knew we had to act. *Fast.*

Todd screamed again, and this time his voice was coated with true pain. I shuddered and tried to focus on Harper, all while keeping my peripheral on the moving sand on either side of me.

Aleksy shot at one of the monsters that was close to double the size of the others I'd seen. I looked away and tried to delete it from my memory. Ian half dragged Todd in the direction of the shuttle, all while one of the worms still clung to his chest and one of his arms. It was a damn good thing that spacesuits would repair and neutralize any foreign atmospheric gasses if we got tears in our suits. Otherwise, every single one of us would be beyond help.

"Cover me?" I asked Jules.

I turned to face her so she could see the seriousness of my request. She stared at me with large eyes but nodded. She raised her gun in preparation while I repositioned the knife in my hand. It turned out that my knife had come in handy much more than I'd originally thought. A part of me didn't think I'd ever let it leave my side again.

"Get it *off!*" Harper belted.

"Trying my best here!"

I didn't know how to kill the ugly motherfucker without stabbing Harper in the leg in the process. I was concerned I'd hit a major artery or hit a bone. Unfortunately for me, I didn't have many options left, because more evil worms were drawing into me. Closer by the second. I jumped when Jules shot at one behind me with a loud crack.

I took in the worm's weaker areas and thought about what would do the most damage. It wouldn't be able to do as much without its head, obviously. Or a giant stinger. Then again, it could simply roll over and impale Harper in more places than one once I decapitated or cut it, and it would all be for naught anyway.

With a shake of my head, I decided I needed to make a choice. Time was not on my side. Jules was covering my ass, and no one was covering hers, except for Aleksy, but he was yards and yards away from us.

"Hurry, please," Jules muttered as she shot at a couple of other areas nearby.

Knife in my dominant hand, I gripped my knuckles so hard around the hilt—as though I was holding on for dear life—and then I stabbed its head. It had been about to lunge at Harper again. My aim was definitely off, but I successfully damaged the side of its ugly head.

The worst hissing sound I'd ever heard erupted from the

creature's fanged mouth. It writhed wildly, fortunately releasing the majority of Harper in the process.

So, I swiped at it again. And again. The other side of its body arched up and struck down. Jules barely managed to drag Harper out of its way, and the stinger missed her leg by a couple of centimeters.

Harper stumbled her way back up to standing, somehow unscathed. As Jules helped her move in the direction of the shuttle, she looked behind them and shot at the wounded worm. The atrocious hissing ceased, but its body still writhed around as the creature slid around in a puddle of what I could only assume was its blood—though it wasn't red. It was a silvery, milky substance.

"Hurry up, Blaine!" Jules ordered. "I can't do anything for you if you just stand there!"

It took me a few seconds to realize that's exactly what I'd been doing. I hastily moved to catch up with them and did my best to ignore the moving sand surrounding us.

By the shuttle, Aleksy was still shooting at the ground. As we grew closer, he turned his attention to us and shot wildly—with a precision unknown to me—in front of us, behind us, and to both sides of us. For a second, I thought he'd been aiming *for* us. My legs grew shakier with each movement I made, but I fought to keep going with the promise to myself that I could rest back on the *Hippogriff*.

Ian dragged Todd up the ramp now, and Raymond met him halfway to help. At least he'd grown a pair and come back to help near the end of the battle. The things were thankfully no longer around Todd's legs. Even in the distance, through his navy space suit, I could see dark stains of blood around his shins. His helmeted head lolled to the side, presumably unconscious.

One of the worms sprung out of the sand and lunged at Aleksy.

"*Umierać!*" Aleksy belted. I had no idea what that meant, but watching Aleksy shoot at one of the monsters while it was still mid-air, and then dropping dead to the ground, was extremely badass, and I hoped I got to make him a drink later to thank him for it.

Finally, the lines and features in Aleksy's face became more prominent, and before I knew it, my boots slammed onto the ramp, and Aleksy was patting my back and shoving me forward, all while shooting one-handed. Jules pushed Harper forward with me. We tumbled back and into the shuttle, both of us landing roughly on our asses and bouncing until we hit the back wall.

"Jules!" Harper yelled, out of breath.

Ian went out to help once more. "We have to shut the ramp!"

"No shit!" Jules fired back. "But how do we do that without one of these hideous things jumping on board?"

"You're going to have to start pulling in the ramp and shoot until it's almost up all the way," Harper groaned. She crawled to one of the seats and pulled herself up.

I glanced around the small confines of the shuttle and didn't see Lata or Darrien anywhere. Raymond and Saba were crouched together on the seats farthest away from the shuttle's ramp, and Todd had been left, still unconscious, in the middle of the seats on the ground. I was comforted by the small rise and fall of his chest. At least he was alive.

"That doesn't sound like the safest plan," Ian yelled as he shot another acid-green beam out into the sand.

"You got a better idea?" Harper said, almost hysterical, and laughing into her mic.

"Uh..." It didn't take Ian long to make up his mind. "No. No, I don't."

My body was unmoving. I wanted to check on Todd. I wanted to go find Darrien and Lata and make sure that Darrien was okay, and I wanted to take his stupid helmet off and kiss him until he was all better. I needed to know that he was alive. But my bones were jelly, and my mind was a haze. I didn't even flinch as the last shots went out into the air, or as one of the monsters almost made it on the ramp and into the shuttle. Its head had managed to get almost to the door, right near my feet, before Aleksy decapitated it with a long knife I hadn't seen him pull out. The hissing sounded again, but thankfully, finally...*finally* —the door to the shuttle closed, and the sand-worm flopped off the ramp and fell to the ground as it did. Immediately after the door closed, Ian went over to the control panel on the side of it and pressed whatever he had to in order to secure the hatch. A much more comforting hiss let us all know we were safe.

ONCE THE ATMOSPHERE inside the shuttle was back to normal, Ian and Jules helped us take our helmets off. Harper took her own off and then sat back in one of the seats with her head back. She was seemingly unscathed, but she was pale and full of shock. Just like I was. Just like everyone was. We hadn't managed to contact the main ship and let them know we were okay yet. No one talked. Hardly anyone moved. Every time I closed my eyes, I saw one of the mega-centipede-worm monsters lunging wildly with its ugly legs. I couldn't get the vision of their serrated teeth out of my head—the way it moved its terrible head back and forth, ready to take our flesh as their lunch. Shivers ran up and down my spine.

I was sitting on the floor, lazily leaning my head back against one of the seats. At first, it had been disorienting not to have the helmet on anymore. I'd hated the confinement, but I guess I'd gotten used to the lights flashing on the screen, my stats, and the weird mics.

Jules and Ian sat on the floor next to me. They leaned against the door that led into the flight deck, both with their knees up. They rested their chins on their kneecaps and wrapped their arms around their legs.

Todd rested on some of the seats, and Aleksy tended to him quietly. Occasionally, Todd would let out a small noise of pain, and Aleksy would remark that he was lucky that the wounds he'd gotten weren't worse. Or, he'd cuss something under his breath. I didn't know much about Todd, but I remembered how dramatic he'd been after we woke from hyper-sleep. I was sure he wasn't the best patient to tend to, but I was still relieved that he was breathing.

Raymond still sat next to his wife on the farthest seat from the door. He held his head in his hands and occasionally let out a very long, defeated-sounded sigh. I wondered if he felt guilty for running when Darrien had been attacked. I would have. Saba lazily ran her hand up and down Raymond's back while she stared at nothing in particular on the wall.

My eyes stung with exhaustion, and my bones ached. The headache that had eased up a bit post-almost suffocating was creeping back. My throat was raw and felt like sandpaper, and I would kill for a glass of water.

My backpack was still strapped on, acting like a pillow for the curve of my back. With a small groan, I leaned forward and shimmied it off. My ribs and calves tightened and protested with the small movement. I opened the pack with my now ungloved fingers and grabbed for the water bottle that had made its way to the very bottom.

I downed half of the bottle in several swigs, then wiped my lips with the outside of my hand. I readjusted the samples in the bag, situated them properly in the encased pack before zipping it up again, and then caught Ian looking at me. I cocked an eyebrow at him.

A small smile spread on his full lips. "We're okay," was all he said.

Jules and I nodded. Todd grunted, and Aleksy let off a dark chuckle.

"Where did Lata and Darrien go?" I asked no one in particular.

Jules pointed at the door across from where she and Ian sat; it was the door I wondered about when we had first boarded so long ago.

"I think they went into the emergency chambers," Jules said.

"The what?"

No one had told us about an emergency chamber before we left. Was that a thing that every shuttle had? I guess it would have to be. And also—is that where the bathroom was? Because, if so, my bladder would greatly appreciate it.

"The emergency chambers," Ian said as he stretched out his legs with a groan, "is exactly what it sounds like. They can accommodate us if we need them to, in some cases for weeks. The door's open if you want to go check on him."

Him. I held his gaze a little longer than normal. He'd said him and not them. Why did he say it like that?

"Are there also bathrooms back there?" I asked, brushing Ian's comment off as swiftly as I could. I stood up slowly, and my legs screamed at me in response. Ian nodded. "Good. Otherwise, this shuttle would be inhumane."

Jules chuckled softly. I walked by Todd and Aleksy and observed the damage. Some of the spikes from each sand-worm had dug into his calves and ankles. Aleksy had to cut Todd's suit at the knee. I wondered if he'd had to use a special tool or something for that, seeing as the suits were prone to stitching up magically after being severed.

Even though the punctures didn't look pleasant, they seemed mostly superficial. Aleksy had him almost bandaged and taken care of. I noticed that Todd's face was completely relaxed, though his breathing was hard.

I stopped behind Aleksy and asked, "Is he asleep?"

"Yes," he muttered. "Fucking finally. Easier to do all of dees and give him de anti-venom widout his complaints every second."

I cracked a grin, then asked, "Is the anti-venom just a precaution?"

Aleksy nodded and turned his head around to meet my face. His glacier eyes looked me up and down. "Do you need someding?"

I shook my head. "No. Just going to go check on Darrien and Lata."

He nodded. "Tell dat woman to come find me when she can." With a wink, he turned his attention back to the unconscious Todd and took out a needle from his kit.

I passed Ray and Saba, then stood in front of the door to the "emergency chambers." I realized I had no idea how to open it. There was no little thumb pad for me to press and magically swing the door open, nor was there a simple door handle because that would've been too easy.

Before I could turn around and ask for help, Ian was beside me. He placed a large hand in the center of the door, and a keypad came to life, glowing a bright cherry red. Ian slowly typed the numbers in front of me so that I could do it myself next time: 2123. Well, it was simple enough to remember the year we were in. Ian looked at me and smiled, then turned to walk away without a word right as the door slid open and revealed a much larger part of the shuttle.

How did I not know this was here? I'd thought where we sat for the shuttle ride seemed cramped compared to the large shuttle before we boarded back on the Mothership, but I never figured there'd be a whole other part to it.

The door slid shut behind me after I stepped into a room several times larger than the seating area I'd come from. There was a small kitchen to the right, and a couple of couches on the other side, next to a couple of doors and a coffee table in between. Everything was less glamorous than what we had on the *Hippogriff* but still clean and welcoming. There was a single door beside the entrance to the kitchen. It had the universal sign which meant a bathroom lived inside: a toilet.

As much as I wanted to find Darrien and Lata first, my bladder directed me into the room. Inside was indeed a toilet, but also a nice, enclosed shower with a bench. I made a note to take advantage of that later if we planned on staying longer.

After relieving my bladder and washing my hands, I made my way back into the weird living room kitchen area. The kitchen had a full refrigerator, and after some rummaging, turned out to be fully stocked with full water bottles, snacks, and beer. Nice to know they gave us alcohol post-disaster. There was a small cupboard full of Meals Ready to Eat and liquor, too.

The two doors by the couches didn't have a symbol on them like the bathroom, so I chose the left one. It was a room, not much bigger than my bedroom back on the main ship, with three sets of bunk beds, made up perfectly with fluffy comforters and pillows left askew from the flight. Besides that, there was a closet on either side. I closed the door.

Darrien had to be in the other room. My heart hammered a little as paranoid thoughts tiptoed into my psyche. What if they'd disappeared and were actually not on the shuttle? What if he was dead, or so hurt that Lata couldn't help him? I swallowed roughly and took a breath before opening the other door.

It was a room almost identical to the other one, only a little bigger. There were still three rows of bunks, but also a couch. To the right of the last bunk bed, I noticed a door that was left cracked open. I was starting to reconsider how large this shuttle actually was.

None of the beds in the room were pulled down. Lata and Darrien had to be in the next room. So, again, I found myself pushing another door open and walking into a new room. But this time, I found what I'd been looking for immediately.

This bathroom was massive compared to the one I'd just used. Three separate, private showers were against the main wall, with doors and concealed walls. Two racks of towels sat on either side of them, also a bit askew from the journey, and there was a foyer portion where the sinks lived, where I stood— and that's where Darrien laid on top of very expensive towels in the middle of a tiled floor, with Lata bent over him.

Darrien's suit had been cut all the way down to his hips. I sat down across from Lata and took everything in: the pool of blood, stale and fresh, underneath his shoulder, the medical supplies were strewn across the floor, Lata compressing the wound in Darrien's chest while attempting to work on the other.

Wordlessly, I took the compression over in my own hands.

Lata looked up briefly, as though she had no idea who I was for a second, and then nodded as if to say *Oh, thank God.*

I wondered if the wound in his chest had been taken care of already, or if I was simply trying to stop the bleeding.

Darrien's eyes fluttered a little—just enough to peek at me through the veil of his thick eyelashes. I could tell he was trying to smile, reassure me, or say something. But he was pale, and he was in no shape to speak. Sweat beaded his upper lip, and gray shadows dusted the space underneath his lids.

His entire chest and abdomen was covered in various layers of blood. A lot of it was dried and caked on, while some meshed with the new flow of maroon. I grabbed the hand of his that was closest to mine with my open one and squeezed.

"Update?" I asked. It came out almost like a beg.

Lata changed her latex gloves and replaced them with a fresh pair, then tore into a fresh suture kit, as well as a tube that I knew contained a gel that would speed up healing by enhancing repair proteins to damaged cells faster than with natural healing.

"He's lucky," she huffed. "The stab to his chest? Missed every major bone and organ. It's almost a fucking miracle." She readied her needle and began to work again. I assumed he was already numb. "And thankfully, this shoulder wound is mostly shallow. That thing got him bloody good, though. It's a damn good thing I got to him when I did."

"Did you already, um, fix his chest?" I breathed.

Darrien was hard to look at in this state; unmoving, weak, tired, and much too pale.

"Mhm." She nodded. "First thing I did. He desperately needs blood though."

"How do we get that? I mean–"

She looked up at me mid-suture and gave me a serious look.

A look that told me to calm myself, or I might worry Darrien even more than he already was.

"Darrien's blood type is O neg," she sighed. "Coincidentally, so is yours, from what your chart said."

In an attempt to joke around like this wasn't happening, I said, "Stalking my chart now, are we?" but it came out weak.

"Aleksy and I looked over and memorized everyone's medical histories and charts as best we could before we left this morning, just as a precaution." She paused. "And now, I'm very glad we did. Because otherwise, I wouldn't know your blood types, I wouldn't know that Darrien is allergic to most antibiotics, and luckily I packed the one he *isn't* allergic to, just in case, right at the last moment." Lata lifted her head and beamed.

I thought of the Captain coming back with more supplies before we boarded the shuttle.

"Wow," was all I could really utter. "Just–wow."

"So, you ready to give Dr. Park some of your good stuff?" she asked.

I blushed, even though I knew she meant my blood and not something...else. I nodded. "What supplies do you need?"

She cocked her head to the gloves beside her inside an airtight bag. "It's okay to stop the pressure on his chest now. If you can, find a blood kit. You'll know when you see it. It might be on the fucking floor, but I think it's still in the bag, in one of the pockets on the inside. Then, glove up."

Cautiously, I removed both of my hands from Darrien, though I didn't want to. His hand was so cold in mine, and I wanted to warm him and give him what little I could offer. I moved around to the side Lata was on and rummaged through her pack after not seeing any kits on the tile. After a couple of minutes of throwing around medical supplies like it was candy in a piñata, I found the blood kit and set it beside her. Then, I snapped on my gloves like I was told, and held my arms up in the air so I wouldn't touch anything and contaminate my hands.

"Great," Lata said. "The gloves aren't super necessary, but the more sterile our environment is, the better." Lata looked around the mess of the bathroom with wide eyes and shook it off with a jerk of her head.

She worked to bandage Darrien up and then ran over to one of the sinks. She took her gloves off once more, and then scrubbed from the petite tips of her fingers, all the way up to her elbows. Lata had somehow managed to undo her spacesuit alone or cut it, and the top part now hung off of her like a wetsuit, leaving her almost bare in a bralette that didn't leave much to the imagination.

"Stop checking me out!" Lata giggled at me from where our eyes locked in the mirror's reflection.

I bit my lower lip but smiled. "Sorry—didn't mean to."

"Yeah, yeah, that's what they all say." She winked. "Okay, come over here."

I got up again and moved over to the sinks beside her.

"Unfortunately, now it's your turn."

Before I could reply, Lata took a pair of trauma shears that I hadn't noticed before, and cut my suit from the neckline, all the way down to my hips. Now, we matched. Sadly, I was heavier chested, and felt more exposed in the thin, scarcely padded sports bra they'd allowed me to wear under the suit; it was nowhere as nice looking as Lata's.

But Lata paid no mind to any of that. She was a freaking doctor, after all. I felt silly for feeling self-conscious about the situation we were in. Lata grabbed for more soap and a towel, and then lathered down my right arm from above my elbow, all the way down. Then, she wiped me off and patted me with a dry washcloth before finding sterile wipes from her pack that were on the floor, and wiping me down yet again.

"You good with needles?"

Her velvety cocoa eyes shot up to meet mine. No, I was not good with needles. Like most sane people. I immediately broke out in a nervous sweat.

I shook my head and bit the inside of my cheek. "I just don't like them. I'll be more than fine. Not like I'm gonna pass out or anything."

Except for the first time I'd had to give blood, where I very much did pass out before they'd even stuck me. I wondered if Lata knew about that because of my chart, too.

Her eyebrows rose. "Go sit down."

She pulled her long, very thick hair back into a high pony-tail, washed her hands again, and came back over to Darrien and me. After throwing on another pair of gloves, she took the blood kit and began to set it all up. I did my best not to look at what she was doing, or think about what was about to go into my arm, and tried to focus on Darrien instead. I knew that he needed my blood, and bad. His eyes were barely open, and his breathing was heavy. His need was my motivator. I could do this for him.

"Stay with us, Dr. Park," Lata said loudly. His eyes fluttered open a little.

"Daph." I thought I'd heard him say my nickname, but it was so hard to hear his almost silent whisper.

"We're going to get some of my blood into you, okay?" I reassured him. I leaned down close to his ear so he could hear me, but my hair fell down into his face, so I sat back up.

"First, I need a small sample of your blood. I have to test it and make sure that your ABO and RH types are compatible." Lata stared at all of the blood on the ground from Darrien. "I have enough of his. I'll need a small sample of yours before we begin."

"How can you test that without a lab?" I asked, my voice a little higher than normal. It sounded foreign to me in my ears.

What if I wasn't the right match? What if no one on the shuttle was? My hands started shaking.

"We have a travel tester for situations like these," Lata said. She held up a tiny box that resembled an eyeglasses case in her hands.

Lata opened the case and took out a glucometer. "Usually, I would take a sample from your finger, but time is of the essence, and I'm running out of gloves." She was on me in a flash, and before I knew it, there was a sharp pain in my hip, and it was done. "Sorry," she muttered.

But she wasn't focusing on me. She was moving at lightning speed, getting my blood and Darrien's blood, putting them in their proper places within the test, and turning it on. A small beep sounded, and she bent over to look at the small device with the most serious expression I'd ever seen on her face. Her lips were turned down, her thick brows knitted together, and she clenched her jaw as she calculated.

Please, let me be a match, I pleaded to no one in particular, but I pleaded nonetheless.

"Yes!" Lata said.

I let out a relieved sigh. Lata even pumped her fist in the air a little with her victory.

"Okay, Daphne, I know you're a lying little shit and you hate needles more than you let on." She smirked at me, and I knew she'd definitely read about my fainting incident in my chart. "So, I need you to focus on your breathing. Got it? And let me know if you feel faint."

Darrien's head moved a little in my direction. His eyes,

only open to narrow slits, looked up at me. "Don't. Pass. Out."
He managed a whisper.

I smiled down at him. "I won't. I've been through too much today to pass out over a needle."

"That's exactly right." Lata managed a small laugh.

So, I did. I focused on my breathing—five seconds in, five seconds out—and I thought about anything and everything other than the stupid needle about to enter my vein. I stared down at Darrien's hand, and I thought about my sweet baby boy, waiting for me back on the *Hippogriff*; how it felt when his slender arms wrapped around me, and how my heart swelled each time he gave me a sassy comeback when we were joking around. I thought about Dad. About how strong he was, and I remembered all of our late nights together, talking and crying and laughing when life around us crumbled more and more every day. I thought about how fortunate I was to have a small family who I'd kill for. I thought about Matthew and Magda, and my mother, wherever she ended up. And then I thought about the warmth and comfort of Darrien's hand, and how it made me feel something I hadn't felt in so long during our ride to planet Virginia.

"Okay, you're done, Daphne," Lata said.

I hadn't even felt it.

"Damn, you're good," I said.

Lata smiled and did a little dance. "Don't I know it."

The crimson blood ran from a small tube down from my arm, and into a bag that Lata held up.

"Won't take long," she said. "Maybe ten minutes or so. I *am* going to take a little more blood from you than I normally would, because he's lost a lot, and he needs it more than you do. You can manage to give a little more than normal, but you're going to feel weak afterward."

I gulped but nodded my approval.

"I'm going to get you both some towels to use as pillows. You're more than likely going to want to lie down soon."

I was beginning to wonder how long we'd all be in this bathroom, or on the shuttle, for that matter. I hoped that someone had contacted Captain Carnell, and let him know we were all, *mostly*, all right.

Lata came back with four fluffy towels in her arms. She set two underneath Darrien's head, and then she put two in place for me. I laid down and situated my neck atop the towels. If I hadn't had a needle in my arm, or if I hadn't been too worried about Darrien's well-being, I may have passed out from exhaustion right then and there.

Darrien and I were side by side, almost as though we were laying down in a bed. I wished for a mattress instead of cold floors. Heck, even a blanket would have been nice. The uncovered portion of my body had begun to grow cold after Lata ripped my suit.

"How long will it take for my blood to help him?" I asked Lata as she checked Darrien's temperature and other stats.

She shrugged with one shoulder and began to scrub the blood that had dried all over him with a wet rag. Her movements were delicate and tender, but precise. Darrien had closed his eyes, but as Lata continued cleaning him, he peeked through his heavy lids at her, then at me.

"No need to thank me, Darrien," Lata said. She pulled out several wet wipes from somewhere nearby and cleaned the areas that she had missed. "You'll be fixed up soon, and you'll feel much better." Lata turned her eyes to me again. "As for how long... well, I'd say an hour or so, but once you're done giving the blood, I'll just have you stay for a little while so I'm sure you don't pass out on me or anything else."

I rolled my eyes. Stupid medical chart.

"Can we get a couple of blankets?"

Lata nodded and left the room. When she came back, she covered both of our legs with a comforter taken from one of the bunk beds.

"Thank you," I said groggily.

"Both of you rest. I'm going to go check on Aleksy and the others, then I'll be back."

Before leaving, she dimmed the lights in the bathroom and shut the door gently behind her.

7

MY BLOOD

It wasn't long before I felt woozy. As the minutes slowly ticked by, I felt worse. Near the end of it, a severe nausea rippled through me in small waves. I had moved to a more comfortable position on my side, facing Darrien, with my legs curled up into a fetal position when Lata finally came back and graciously took the needle out of my arm.

"Good job, babe," Lata said. She brushed my hair back a little, then quickly moved to get Darrien set up.

I'd been gone for a while and was surprised no one else had come to check in on us.

"Aleksy wanted me to send you," I said. Talking to Lata was a good distraction from the dizziness. Watching as she set up Darrien's IV, however, was not. I squeezed my eyes shut.

She snorted. "Of course. And I will go out and check back in later, but there are more pressing matters currently."

"Don't we have to leave soon?"

Lata didn't respond for a bit, but I knew better than to open my eyes. Instead, I focused on counting backwards from one hundred, and taking deep breaths through my nose.

"Hmm," Lata finally sounded. "I don't know. Probably? I am as new to all of this science fiction, NASA crap as you are."

She paused once more, then I heard her rustling around. "He's all set up. It'll take a bit, like I said, but he should be feeling better after a while." Lata exhaled a deep sigh of relief. "I also gave him some painkillers, so he might be loopy here in a while, which I personally cannot wait to witness."

I grinned and opened my eyes. Lata was standing and disposing of packaging and everything else she no longer needed into a biohazard bag that I guessed was in her med kit. Instead of cleaning herself up, as she was *also* very covered in blood, I watched her pick up all the things that had rolled and shot out of her kit, and put them all back where they belonged. After that, she went and washed her hands for what felt like the fiftieth time, splashed some water on her face, and then came back to my side.

"Are you good to stay here with him? Are you okay?"

I wanted to tell her I was still a bit nauseous, but more than that, I wanted her to go and see if she could help Aleksy with Todd. I wanted Darrien to feel better, and I wanted everyone to be fine so that we could get off of this stupid planet as soon as possible.

With a small nod, I said, "Of course. We're good here."

She patted me on the shoulder, then walked away. "Be back in a flash. Aleksy needed some more gauze. I'll check in with Harper, too, and see if we'll be leaving soon or not."

I waved to her, and she blew me a kiss. The door opened and then closed, and it was just me and Darrien again. I shivered a little, and though I wanted to pull the comforter up to my chin, it couldn't go over Darrien's hips. The cool tile did help with the nausea a bit, luckily. The baby hairs closest to Darrien's hairline stuck to his head, secured there by his sweat. His long lashes were still, and I knew he was finally resting. I took the opportunity to take in the sight of him fully, without fear he would catch me staring.

His skin was still much too pale, which made his freckles seem darker than they actually were, and that unnerved me. I wanted his sun-kissed, warm skin tone to return. I wanted Darrien alert and cracking jokes, not on pain meds and covered in his own sweat and blood.

More than that, I wanted to lean over and kiss him.

But, I stayed put from where I laid on my side while making sure his chest continued to rise and fall with each breath, just like I'd done when Jaxon was a newborn when I'd been terrified he would simply cease to exist because he had been much too perfect to be real; so small and fragile and breakable.

It really had been miraculous that the weird flower's spear hadn't penetrated Darrien in any vital organs. As soon as I'd seen him get stabbed the second time, I thought for sure he would meet his end. But here he was, getting fresh blood pumped into his system. Breathing.

Darrien let out a low moan and shifted ever so slightly. The floor was not the coziest place, but the makeshift pillows helped a little. I wondered if Lata came back with Aleksy or someone else if they could move him to one of the beds in the other room.

"Are you okay?" I asked softly, in case he was asleep.

He shifted his head in my direction and opened those captivating eyes. They were wider now, and more alert. I couldn't see how much blood he had taken so far in the dim light, but it seemed it was starting to make a difference.

His slightly curled hair toppled over onto his forehead and stuck to his sweaty skin. Without much thought or hesitation, I reached out a hand and pushed the thick locks from his face.

"Did today ruin swimming for you?" he whispered.

I drew my hand back to rest on my hip. That was not what I had expected him to be concerned about. He had a way of always catching me off guard. I was about to reassure him that it hadn't made a difference, but I truly didn't know if it had or not.

"Maybe. I hope not," I said honestly. "Darrien. Please. Are you okay?"

A small smile tugged at one corner of his lips. "I've certainly been better." His smile faltered a little. "You and the others were right."

"What? What do you mean?"

He motioned weakly at his chest with a hand. "We should have waited. Done more research. Had more precautions in place."

"So, you're saying I was...right?" I said, unable to stop my smile.

"Yes," Darrien said. "Which is a very hard thing for me to admit."

I couldn't help the small snort of a laugh that came from my chest. He smiled fully, then. I hadn't done it on purpose, but as we looked at each other, I realized my bent knees touched his hip. My upper body was only a few inches from his wounded shoulder. I scooched back a little. The last thing I wanted to do was bump into him and hurt him even more.

"I'm fine," he said in a throaty voice. "Come back."

I stared at him but did what he said. I moved in closer so that there was hardly a centimeter between our bodies. His lips were parted like he wanted to tell me something important.

"Daphne."

"Darrien?"

He took in a large breath and inched even closer to where our noses could almost brush up against each other.

"As soon as I'm better, I am going to kiss you so goddamn hard."

My heart pounded uncontrollably. I could feel each beat on every inch of my skin.

"Would you be alright with that?" he whispered, as though he was uncertain.

I nodded and traced his lower lip with my shaky thumb. His lower lip was plump and chilled and I internally begged his body to warm.

"But, I don't want our first kiss to be on the floor of a bathroom while your blood is being pumped into my body," he noted with a toothy grin. The color was beginning to come back into his cheeks.

"Okay," I agreed.

I was fine with that. I didn't want it to be here, either, on the cold floor, blood all over the tile. Every part of my body throbbed and felt weak, too. Still, I couldn't help it as I stretched my neck over and kissed down his sharp jawline. A jaw wasn't a mouth. It didn't count.

His eyes closed, and a pleasant, deep sound erupted from his chest which made my knees weaker than they already were. My tongue trailed down his jaw, to the soft area right beneath his earlobe. I swirled my tongue around that soft patch of skin, and then nipped at his lobe softly. My hand rested on the other side of his neck, caressing and in need.

The door to the bathroom opened, and I stopped—which was great timing. I'd needed to be stopped. The poor man had just been stabbed twice, and I was trying to eat him up like dessert. My hand retreated, and I moved away from his body, immediately missing the feel of his arm and neck against mine. His eyes opened again and flashed to mine with desire, and his cheeks were fully flushed. He exhaled shakily and winked at me before closing his eyes once more.

Lata, Aleksy, and Jules came in and looked down at us. Lata bent down and checked on Darrien's blood bag.

"You two seem cozy," Aleksy laughed in that husky way that he did.

A blush made its way up from my stomach all the way to my neck and to my cheeks. "Any word from the Captain?" I asked, hoping to pull all of the attention off of Darrian and me.

Jules leaned against the wall and crossed her legs and arms. Instead of her usual neutral or happy expression, her eyes were cold, and her mouth was turned down. There was something wrong. Lata and Aleksy didn't answer me, either. I did my best, even though I still felt weak, and moving made my nausea return, to prop up to a sitting position.

"What?" I asked again. "What is it?"

Jules sighed and slipped down the wall to sit on the floor. "Once Harper got over her shock, she began going over the launch status precautions that we always do before lift-off. We both communicated with the Captain back on the Mother-ship, as well."

She stopped and closed her eyes. Lata busied herself with cleaning up more medical supplies, and Aleksy walked over to the sinks, as he was covered in Todd's blood.

"Jules?" I begged.

Darrien didn't take his eyes off me. One of his fingers brushed against my thigh and moved in a fluid back-and-forth motion.

Jules looked up at the ceiling as she explained. "Something is wrong with the shuttle. Harper wanted to go back outside and check it out, but Ian and I wouldn't let her. Obviously." She chuckled darkly. "That woman is hard to tame, as you all know, I'm sure. Anyway, we think that those—centipede things—did damage to the shuttle."

I paused with my mouth hanging open. Lata rubbed at her

eyes with her fingertips, and Aleksy came back and sat by her. He gently placed a large, meaty hand on his wife's arm.

"So," Jules continued, "The good news is that those fuckers seem to have gone elsewhere. At least for now. The camera footage we had showed us that they retreated back to whatever hellacious part of the planet they came from about half an hour ago. They didn't damage anything that will make our oxygen run out, so that's really good. But, they *did* puncture a considerable amount of the main engines, and some of a rudder, which essentially means–"

"Essentially, we are fucked," Aleksy finished for her.

Jules rolled her eyes and Lata swatted at the top of Aleksy's head.

"The *shuttle* is fucked, sure," Jules snapped. "But Captain Carnell is sending another one."

Thank fuck. I exhaled the breath I'd been holding and eased back onto my elbows.

"Unfortunately," Jules started again, "the star has set on this planet already. We thought we'd have more light, but it turns out that planet Virginia gets about two hours less daylight than Earth."

"So, that means we have to wait until morning for the other shuttle?" I guessed.

Jules nodded.

"Wonderful," I muttered. "So, as soon as the sun rises, Carnell will come with another shuttle?"

Aleksy shook his head as Jules avoided my gaze to look down at her feet.

"No," Aleksy said. He turned to look at me. "Carnell must stay on de ship. He cannot leave Emma and your father alone dere."

It took me a moment to realize what he meant. Even

Darrien's fingers halted in their caress for a few seconds. *No. Absolutely not.*

"Are you telling me that my father, who hasn't been on a spaceship in over three decades, is going to be the one to come get us?" My voice was sharp and demanding and cut through the room like a jagged shard of glass.

No one answered me. I had my answer.

"Are you fucking with me?" I laughed darkly and blinked away hot tears.

"Daphne, it's the only option we have," Jules said softly. "You were chosen for this mission, but so was he. He was an amazing engineer back in his day."

The sudden urge to punch something overtook whatever rational thoughts I had left. My jaw clenched, and I tried to breathe, but I couldn't. I didn't even know if Dad had ever flown a ship. I knew he'd been on the *Griffin 3* with my mother as an engineer, but I had no idea what his job was other than to work on and maintain the engines while in space.

"Does he even know how to fly one of these things?" I gritted. I wanted to talk to Carnell and yell at him myself.

"Um, I think the Captain is going to give him an extensive run down tonight," Jules said. Before I could snap again, she quickly added, "But, Daphne, he used to design and test the ships. He knows how it all works—the technology of flying isn't much different than it was when he worked for NASA. And, truthfully, the shuttles are pretty easy to fly. I talked about it with him and the Captain. He sounded confident."

Of course, he would sound that way. Because I was stuck on a strange planet, and he was up in the spaceship and he wouldn't allow that. Dad would do anything to get me back safely, and I knew it. Otherwise, he would have given everyone the middle finger and that would be that.

My eyes stung, and I wiped at a tear before it could roll

down my face. No one spoke for several stressful minutes. Darrien closed his eyes, but I knew he was still awake. I wanted to lay back down with him again, and I wanted everyone else to leave us.

"So, we're stuck here for the night," I said once I calmed down and my body stopped vibrating with fear and fury.

"Mhm," Lata grunted.

"And those things are out there," I said. "And they might come back and fuck with the shuttle again. Or worse."

"Yes," Jules said. "But we're probably going to be fine."

Probably.

"Well, aren't those just incredible odds?" I asked humorlessly before laying back down.

8

DIHYDROGEN MONOXIDE
EROTICA

The rest of the crew moved from the main shuttle and into the emergency chambers. It was five in the evening the next day back on the *Hippogriff*, but on planet Virginia, our day was just coming to a close. From the holographic camera feed that Harper had displayed on the main wall's room/kitchen area, all was still outside—at least, it seemed to be.

Todd was placed in the smaller of the two bedrooms, passed out on one of the lower bunks, still covered in blood and wearing his space suit. Darrien had been moved to one of the bunks in the bigger bedroom, and was in a similar position; lying in his blood-ridden space suit, or whatever was left of it, and covered in dried sweat and blood. He had luckily fallen asleep not long after. The pain meds made him extremely tired, but when he occasionally came to, his eyes were glazed over, and he would just smile at me like everything was hunky dory.

Lata told me that the blood I'd given had done wonders for Darrien, and that the healing agents, along with the painkillers she had administered helped him out a lot. Now, he just needed his rest so he could let the medicine work its magic.

I looked at the rest of us in the living room and thought it was close to a miracle that we had all made it back to the shuttle relatively unscathed. Raymond, who had apologized to Darrien more than once already, turned his guilt into acts of service, and worked to prepare us all some food from what he could scrounge up in the kitchen. Saba had asked if he needed help, but he had shooed her away. I couldn't tell what he was making from where I sat on one of the couches, but it smelled decent.

Lata had found extra clothing stored in the closets of both bedrooms, and I had changed into a pair of black sweatpants and a matching sweater top that had the Todd Darcy logo etched tastefully above the right breast. Lata wore the identical set in gray, and Aleksy had found a pair of athletic shorts and a simple t-shirt to replace his dirty suit.

Once Ian had made sure everyone was okay for the time being, he had practically raced into the larger of the bathrooms to take a shower. Jules and Harper, still in their suits, sat side-by-side on the couch next to ours looking debilitated but still alert. Harper wouldn't take her eyes off of the outside video cam, and Jules had her head leaned back. She wouldn't close her eyes or really rest, though. Not even for a minute.

My mind was racing. About Darrien, Dad and Jax, why we were even in the situation we were in, how NASA could be so fucking stupid to send us down to the planet so fast, how Captain Carnell was really going to send Dad to get us, about those fucking creatures outside and whether or not they'd come back, or if something worse would come and hunt is in the night.

I pondered whether things would have been better if Mars hadn't closed its borders in 2088. I wondered if the people who lived on the planet were still alive, or if they were all dead. I thought about how close science had come to saving us all when we'd discovered that one of Jupiter's moons was very similar to Earth, and how that sliver of hope had gone down the drain not long after, when the atmosphere turned out to be too toxic. I remembered all of the possible planets that NASA and the other space centers had thought were "it" throughout my lifetime.

And I remembered how each time they thought they'd had it, they'd failed.

What Darrien said earlier was true: there should have been more precautions set in place before we set our feet on a planet. Dad and I were right. This was lazy work; more research needed to be done in the future, if we were to leave the Mothership.

I understood that the Earth was dying and that the clock was ticking, but something about the hasty orders to come to planet Virginia didn't feel right to me. It hadn't felt right since our initial meeting. It was odd how the Captain had pushed. What good would finding a new planet to live on be if the majority of the space crew died?

I wanted to throw a fit after simmering in my thoughts for a while. I wanted to yell at Todd and at Harper and Jules, and even Ian a little bit. They had to know more than the rest of us did. Right? If Carnell knew something, they surely had to know about it.

Saba, who came around to sit near me, suddenly asked, "Is your head feeling better?"

I blinked at her. I'd forgotten everything and everyone around me for a few minutes, and coming back down to reality took me a few drawn out seconds. So, I nodded, even though there was still a dull pounding at the base of my skull.

Lata and Aleksy were making me drink water and eat a protein bar. I'd barely nibbled at the bar, but the water had helped a little. Whatever Ray was cooking now smelled very unappetizing. I should have been more hungry, but I wasn't. Instead, I was just pissed off. I didn't want to be in the room with any of them, really. Not even Lata and Aleksy were helping my mood.

"It's getting better, thanks," I managed. "I think I'm going to go check on Darrien and Todd," I told Lata. Which was only half true, because I didn't see the point in checking on Todd, nor did I particularly want to if he was sleeping. "I might just lie down for a bit, too."

Saba scrunched her brows. "Aren't you hungry?"

I glanced at the uneaten granola bar. "No, not really."

Lata took the bar from my hands but made sure I took the water with me.

"It's been a rough day," Lata said. "I'm sure you will want to eat later. If Darrien is awake and feeling better, let him know of the food?"

I nodded in agreement, though that didn't seem likely, and stood from the couch. Saba took my place next to Lata, and they began chatting about something meaningless as I made my way into the room where Darrien was.

As I closed the door behind me, Ian emerged from the bathroom wearing pajama bottoms and a long sleeve shirt. He waved at me and motioned for us to be quiet because of Darrien, who was breathing deeply on the bunk closest to us. In one hand, Ian held up his space suit and looked at me with a question in his eyes. I jerked my head toward the closet where an airtight hamper was. He gave me a smile and patted my shoulder, then dumped the suit and tiptoed out of the bedroom to the living area.

The room was almost as dark as the sky outside. The only light was that coming from the crack in the bathroom door, and even then, it was a dim one. I couldn't see Darrien very well, so I decided I'd just climb on the top bunk above him and rest until he woke up, and then I could ask if he needed anything. I was still pissed off at almost everyone on the shuttle, but I was especially angry with the Captain, and this time he wouldn't be able to schmooze me over so quickly. Things had to be different next time. If there was a next time.

I had climbed up a couple of rungs on the ladder when I felt a hand around my calf. I stilled and my breath turned shallow.

"Daph?" Darrien said quietly.

I jumped back down from the ladder and found his hand in the dark. My eyes had adjusted enough to see his outline a little in the dark blue-hued room. I managed to sit on the edge of the too-small bunk.

"Hey."

"Hi."

Neither one of us said anything more.

I attempted to clear my throat which had gone dry. "Are you okay?" I asked. "Do you need anything?"

When he spoke, I noticed that his voice was thick from sleep. "No," he murmured. "Unless you want to help me to the shower?"

"I–I might need help to move you if..."

His hand caressed my knee lightly. "No, I'm stronger. I can make it for the most part, I think." He paused. "But, if you want to rest, can you maybe get me Aleksy or Ray?"

"No," I said a little too fast, but I didn't want to sleep now that he was awake. I didn't want to ask anyone else to help him. "I can do it."

"Thank you," Darrien said as he moved himself up into a sitting position with a small groan. "I feel very, very gross. My body is making it hard to rest."

Despite his concerns, he didn't *smell* gross. His face was closer to me now, and he still smelled of sunshine and Earth. I lingered for a moment, then forced myself off of the bed. I rounded the bunks and opened the door to the bathroom wider, which let in enough light for me to see where our surroundings were so I could help him walk.

When I made it back to him, he was standing, but leaning against the bunks. The shadows that danced around the room from the bathroom accentuated the muscles of Darrien's chest. Despite the bandages, each muscle was hard and defined. The biceps in his unscathed arm tensed as he grabbed onto the top bunk for support, and his abs contracted ever so slightly with the movement. He was looking at me, eyes brighter than they had been before he slept.

"I like your pajamas," he joked.

I smirked. "Yeah, you'll like a pair of your own after the shower, I'm sure."

"Perhaps. I have trouble sleeping in clothes, though..."

Heat seeped into my cheeks at the thought. I shook my head and took a couple of steps toward him. When I closed the gap between us, he wrapped a long arm over my shoulders. He led me slowly to the bathroom as I supported some of his weight. When we entered the bathroom, the light was harsher. We halted by the wall of the door, and I adjusted the light to a dimmer setting on the small screen, then I made the light darker and more violet-toned. The white light was too much on my head.

Darrien felt relief, too, as the lights went down. His body shifted and eased against mine.

"Thanks," he said.

"Mhm. It was hurting my head too."

We walked over to the large showers.

"It still hurts?"

"A little," I admitted. "I know I should have asked Lata for some pain meds, but I just. Didn't."

Steam rolled out of the middle shower of the three from Ian, so I guided Darrien to the last stall farthest from the bathroom door. I pulled on the shower door and helped him in. The stall was decent in size, and luckily had a large bench in the middle, against the wall, where Darrien could sit and still feel the water. Shampoo bars, body wash, wash cloths, and just about everything else he could need was on a shelf adjacent to the impressive shower head.

Darrien sat down on the bench and leaned back against the wall with a heavy sigh.

"Uh," I said awkwardly. "I guess I should get you a towel. And some scissors, to, um, you know." I gestured to the remnants of his space suit that he wore on his legs.

Lata's medical kit was still in the bathroom, resting on a stool near the sinks. She had organized it and put everything back in its place, so it was easy to find the pair of shears we'd used earlier. Then, I grabbed a towel from one of the racks and made my way back into the stall.

Darrien's eyes flashed to mine, and then I looked down at the bandage in the center of his chest, and the other one on his shoulder. I didn't know if they needed to stay on, but I'd assume so. They looked like they were cemented onto his skin with some sort of medical tape.

"They're waterproof," Darrien mentioned.

"Oh. Good."

I sat the towel down on the floor, near the door where he could reach, and handed him the shears.

"Do you want me to start the shower for you?"

The way he was looking at me had my pulse thready and my limbs jittery. His eyes took in the swell of my breasts underneath the sweater, and the skin of my stomach from the somewhat cropped top as I reached up to turn the shower on.

He gave me a terse nod as my fingertips reached the nozzles. The shower was nice and large, but not nearly as high-tech as the showers on the *Hippogriff* with their touch screen water temperature settings. I turned on the hot water and a little of the cold, running my hands through until it was hot enough, but not scorching.

When I turned back around, Darrien had managed to cut the space suit all the way down to his knee but had trouble bending over any further. I turned the water on full blast and allowed it to hit his chest, then took the shears and worked on getting the rest of the damned suit off of him.

The hot water ran from his neck, down his chest, and into the suit that remained. Luckily, his boots had been taken off earlier by Lata. I cut down from his knees, all the way down until there was no more suit. After peeling off the suit and throwing it near his towel, I hesitated, looking at the pair of briefs Darrien still wore.

I looked up to find him watching me.

"You can take those off, too," he murmured softly. His voice was buttery and created flutters low in my stomach.

I tried not to focus on the warm, smooth skin of his hip underneath my hand. I tore my gaze from his and grabbed the towel I'd laid down on the floor, then threw it over his lap and smoothed it out so that he could keep some level of privacy.

"Is that okay?" I asked.

He nodded and continued to look down at me as I began pulling his underwear off and down his thick thighs. The hot water drenched the braid I'd put in my hair after I changed earlier, and flowed down from my neck, under my sweater and sweatpants, leaking into my own undergarments. After several tugs, I finally got his briefs down around his ankles and pulled them off.

"Are you okay?" I asked as I stepped over to the door, out of the shower's aim.

It was hard not to keep my eyes locked on his body, even in the dim violet lights. I liked how the water clung to the slight dusting of chest hair he had, how his arms folded over the towel in a seemingly relaxed pose, and I liked that I knew he was anything but relaxed because he was still looking at me with hunger in his eyes. He stared at my wet sweater top which stuck to my breasts.

He nodded slowly as his gaze traveled back up to my face.

"I'll, um, stay outside of the stall until you're ready to get out?" The voice that came from my lips sounded like a mousy version of my own. "And then I can get Aleksy or someone to come to help you out, and get you changed."

Darrien chuckled darkly. "I think I'm capable of changing and walking a few feet."

"Oh, okay. Well, I'll get you another towel, and–"

He wrapped his long fingers around my wrist closest to him as I turned toward the door to leave, and I froze.

"Daphne?" His voice was deep and throaty, laced with spice, and my head was spinning.

His fingers dug into the waistline of my sweatpants and tugged; a silent plea for me to come closer. To go back to him.

"Darrien, you're hurt," I pointed out the obvious as I turned back to him.

"Right."

"Mhm."

"Stay, please? I'll be good. Just–stay?"

I wanted nothing more than to stay, but I also didn't want to hurt him.

Darrien's hands gripped my waist with longing. He pulled me down on top of his lap so that my legs were draped over his legs. The hot stream splashed our faces and our necks. Steam rolled in between us and all around us in the small space, and I couldn't fucking breathe, because I felt like I was going to die if he didn't touch me.

"Your clothes are wet," he said, only an inch from my mouth now.

"They are," I agreed breathlessly.

"Should we take them off?" he exhaled roughly.

Droplets from the shower meshed with his hair, and semi-straightened curls stuck to his forehead and temples as he peered down at me. Water ran down his nose and moistened his lush lips. His hands traveled underneath my top and played teasingly with the snaps on my bra. The towel underneath us, also drenched, allowed me to feel almost every inch of him. His desire was more than apparent underneath my quivering thighs.

"I thought," I managed to say, "you were going to behave?"

Darrien's head nuzzled into my neck, and a low, contented sigh escaped his lips. His breath was hot against the area right below my ears.

"I will be good, Daphne," he murmured in my ear. He nipped at my earlobe, and my thighs clenched together. My head fell back from his touch. I needed more of that, but we couldn't go there. "I can be good and still play a little, right?" he whispered.

The moan that I let out couldn't be helped as he kissed all up and down my neck; his tongue mixing with the warm water. I would surely explode from my overstimulated nerves at any moment. My eyes closed, and I sank as deep as I could into his touch.

What was I worried about, again? He paused just a little, and I remembered the bandages as my fingers ran down his barren chest.

"You're hurt," I gasped.

"Yeah," he agreed, "and getting better by the second."

Though he couldn't bend forward very well, he was able to

strip me of my top and throw it over the side of the stall using his uninjured arm. His other hand moved from my back, and up to cup my face. He pressed our noses together, and his gaze didn't falter for a single second from my own. Darrien took my hair out of my braid and gently ran his fingers through my long locks, then moved all of it out of my face, behind my ears.

"Stunning," he whispered. "Daphne Blaine, for the love of God, please let me touch you," Darrien breathed heavily.

I paused, and his hands didn't move at all. He waited, body tense, his breathing rough and ragged. The water beat down on us as he held me. I couldn't help it. Whatever control I'd had, which was already close to none, ceased to exist altogether. I stared down at those beautiful, wet lips only inches from my own.

"Kiss me like you would have in the cavern," I said with my heart pounding in my ears.

I had expected him to crush his lips against my own, but first, he grinned, dimples coming to life, and fuck, I never knew someone could be so beautiful. For a second, I felt horrible when I realized it'd never been like *this* with Matthew. But I wouldn't think about that. Not when Darrien Park was grinning at me, calling me stunning, and touching me.

I took in his convincing smile, and a smile of my own crept up. Gently, I ran my fingers through his wet locks. Darrien brushed his nose against my own and inched in closer. His thumb ran over my lower lip, teasing, and then every thought and worry disappeared as his lips met mine. Darrien kissed me gently at first, barely covering my lips with his own, and I felt his kiss as though it brushed against every inch of me. My nerve endings burned and exploded, and I gasped as his lips parted from mine.

Before I could take a steadying breath, Darrien managed to pick me up enough with his good arm around my waist. He

B. G. THOMAS

moved my legs on either side of him in a straddle that allowed me to feel him right where I wanted him. And there was...a *lot* of him.

He cupped my face again, this time with both hands, and kissed me deep and slow. My arms wrapped around his neck as he slipped his tongue into my mouth ever so slightly, swirling the tip of my tongue with his own. And then he was kissing me fast and hard like I was his oxygen; like he'd die without me.

The feeling was more than mutual. My hips rolled against him. Towel be damned. His fingertips dug into my waist as he bit my lower lip and tugged at it with his teeth. A moan escaped from both of us as one of his large hands slipped into my pants and underwear to squeeze my ass.

Darrien broke away from me and unclasped my bra in one fluid motion. His eyes didn't leave mine for a second as the bra fell from my breasts, down to the floor.

"That's much, much better," he purred.

I nodded in agreement, unable to find the words. I was careful not to graze the regions near his bandages as I moved forward, my belly against his chest so that he could get a better view of me. Normally, I would be trying to cover myself up, self-conscious or worried about my appearance. With Darrien, my body burst into flames when he stared down every inch of my exposed skin. And he *did* stare.

"Fucking *hell*," he said as his head dipped into my chest.

"You said you wanted to play," I said. "So, go ahead and play, Dr. Park."

A rumble came from his lips, and as I ground harder onto his cock through the towel, Darrien licked one of my nipples lightly with the tip of his hot tongue while his other hand lightly caressed the other. His hands massaged and explored every inch of my breasts, leaving me struggling for breath. He sucked harder, and I gasped, almost coming right then and there, with my pants still on and all.

Darrien fisted my hair and brought my face back down to meet his and he kissed me over and over and over—with tongue, without. His hands were only on my face and my hair, and many minutes went by with us just kissing and memorizing how the other's lips felt on our own. His lips were my new favorite things to taste. Each time we broke away for air, I was desperate for him to come back to me.

The water was still hot, but neither of us had done any bathing. I stood up, unable to take it anymore, and stripped off my sweatpants along with my drenched panties. Darrien looked up at me like I was a goddess; his lips were parted, and those brown eyes consumed my body and soul.

I grabbed the towel with one hand, and slowly removed it from his lap. A smirk fell on my face as I took him in. It was my turn to stare, to memorize every inch of his bare skin. I crawled back onto his lap. The warmth of his skin on my own was nothing short of phenomenal.

"You're so fucking gorgeous, Darrien," I said against his lips. It was true. He was, and I'd noticed from day one. And now his body was against mine, and my fingers could caress each tight groove of his muscles. I could suck on him and wrap myself up in his sweet scent of sun and pine.

I kissed him gently, and his hands slid up and down my bare, slick back. Then, his dominant hand moved from my back to my waist, my stomach, and then down, down to the center of me.

Oh, God.

And it was then that we heard the bathroom door open. The lights grew brighter, and footsteps made their way over to the shower stalls.

Darrien smiled wickedly at me. He didn't stop moving his finger over my clit. I clenched my teeth, and he covered my mouth with his free hand. As the footsteps got closer, he slipped one of his long fingers inside of me. I couldn't help but bite the hand that covered my mouth; every part of me was on the edge of coming undone, and that beautiful, devilish grin of his was not helping.

"Darrien?"

It was Aleksy, and he was right outside the door of the shower.

Darrien picked up the pace of his finger inside of me, staring down at his glistening index finger each time he plunged out and back in.

"Yeah?" Darrien asked; somehow his voice seemed completely normal like he was actually just taking a shower like he wasn't fingering me and looking at me like he wanted a taste.

"Do you need any help in dere?"

"Oh, no. I'm fine," Darrien called. "Thank you."

There was a pause. "Well, I am certain Daphne is being of great help to you," Aleksy said.

Embarrassment crept up, but pleasure curled deep inside of me, washing whatever embarrassment away because Darrien didn't stop. He slipped a second finger inside of me and picked up his pace.

"She's just helping me wash up."

"Right." Aleksy chuckled. "Daphne, I believe you left your shirt out here. It seems quite—*wet.* I wonder how dat happened?"

Darrien didn't reply. His hand still covered my mouth, but a small laugh came from his swollen lips. He licked his bottom lip as he circled my clit without abandon.

Aleksy cleared his throat. "Lata wanted me to, er, tell you

dat you should take it easy, as you heal. And to not let your heart rate get too high if you get de gist. Yeah?"

"Understood, Aleksy," Darrien said.

There was another prolonged pause before Aleksy's footsteps slowly walked away. Finally, the door closed in the distance, and we were alone again. The lights remained brighter but I didn't care, because now I could see more of the beautiful man underneath me as he worked me with his talented fingers. He moved his hand from my mouth.

"Darrien," I begged. "We have to stop."

His head dipped into my neck. "And we will. As soon as I feel you come."

Darrien sucked my neck and moved his fingers in and out at the speed of light. After a few seconds, he took his fingers from me and swirled them around my clit at a devastatingly fast pace.

It didn't take long at all for me to come undone all over him, shuddering and shaking, and kissing him deeper in between panting and moans I couldn't help but let out. I wanted more, but I knew Aleksy was right. I gazed up into his eyes as he took the two fingers he'd used on me, stuck them in his mouth, and sucked them clean. He groaned, and it took every ounce of my self-control not to slip him inside of me right then and there.

My forehead pressed against Darrien's. I tried to steady my breath. I could feel his desire in between my legs—his cock was hard and slick, and I was more than ready for him. All of him.

Aleksy and Lata were too fucking smart. Then again, we'd been in the shower for what must have been a long time, and as soon as someone came to look for us, I knew it'd be obvious what we were doing.

"We can't," I whispered against his lips.

He nodded. "I know."

"I'm sorry."

He kissed me hard and caressed my ass and back as I pressed into him.

"Don't be sorry, Daphne." He smirked. "Now, I get to think about everything else I'm going to do to you next time. I'm dying to get my tongue in between your legs."

9

TREPIDATION

After finally breaking away from the comfortable confines of Darrien's lap, I washed my hair and my body. I had planned on taking a shower sometime after dinner, anyway, and showering with Darrien was much more fun.

He watched every move I made with bright caramel eyes and a coy smile. As I washed my chest facing the shower-head, he leaned forward and nipped at one of my ass cheeks from where he sat on the bench.

It felt so natural to laugh and play in the water with him, both of us totally exposed to the other. I didn't even mind that the lights were brighter. I wasn't as skinny and toned as I once was, and I still had stretch marks from when I'd been pregnant, but all of the things I was usually self-conscious about fell to the wayside because the way Darrien looked at me had me feeling like a goddess.

After I bathed, I helped Darrien wash his chest, careful to maneuver around his wounds and bandages. Then, I washed his hair. Darrien leaned into my hands as I did so, closing his eyes as though my touch was the best thing I could have ever done for him.

It was hard to leave the comfort of the stall, but finally, I got out, wrapped myself up in a fluffy towel, and then tiptoed through the bathroom to the closet in the bedroom where I found some clothing in a hurry. I didn't want to run into anyone. The sweater I'd gotten him was too large, and so were my sweatpants, but they would do.

After I got dressed, this time entirely panty-less, I helped him out of the shower. His skin glistened in the light with stray water droplets that the towel couldn't catch. He scrunched up a towel in his hair to dry it some, and then I helped him into his pants and shirt.

"Clothes are no fun," he said. "Not with you around, anyway."

I smirked and bit my lip, then helped him out of the bathroom. It was apparent he was feeling better, though, because he didn't need as much of my bodily support. Darrien was a full foot higher than I was now that we were standing again, and his swollen muscles brushed against me as we moved back to the bedroom, which made me want to drag his injured ass back into the shower stall all over again, but I knew Lata or Aleksy would find us and give me their wrath if I did.

Darrien got back into the bottom bunk where I'd found him initially, and I was glad to see that we were still alone in the room.

"I'm going to rest a bit," he sighed contently as he got comfortable. "You should go eat."

"*You* should also eat," I shot back. "Build up your strength."

He chuckled. "Fine. I'll try to eat a little later, but I'm afraid someone has exhausted me and I'm in dire need of a nap." Darrien winked at me, and I wanted nothing more than to stay there with him, even to join him for a nap. But, he was right. I needed to eat, and one of us probably needed to make

an appearance to the others, even if it was just to assure Aleksy
—well, Lata—that we were behaving.

"You're right. I'll be back in a bit."

I turned to leave, but he tugged on my wrist, just as he'd
done in the shower, and pulled me down to sit on the bunk.

"Are you going to get me into trouble again, Darrien?" I
laughed.

He shook his head. "Absolutely not. Though, trouble
sounds wonderful. I can't wait to get into more trouble with
you."

He tugged on my sweater sleeve, and I bent down to meet
his lips. Darrien's kiss was soft and slow. He tangled his hands
in my hair, then cupped my chin before letting me go.

"Mmm," he sounded. "Now I can go to sleep."

I stood up and covered him with a blanket before leaving
him in the quiet room.

The last thing I wanted to do was go and be with the
others. I didn't want Lata and Aleksy's looks or Lata's repri-
mand. Though, knowing Lata, the scolding would only last for
so long before she started to ask me other, much more inappro-
priate questions. I also didn't want to make small talk with the
others or begin worrying all over again about the situation we
were in.

But what I wanted was no longer an option. Not anymore.

As I entered the common area, I noticed that I *was* hungry.
My stomach began to grumble. I had no idea what time it was,
either. I looked down at the bracelet I was allowed to put back
on after we'd changed out of our spacesuits and realized it was
close to nine.

Harper was still studying the footage outside, now with a
steaming cup of tea in between her hands. Jules was curled up
next to her, asleep. Raymond and Saba were gone, so I
assumed they'd gone to sleep early in the other bedroom.

However, Todd was awake and on the other couch beside Lata.

Lata turned her head to me and gave me a knowing smile. "Hi. Nice nap?"

Todd looked at me, then. "Nap? Or shower?"

"I, uh, took a small nap, then decided to take a quick shower. Just got out." Lata moved to speak, so I cut her off. "Where's Aleksy?"

"He didn't want to disturb you or *wake* Darrien, so he's taking a shower in the small bathroom," she said, motioning to the bathroom near the kitchen.

"Oh, okay."

Todd's legs were propped up on a pillow atop a small coffee table. He wore a pair of sweat shorts that showed off the bandages Aleksy had put on him earlier, which came close to reaching his knees. Some blood trickled through on the underside. It certainly didn't look pleasant.

"Feeling okay?" I asked Todd.

"Hurts like a bitch," Todd commented with a half-smile. "But, a bit better thanks to strong pain pills."

I couldn't help but compare Todd and Darrien. Where Todd complained about most things, Darrien hardly brought up his discomfort, even in the worst circumstances. And though Todd was gorgeous and brilliant, I couldn't help but notice that he was nowhere near as attractive to me now as he'd been the other night.

I made my way to the kitchen a few feet away. Unsurprisingly, Lata got up from her spot on the couch and joined me. She leaned against one of the counters in the small space and stared at me as she played with the end of her ponytail.

"Raymond attempted to make some sort of chili earlier, but it tasted more like cat food than anything. Or, what I would assume cat food would taste like. I've never actually tried it, thankfully," Lata snorted. "But, there are some things in the cupboard, or you can have some instant noodles."

The cupboard was full of protein bars and the so-called instant noodles in two flavors: shrimp and chicken. Other than that, there were several unappetizing Meals Ready to Eat packets, nuts, and some dried fruit. I opted for the chicken noodles.

As I prepared the noodles and put them in the old-fashioned microwave and set the time, I could feel Lata's eyes on my back. It came to the point where I couldn't avoid her anymore. I turned around and leaned on the counter that divided us.

"You were bad," she said with a snicker.

My eyes rolled far back into my head.

"You were!" she whisper-yelled at me. "If his heart rate had gotten too high, or–"

I sighed and rubbed my eyes with the tips of my fingers, but nodded. "I know, Lata. I know. Thank you for sending Aleksy in to... break us up." Even as the words came from my mouth, a smile spread across my face that I couldn't help. I laughed. I could still feel Darrien on every part of my body, and I didn't have a single regret. We really *should* have been more careful, but things could have escalated way more than they had, too.

"In my defense," I said after retrieving my noodles from the microwave and stirring them on the counter. "I did not start it."

Lata gave me a wicked grin. "You didn't have to. You two have wanted to jump each other's bones since the second we boarded the *Hippogriff*."

My brows shot up. "Is that so?"

She ignored my questioning gaze. "Can't say I blame you. Or him. You're both hot as hell, single, and the Earth is dying and all." Lata sighed. My fork was frozen in my cluster of noodles. "Though, Todd might get jealous."

My eyes bulged as Lata giggled and started stirring my meal for me.

"Todd asked where you were about five times after he woke up," she whispered.

"Christ," I muttered. I took my noodles back and added the flavor packet. "Can we talk about something else, please? Anything else. I'm begging you."

Lata's eyes were playful, but she pursed her lips. "Fine. But I want details later."

"Fine, fine."

She motioned over to the others on the couch. "We saw a couple more of those centipede assholes about thirty minutes ago, but they left the shuttle alone. Other than that, it's all just sand. I doubt Harper will get a second of sleep tonight. She's obsessed with making sure nothing else is out there."

"Well, I don't entirely blame her after the events of today."

She shook her head. "Me neither. I don't know if I'll be able to sleep."

"I hope you try. Maybe raid some of the drugs you and Aleksy have in your kits. You both had a long day, too," I pointed out.

Lata shrugged. "I don't usually get the best of sleep anyway. Aleksy, on the other hand, well, he can close his eyes for two seconds and be snoring."

That made me think of Matthew, and as I took my first bite of the noodles, my body tensed. Guilt washed over me in a cold blanket. I forced myself to chew and breathe. *Matthew is gone.* It was true. But it was more of what I'd realized as soon as Darrien had kissed me; Matthew and I had never had that kind of chemistry. We had chemistry, sure, but not like *that*. Just thinking that while being with Darrien made me feel like the worst widow in the world.

And then there was the whole Todd thing on top of it.

I didn't regret what I'd done with him, but I didn't want it to happen again, either. I'd known that this morning, before me and Darrien's relationship escalated. Todd wasn't my kind of person, and I was beginning to realize that after being solo for so long after Matthew's death, that I didn't want anything casual. I didn't want him to surprise me in my room just to get laid. No. I wanted Darrien's forehead pressed against mine, I wanted the playfulness of him biting my ass when I wasn't looking—I wanted *Darrien*. My shoulders tensed even more as I pondered whether or not I was something casual to him. Was I? Or did he also want something deeper?

"Your noodles are going to get cold if you don't eat dem soon," Aleksy said. He joined us in the kitchen and leaned against his wife. She ran her hands over his bald head and gave him a half-hug. He kissed the top of her head. "Is de bathroom good to go into now?" Aleksy grinned. "It was so stuffy in dere, I could almost not breathe."

Todd most definitely overheard Aleksy's joke, so I focused on flipping Aleksy off and shoving more noodles into my mouth.

"Did you get de details yet?" Aleksy asked his wife with wiggling brows.

Lata slapped his shoulder playfully. "Shut your gob, darling. We'll ask her everything *later.*"

Aleksy walked away after shooting me an overly dramatic pout.

"I'm sorry we are such gossips," Lata said. Her London accent was thick. I noticed it became thicker as the day went on, and the more tired she became. "We're both just hopeless romantics. It's bloody annoying, really."

They were definitely gossips, but I knew that was because they actually took a liking to me. I liked them, too. If things were normal, and I'd met them under normal circumstances back on Earth, I'd think we'd have been great friends. I hoped we could still turn out to be great friends while also working together as we continued our mission.

"How did you two meet, anyway?" I asked.

Lata ran her brown fingers through her dark hair, making the few strands of silver glitter in the light. She smiled sheepishly. "Ah. Well, Aleksy originally came to America and married someone else."

I lifted a brow, intrigued.

She nodded. "It's nothing too crazy. Aleksy married this woman who ended up being a total nutter. They were divorced after a year or so." Lata rolled her eyes. "Crazy bitch, I tell ya. But, I'll go into that another time, when we have wine and aren't stranded on a shuttle. Anyway, after they divorced, Aleksy worked and went to school, and stayed in the states. He eventually ended up at the Mayo Clinic where I worked in the Infectious Diseases department. He obviously was not in the same department." She laughed. "But, we bumped into each other one day. He made me laugh. I needed to laugh."

I understood that. "Did he ask you out?"

She shook her head. "No, no. After we kept bumping into each other, I finally asked him out after a few months. Believe it or not, the man is quite shy when he likes someone in *that* way."

Aleksy was on the couch, inspecting Todd's bandages while Todd fidgeted. I could see him being shy. He was gentle, despite his lighthearted demeanor, and I could see that a part of him wasn't as confident as Lata was. Especially after a divorce, I figured.

"How long before you got hitched?"

I turned to throw away my noodles, only half eaten. I made a note to grab Darrien a protein bar or something before I headed back to the bedroom.

"Two months."

My jaw dropped, and I whirled back at her. "Two months?"

"Mhm." Lata's smile grew large and genuine as she looked over at her husband. "I decided I never wanted to stop laughing again. And I haven't stopped since."

10

MONSTER ANTHROPODA

Saba, Raymond, and Todd slept in the smaller of the two bedrooms. Harper refused to stop watching the camera, so Jules had to bargain with her and convince her to at least take shifts so that she could get some much-needed rest. By the time I had left the common area, Harper was passed out on the couch. Jules groggily studied the feed with a blanket wrapped around her shoulders. I decided to stay up a little longer and keep them company because my body was still buzzing from the shower adventure Darrien and I had.

"She's the most stubborn person," Jules muttered to me as I sat beside her.

I snorted. "You don't have to convince me. I've noticed."

Jules yawned. "Are you holding up okay?"

I shrugged. "Yes and no. It's a lot to process, I guess. What about you?"

She shook her head slowly. "Yes and no. I'm happy we're all alive and mostly unscathed. Never in my wildest dreams did I think we'd ever encounter the things we saw today," she said as a shiver worked its way through her.

"Yeah, no kidding."

We sat in silence for a while, both of our eyes glued to the screen. After half an hour, I bid Jules goodnight and retreated into the larger bedroom. I was still high on adrenaline, but my eyes were heavy, and I knew I needed to take advantage of the rest being offered to me before I stayed up all night.

Ian had gone to sleep before most of us and had taken one of the top bunks across the room from where Darrien and the door to the bathroom were. Lata and Aleksy, despite Aleksy's large size, shared the bottom bunk in the middle of the rows beside where Darrien lay down. Everyone was fast asleep, from the sounds of the breathing (and snoring from Aleksy) around the room.

After eating a little, I'd grabbed Darrien a protein bar and a small package of dried fruit, not knowing which he would prefer, but when I got back to the room, I found him passed out, happily dreaming from the looks of it. I didn't want to wake him from his slumber, so I climbed up to the bunk above him after leaving the snacks by him on the floor.

I had tried for ages to calm down and fall asleep, but even through the thick walls of the shuttle, I could hear the howling of the winds outside, and despite my very *fun* evening, every time I closed my eyes, images of Darrien stuck under the water, or the flower stabbing him, or the fucking sand worms flashed across my mind, and after that happened on a loop for a while, I couldn't find the peace within myself to fall asleep.

That, and Aleksy snored really, really loudly. I didn't understand how everyone else could sleep through it, but then again, it had been an eventful and stressful day. Lata must have been a deep sleeper once she went to sleep. Or, maybe she was just used to her husband's snores.

As more time ticked by, I began obsessing over the fact that Dad would be navigating a shuttle to our rescue—all by himself—in mere hours. If he wasn't already on the way. And then I began worrying about what would happen to Jaxon if he didn't come back. Or I didn't come back. Or worse, what would happen if neither of us did. The last thing I wanted to do to my son was what my mother had done to me, even though it hadn't been her fault. Jaxon had already lost Magda and Matthew, just like I had. He didn't need more loss in his life.

I knew Dad was more than competent. He was one of the smartest people I knew. He had taught me algebra, trig, and geometry before I'd even entered middle school, before I went to public school when he still taught me at home. He'd read me Shakespeare's sonnets aloud, and we'd had long, drawn-out conversations about the work of renowned novelists from the twenty-first century, like Atwood, Tan, Adichie, and Butler. He taught me the importance of taking care of Mother Earth. We composted at home and volunteered at local environmental organizations, spending weekends picking up trash and protesting. Dad had explained to me every question I'd had when I was young in as much detail as possible, which resulted in giving me many history lessons about the COVID-19 pandemic, the separation of the United States of America from the Old Glory States, and so much more. He was the reason I'd graduated high school early and gone on to college when I was barely sixteen.

Dad was an aerospace engineer, but he hadn't been in practice since I was a toddler. When we moved from Florida due to the country dividing, he had been let go from NASA almost immediately afterward. For a long time, he didn't work at all because NASA gave him a shit ton of money because of what happened to my mother. Then, after volunteering at the conservation for so long, he eventually became the financial advisor and main accountant for them. Yet, I was still worried. Dad was never the best driver, either. Many times, he would get distracted and almost crash the car into the car in front of him, or worse. I didn't want to think about what he'd be like while flying a space shuttle.

I placed a hand over my heart and felt the fast beating. *Thump, thump, thump, thump.* It was too fast. My breathing was shallow, and tingles slowly started emerging at my fingertips and eventually made their way up my fingers, all the way to my palms and wrists.

I'd grown up with panic attacks and knew what was happening to me. No amount of careful breathing could help me now. Typically, I had an emergency stash of my medication with me for when this happened, because it always would happen at the most inopportune moments. As a pre-teen, the attacks felt like the end of the world. Like a heart attack or something worse. I'd often throw up in the middle of my more severe attacks and then lay on the floor in my sweat—waiting and begging my body to come down and level out. As an adult, the attacks still happened, but less often. I could normally talk myself out of them, but apparently, that wasn't an option tonight.

Feeling alone on a space shuttle that no longer worked while my dad and son were miles and miles above me did not help. Thinking over the events that had happened on planet Virginia, and worrying over what would happen next in the morning made it all worse.

As quietly as possible, I made my way down from the ladder and onto the floor, then padded into the adjoining bathroom. Luckily, Lata had left her medical kit where it had been earlier next to one of the sinks. I sifted through her kit in the very dim light, with shaky hands and numb limbs. I knew I probably should have just woken her up and asked for some meds, but I couldn't bring myself to do so. She needed her rest, and I was strong enough to try and find some sort of benzodiazepine to help my attack fade away. If I didn't find anything, oh well. I could lay on the bathroom floor, the cool tile against my skin, and wait it out. I'd done that many times before, and I could do it again.

A giant sigh of relief escaped me as I found a box of meds. It normally would have been locked, but with the chaos that transpired earlier in the day, Lata had left it open. I used the emergency flashlight on my bracelet and looked through the different medications listed. I finally found one named *prohizepan*. It was a newer kind of benzo that was created a couple of decades ago, and it was known to shut down panic attacks almost immediately. I had been hoping for a simple Xanax, but took the prohizepan and popped one in my mouth. It dissolved instantly and filled my mouth with a pleasant citrus flavor. I leaned my trembling body against the sinks, and within a minute, I was less clammy, and I felt like I could breathe again. As more minutes passed, my heart returned to a steady, comfortable rhythm.

I wasn't one to pray to anything in particular, but I thanked whatever I could that I had found the drug, and that I was able to come back down and resume some sense of normalcy.

After splashing some water on my face and re-braiding my hair down my back, I went back into the bedroom, but instead of climbing back up to the bunk above Darrien, I carefully hopped over Darrien so that I was facing the wall, and wrapped my arms around him.

Darrien let out a deep, contented sigh, then turned to face me. He wrapped his arms around me, and I breathed deeply into his neck, smelling the sunlight I missed so much, right here in the middle of outer space.

"Daph?" he murmured to me.

"Mhm," I confirmed.

"Thank goodness. I was worried Harper was trying to come on to me."

I rolled my eyes in the dark, but a smile crept up on my lips nonetheless as he chuckled.

Darrien was half asleep, but his hands shoved me closer to him so that my leg was propped over his on top of the blanket so that our chests could merge into each other. He was so warm and cozy. Whatever anxiety and ache that was leftover from my sudden attack eased away as he squeezed my thigh, my ass, and then nuzzled his face into my neck.

"I was dreaming of you," he said softly.

I desperately wanted to dream of him. "I hope it was a good dream," I said playfully.

"We were swimming," he said sleepily. "And you were educating me about some kind of shark."

Well, that sounded pretty accurate. My smile grew. "You're warm," I said.

His face came up to meet mine. "Are you cold?"

I wasn't too cold, but I wasn't complaining about the warmth of his body, either. "A bit," I said.

I could tell he was still half asleep, yet Darrien still managed to lift up the covers for me so that I could slip in next to him. Darrien hugged me and pulled me into him as closely as he could, then traced lazy circles along my backside. He didn't even know how much I needed that. He just...did it.

"Kiss me?" I asked.

"Daphne Blaine," he murmured in the dark, "I will kiss you whenever you want me to. Whenever, wherever."

Darrien's lips met mine in a soft kiss, but it quickly turned deeper, and then he was devouring my lips completely without restraint.

"I know we can't misbehave again," he whispered into my

ear. He was more alert now. "But, I want you to kiss me for however long as you want."

So, I did.

A SMALL RATTLING NOISE, similar to the annoying rattle of a broken dishwasher, stirred me awake. I must not have been in a deep sleep, otherwise, I don't think I would have noticed.

Darrien and I had kissed and touched and moved against each other in the silence, careful not to wake the others, for what felt like eons. How long ago had that been? The last thing I remembered was the natural slowing of our kisses in the darkness, his hands pausing on my back, and how I fell asleep nuzzled into his chest while he rubbed my shoulders. We must have passed out at least a couple of hours ago, but time in and of itself was disorienting.

I removed my arm from Darrien's chest and checked my bracelet. It still read the time back on the *Hippogriff*, but several hours had gone by since I came into the bedroom.

My lips were still swollen from our middle-of-the-night make-out session and Darrien's scent lingered on my skin, overwhelming my senses in the best way. His heavy arms were still wrapped around my body, which almost made me fall back asleep and forget why I'd woken up, and then the rattling noise sounded again—but this time it jostled the shuttle, and the noise radiating through the ship was loud enough to wake Darrien and some of the others.

"Are you okay?" Darrien asked immediately after his eyes popped open.

I nodded, sitting up fully in the bunk.

"What the hell was that?" Ian asked groggily from somewhere in the dark. He was making his way down from the top bunk, from the sound of feet hitting the ladder.

"Mmm? What?" Aleksy stirred.

Lata groaned from under the covers. Maybe she hadn't gotten much sleep, after all.

Darrien sat up alongside me, and despite the fact that the shuttle was literally rocking us now, Ian gave us a very long, pointed look after dimming the lights.

"I'm going to go check with–"

Ian broke off mid-sentence as Jules busted into the room, the same blanket over her shoulders, braided hair in stringy wisps, and with dark circles under her eyes.

"Everyone get up and get dressed! Stat!" Jules barked in a way that reminded me of Harper. "Don't ask me what's going on, I don't fucking know, so just get ready."

And with that, sleep-deprived Jules slammed the door and was out of sight.

"That can't be good," Ian muttered.

Ian didn't second guess her. He immediately made his way into the bathroom, as did Aleksy. Lata groaned again but managed to sit up in bed. It was perhaps the one time I'd ever seen Lata *not* look naturally beautiful. Instead, she was straight-up adorable with her tangled hair, slits for eyes, and crumpled shirt. It took her a moment to realize that she had taken her pants off.

She looked down at her lower half, then up at me and

Darrien. "I don't care. I'm a doctor." Lata rubbed at her eyes and yawned. "So, no idea what the bumping is?"

We shook our heads. Another wave of jostling hit us right as she tried to get up and put her pants on.

"Sure doesn't seem like a *good* thing," I said.

Lata came over to us. "No, I wouldn't say so."

She motioned for Darrien to lift his shirt, which he had some trouble doing, so I assisted him.

"Well, aren't you two cozy over here."

I coughed a laugh. Ignoring her, I said, "I don't know how you sleep next to Aleksy with how that man snores."

Lata smoothed her hands over Darrien's bandages and then checked his vitals.

"I am an insomniac, but whenever I do sleep, not even the shaking of this space shuttle will wake me up. I'm one of those annoying people who have to set, like, twenty alarms if I need to be up at a specific time. Sadly, I don't think I was asleep for long before Jules came in." Lata huffed and then pulled down Darrien's shirt. "You need to drink water. And eat food." She pointed at him.

Darrien nodded.

"How long do the bandages on his chest stay on for?" I asked, truly just curious, while trying not to focus on the rattling beneath us. I stood up and unbraided my hair, running my fingers through my long locks in the hopes it wasn't a tangled mess.

"They will dissolve when everything is done healing, or close to it. And they are waterproof—but I think you two figured that out already?" Lata winked.

With that, she also went into the bathroom. I figured I would let everyone else get ready and take care of their needs before I followed.

"Those two are really into what we do in the shower,"

Darrien murmured as he moved to sit up and adjusted the drawstring of his pants.

I began a French braid and also adjusted my very askew clothing. We had both gotten tangled up in each other and the sheets and blanket. Darrien casually shook out his hair and ran a hand through it. Somehow, it came out looking even better than it had yesterday, despite the occasional loose strand and cowlick.

A loud bump sounded on the side of the shuttle wall where the head of the bunks rested. The bump made me jump about three feet into the air. I expected Darrien to laugh at me for being spooked.

Instead, he asked, "What the hell is that?"

"I just hope it's not the fucking sand-worms again."

He paused, and when he didn't respond, I remembered that he had been inside when the worm attacks had happened, and he probably had no clue what I was talking about. I looked down at him and met his pensive eyes.

"After the whole flower thing," I said, "they took you inside the shuttle, but then Todd got attacked by these..." I didn't know how to explain the horrible creatures to him without being totally blunt about it, but I didn't want him to get spooked, either. "Worms. Kind of. Picture a big worm-centipede hybrid. With teeth?"

Well, shit. That was probably not what I should have said, but sugarcoating it might have made matters worse. I didn't want to lie to him or have him go outside unprepared for whatever reason.

"I don't like the flora *or* fauna on this planet," he said. His beautiful, up-slanted eyes widened. "Is Todd okay?"

My cheeks burned. Was I supposed to tell him about Todd? If I didn't, I was sure that Todd would let it be known soon enough. Then again, Darrien and I hadn't talked about anything regarding where our relationship stood. But not telling him about what had happened with Todd somehow felt like a lie. I would have to tell him at some point if only to clear my mind but now was not the time.

I nodded. "One of them also got to Harper, but by some miracle, she wasn't harmed. Todd has some injuries on his calves."

Aleksy came out of the bathroom then, with Ian trailing behind him.

"Do you need help to the bathroom?" I asked Darrien. I would have the guys help me if that was the case. It would take much longer for me to help him alone.

With a small grunt, Darrien held on to the bunk for support but managed to stand. He used the bunk all the way to the bathroom door, and then let go cautiously.

"I think I'm good. But I'll have Daph call you if I fall off of the toilet or something," he said. He turned over his shoulder and gave the guys a grin.

Meanwhile, I replayed the way he'd said *Daph* so casually over in my head.

"Great. We will meet you in the common room, den," Aleksy said. "Make sure Lata is okay, Daphne, yeah?"

"Of course."

With that, they left, and Darrien and I made our way into the bathroom. Darrien moved impressively fast for someone who had been stabbed one day prior. Modern medicine was nothing short of a miracle.

Darrien retreated into a stall as I went to one of the sinks. Lata was packing up her kit next to me.

"I took something from your kit last night," I said. I didn't want her to be confused if her count was off for whatever reason. If they even did that. "Just to help with–my anxiety."

At the sink, I turned the water on and grabbed one of the

toothbrushes from a cup that was there for us to use. I squirted some toothpaste on it from the dispenser in the wall and quickly brushed. Jules had told us to hurry, but I was going to wait for Darrien no matter what. It wouldn't make much of a difference.

Lata patted me on the shoulder. "Don't worry about it. I'm glad you helped yourself." She sighed and turned on the sink after shouldering her med kit. She splashed some cold water on her cheeks, waved, and then walked away to join the others.

By the time Darrien was done and at the sink to wash up, I went to one of the stalls and relieved my bladder. I hadn't realized how badly I had to pee after the abrupt wake-up call. When I met him back at the sinks, I washed my hands faster than I should have, but the urge to meet with the others and find out what was happening grew every time the shuttle made a weird noise or shook.

"Ready?" I asked.

Darrien leaned against the sink. The coloring in his cheeks was back to normal, and they were even a little rosy, perhaps left over from how warm we'd been in the small bed. He nodded and gave me a small, coy smile.

"What?" I asked.

He shook his head and motioned for me to lead the way. "Nothing, nothing," he said, but I could hear the low chuckle behind me as we walked to the common area.

Everyone was there except for Raymond, I noticed. Harper and Jules were showing the crew something on the screen, and my stomach flipped, leaving me with the too-familiar feeling of nausea. Todd sat in the same spot on the couch as he'd done the night before, with his feet propped up.

"Let me guess. The worms?" I asked. My voice didn't sound nice at all, but a bitter rage started coursing through my veins as soon as I remembered the situation—how we should have waited, how my father was coming to rescue us because no one else was able to. Everything combined made my temper flare. The flower that had stabbed Darrien flashed through my memories, as well as watching Todd being dragged by the worms, and when Harper had been taken face-down in the sand.

Saba was the one who turned her head from the screen to me and nodded. "It doesn't look like they are happy. They are attacking both ends of the shuttle. And–"

"And there's something else out there, too," Harper whispered.

Great.

"What is it?" Todd asked, eagerly trying to get a better angle to look at the screen.

"Jesus, Darcy, fuck if I know," Harper snapped as she examined the holographic screen on the wall. Her arms were crossed, her body rigid, and her shoulders tensed. Her face was only a couple of inches from the holograph, and she was studying the area that was barely in the camera's view, which was right underneath the flight deck.

Saba pursed her lips and didn't say anything more. Todd ground his teeth together and crossed his arms defensively. I had a feeling that not many people talked to the famous Todd Darcy in that manner, and the rest of us knew better than to get involved. Everyone hushed after Harper's comment. Jules had fallen away from Harper and the camera feed but remained near Harper with nervous, inquisitive eyes.

"There!" Harper belted. She pointed her finger right underneath the area underneath the nose of the shuttle. "I saw something. Bigger than those worms."

Fucking great.

"Did you see anything at all last night?" I asked. Every muscle in my body vibrated with uncontrollable, seething anger from the situation we were in, with fear acting as a close second.

"No," Jules interjected. "Except what we thought were a couple of worms here and there. The fuckers don't have good aim, though. Occasionally, one would fling into the shuttle, but nothing other than that."

"Where's Raymond?" Darrien asked from where he was seated beside Todd.

Jules shook her head. "He hasn't come out of his room yet."

"He seemed to still be resting when I got up," Saba mentioned. "I tried pushing him some to wake him. I figured he'd be out here by now, though..." Worry laced her words as she glanced over to the smaller bedroom's door.

I stared at her. "Well, did he *move* or get up after Jules woke us all up? Anything?"

Saba's eyes first looked hurt, but then they turned into panic. "Well I–I don't know. Todd, did you see him get up? I thought he would..." she trailed off.

Todd continued to stare at the holograph and shook his head.

"Bloody *hell,*" Lata cursed as she shot up alongside Aleksy from the couch. They rushed into the smaller bedroom.

I didn't bother to rush in after them, or the others who followed. Soon enough, it was just me, Todd, and Darrien in the common area. Darrien got up to sit on the coffee table with his head turned toward the bedroom, waiting. I hoped that Raymond was still asleep after the events of yesterday, but something in the pit of my stomach was gnawing at me, telling me that something was wrong.

A couple of screams confirmed my suspicions. I closed my eyes and exhaled the breath I'd kept in.

"What?" Todd asked, mindlessly.

Darrien shook his head at Darcy. "Dude. Pay attention to the people around you. Yeah?"

Todd rolled his eyes and returned his gaze to the feed. Before I made the decision consciously, I was sprinting into the room and standing next to the others. After looking down at Raymond's body in one of the bottom bunks, a scream almost detonated from inside my chest.

Stupid fucking NASA. Stupid Captain Carnell, Jules, and Harper. Stupid.

Somehow, one of the worm aliens had found its way inside the shuttle, without Harper or Jules, or any of the rest of us noticing. Even Saba hadn't noticed. What stopped the thing from attacking her or Todd next?

The brilliant, genius, spineless academic lay limp in the bed, his complexion a horrible combination of blue, purple, and dark brown. Beside him, was a dead centipede monster, frozen on its back. Raymond's body was bloated from where it was tangled in the sheets and comforter, and his normally chocolate brown eyes were completely dilated to the point that all color was lost. The whites of his eyes were a deeper shade of red than blood. Dried vomit and blood coated his mouth, chin, neck, and down his sweater. Somehow, his puffed-up face looked serene, as though he didn't realize that he was about to die. I hoped that was the case.

"He–was–face down when I–" Saba's voice trembled uncontrollably. "I di...didn't hear anything. Didn't *feel* anything. How...I slept in a different bunk–oh my–" She couldn't speak any longer. Saba crouched in front of her husband's corpse and wailed, burying her head in her hands.

No part of this was Saba's fault, and I knew she'd feel guilt over it no matter what. I shushed her and stroked her thick locks of hair which were suddenly pressed against me as soon as I met her on the ground.

Aleksy got down on his knees alongside us and took out a pair of trauma shears. He looked down at Raymond's body and shook his head. "Anyone who doesn't want to see dis get worse may want to leave de room."

Saba rushed from my arms, a sob lodged somewhere in her throat and exited the room. Harper, who had turned several shades paler than her usual light brown complexion, walked after her with eyes that were empty and cold. I supposed that looking at how she had almost met her fate was petrifying in more ways than one. Ian followed them shortly after.

Jules leaned against me with a hand over her mouth as Lata kneeled down to assist her husband.

"Wait, you moron," Lata swatted at Aleksy's large hands. "Masks."

That was a *very* good idea. Luckily, Lata still had her med kit strapped around her. She dug inside of it and passed us all old-fashioned KN-95 masks. As she gave me mine, I noticed it was the fancier version that would seal off our mouths and noses completely. We would only be able to wear them for a few minutes before the oxygen that aided our breathing ran out, but they were much better than wearing nothing.

"Okay, now," Lata gave her husband her permission.

Aleksy rolled his eyes at her. Jules and I got up and stood near the bed, but made enough room for Aleksy and Lata to work. It was hard to breathe in the mask, and I don't know if it would have been any easier without it. I glanced down at Jules, who was an inch or two shorter than me, and noticed that she looked peaked and clammy. The shock of the initial rocking of the shuttle, along with getting close to no sleep, and then more chaos after finding Raymond in this state had thrown her.

"Are you sure you want to stay for this?"

She looked up at me and nodded. "I want to know so that we can be prepared."

Though her words were strong, her voice shook. I wished I could convince her to rest, but there was no time for that. Lata laid down a blanket from one of the empty bunks around us on top of Raymond's face and chest, all the way down to his thighs. Aleksy cut Raymond's pants slowly and precisely. After each cut of the material, he paused and examined what was underneath. I wondered what he supposed had happened— what he thought would be under the pants, where the worms had latched on.

After a few moments and more cuts, Lata let out an impatient sigh.

"Oh, my God, what?" Aleksy fussed at his wife.

She sighed again. "You're taking forever, babe."

Aleksy huffed, and gave her a look of annoyance, but passed over the scissors and switched places with her without another word.

Unlike Aleksy, Lata's approach was the total opposite: she took the scissors in a gloved hand, found the spot where Aleksy had left off, and then glided the scissors down the rest of the intact pant leg, making one long gash in the fabric.

"*Niecierpliwa kobieta,*" Aleksy muttered.

Lata handed the scissors to Aleksy and replied with, "*Bądź cicho.*" I had no idea that Lata spoke Polish too. The pair always seemed to surprise me in the oddest ways.

Aleksy peeled back the ripped layers of clothing on one side, and what we discovered had left me wanting to vomit, run from the room, and get closer all at the same time. I'd never seen anything like it. Lata finished cutting open the other side through a very evident gag.

Jules had apparently mostly felt the need to puke, for she covered her masked mouth with a hand and left the bedroom as fast as she could, muttering something about how she couldn't stay.

It was a wonder how the pants had even stayed on Raymond's legs. Both of his shins were covered in purplish brown rings that began above his knees and twisted down the rest of his legs. Planted on both legs was a giant, bubble-like sac, that was filled with clear fluid and small particles that glowed silver and yellow. The nausea circling my intestines and stomach grew to an intense level as I realized what the sac reminded me of.

"Millipedes and centipedes lay eggs," I said cautiously. "And they look, um, similar to—"

"That's the most disgusting thing anyone has ever said out loud," Lata said. She turned to meet my gaze with her large eyes.

"I know," I agreed. "But it looks like just...two? I think."

Aleksy laughed. "*Just* two."

We stared at the corpse under the blanket, and at the decorated legs with the two egg sacs in silence. I didn't understand the swirls. I could hardly comprehend the sacs. Had the centipede-worms been trying to kill us so that they could lay their eggs on—or, worse, *in*—us?

"Are there any puncture wounds?" I asked. My view was blocked by the others, but I didn't dare get closer.

Lata tilted her head to the side as Aleksy took off Todd's socks and shoes. "Mmm," she sounded. "Yes. Good call, we may have missed them. Here, right in between the Achilles tendon and heel."

Lata tapped at the area, and I shifted my body to see. Unlike a regular centipede, which would typically leave two holes in the skin, the puncture wounds that Raymond had endured were six...and much, much larger. He had several sets on either side of his ankles, almost hidden from sight.

Though he hadn't made a sound, I sensed his presence almost immediately from behind me. I whipped my head in the direction of the door, and there was Darrien, leaning against the door frame, arms crossed. He stared at Raymond with tears rimming his eyes.

I suddenly wondered if the wounds that Darrien had endured would turn into something like what had taken over Ray. I hastily threw one of the masks that were on the floor next to her to Darrien. He gave me a look but secured the mask. I scooted back against the wall so that I could stand near him, more worry lacing every breath I took.

I turned my head in order to look over and up at his tall figure. He was unreadable, with a face like that of a statue, aside from the tears. He stared straight ahead at his deceased friend, but it didn't take long for him to look down at me. Despite the mask that took up the majority of his face, I could tell by his eyes that he was giving me the best smile that he could, despite the circumstances. Using his hand closest to mine, he intertwined his long fingers through mine, then bent down to whisper in my ear.

"I will be okay," he murmured. His mask grazed my earlobe softly.

A slight chill ran down my spine. "You'd better be."

"And the sacs are...?" Aleksy turned to me, and despite the severity of the situation at hand, his eyes went down to take a look at whose hand I was holding—well, gripping.

"They're, um," I cleared my throat. "I can't tell for sure. On Earth, Centipedes and Millipedes have one sac per organism."

Darrien gaped at me. "Well, that's gross."

I sighed. "These are grosser than what I've ever seen. Typically, they lay their eggs like normal. You know, somewhere else. Not attached to a host..." I stared at the sacs and the glowing particles that swam within them. "And, to be completely honest, I'm not sure we're dealing with just beings here."

Lata whipped her head around and gave me a terrified look. "What do you mean? You said that there's one organism per sac."

Aleksy and Darrien had their eyes glued to the sacs. After a prolonged moment, understanding twisted up their faces.

"But, Lata," Aleksy said as he turned his wife back toward the body. "Dere are dings floating within. Yeah?" Aleksy turned back to me to see if he'd understood me.

I nodded. "It's hard to know for sure, but that's my best bet. And due to the radical progression that has already happened, I'm worried about how long it will take for them to..." there really wasn't a better word for what I had to say, than "...hatch."

Lata stepped back from Raymond's body in a rush. Aleksy joined her and put a beefy arm around her shoulders.

"But they didn't even *lay* the eggs," Lata said. Her eyes were the largest I'd ever seen, and her lips parted in understandable terror.

"Well, maybe they didn't lay them how the similar animals did on Earth. Maybe in this world, they lay their eggs by injecting them into a host."

Darrien sighed. "I'm beginning to think I should have caught up on some sci-fi alien movies before boarding that damn ship." I squeezed his hand in mine.

"So, what do we do?" Aleksy rasped through his mask.

We stood in silence. I was happy that Lata had taken the time to cover up the rest of Raymond's corpse. When I closed my eyes just to blink, I could see the hazy image of his bloated face, the red eyes, the vomit. For some reason, all three pairs of eyes turned to me.

"What? You think I know what to do?"

Lata shrugged. "You're the animal person."

I chuckled. "Yeah—*animals*—not weird aliens on a strange fucking planet that none of us knew anything about. And besides that, I mostly work with mammals, marsupials, and reptiles. Not arthropods. So I'm definitely out of my league here."

Another long moment of silence went by.

"We're going to have to get him off the shuttle," Darrien concluded.

I sighed. "Don't see any way around that."

Lata shivered, shook her head, and took off her gloves. "How the fuck did the damn thing get *in* here?"

I didn't answer because I didn't know. Raymond was dead. Perhaps we would all be dead soon. Surviving until Dad came to rescue us was our only hope now.

11

A UNIVERSAL FESTER

We left Raymond in the room after we covered him up with more blankets. Lata immediately took Darrien back to the bathroom for an extensive examination and more blood tests and who knew what else. Aleksy, Saba, and I sat on one of the sofas in the common room, sipping on instant coffee in silence. The coffee sucked, but it was better than sitting on the couch, doing nothing at all.

Saba looked like a shell of herself. Though her loud cries of peril had diminished, tears still flowed steadily down her face as she clutched her untouched mug of coffee in between shaky palms.

We had all come to the conclusion before leaving Raymond on the bed that we would have to find a way to move him. We had no choice but to get him outside before too long for fear of those... *things* hatching and wreaking havoc. Aleksy said that as soon as he finished his coffee, he would try to find something to move Raymond with—or *in*. He had also been waiting for Ian to come back from wherever he'd gone off to so that he would have help. Raymond's body was heavy, and we both knew without even mentioning it that Darrien and Todd wouldn't be able to help. Normally, I would have volunteered to assist Aleksy, but my body was screaming for me not to move after the way I pushed it yesterday.

Harper and Todd still studied the hologram. Neither one of them had seen any other creatures since our abrupt awakening. I supposed that hyper-fixating about what the monsters were doing outside was better than dwelling on wherever their thoughts would roam otherwise. Jules had returned to sit with us after a bout of puking and some anti-nausea medication from Aleksy and leaned on the second couch next to Saba, who sat there, eerily staring at nothing in particular, deep in her shock.

I hadn't seen Ian in a while, and I was beginning to worry about his well-being when finally he came back in through the door that led to the flight seats and flight deck.

He smiled gently, but it didn't reach his eyes. "I just talked to the Captain. William left a few minutes ago, and he should be here in a little over an hour. He is going to try to land as close to us as possible, so we won't have to walk very far."

Somehow, I hadn't thought of the fact that we would have to go back outside. I hadn't thought of the fact that my father would have to open up a hatch and wait for us to enter, which would put him at risk, too. I'd been so worried about him flying the shuttle to begin with, I hadn't considered what would or could happen once he got here.

Before I knew it, I'd come undone. The coffee mug shook in my hand. "This is just so completely fucked," I said, louder than I had meant to. "Why the hell are we here? Why did *no one* take the time to do some digging into this planet and this stellar system before we were dropped down here, essentially blind?" I started laughing, purely caught up in my frustration. "Did NASA literally just find this random fucking planet and go, 'Wow, look! A planet! Let's send some of the only people we have left down there and just see what the hell happens?'" I dug my fingertips into my eyelids. Tears were forming, and not from sadness, but from total fury. "No one briefed us on anything. No one told us what to expect. NASA didn't even research this place at all, did they? Are you guys trying to fucking kill us? I get we're literally in the middle of the apocalypse, but I don't think any of us will get anywhere if everyone on this mission keeps acting like goddamn morons!" I huffed and slammed my coffee mug down on the little table in front of me.

Harper ripped her gaze away from the footage at my outburst. She looked at me and then sought after Jules's gaze. Ian shook his head and crossed his arms as he leaned against the wall.

"Well?" I demanded. "Tell me why. Tell me. I know that NASA isn't this stupid. But I also know that NASA can be a total bag of assholes, too. Did they send a search ship out when my mother and her crew got lost? No. They fired my dad for asking too many questions and for trying to find out what happened to her so that we could move on, at least. But they wouldn't even grant us that. No, instead they gave us money to shut Dad up. Every single fucking thing that NASA does and creates is on purpose—I know that much from my father. We might not know *why*, but we know that much. I'm not a fucking idiot, and neither are the rest of the people here.

"Carnell sent us down here without any briefing. You all didn't even teach us how to use the suits or the gear probably, for fuck's sake. Something is off, and I know I'm not the only one who has noticed. So tell us. Now."

Lata and Darrien came back in then, and shot their heads confusedly around the room, obviously picking up on the tension that I had created and the fact that everyone was turned toward me.

I dug the fingers of my left hand into my right forearm to

keep from speaking again or doing something rash. My lungs were burning from the built-up emotions I'd kept in, and I wanted to throw something. I had agreed to this. I had agreed to help. I did *not* agree to go in blind, get attacked, see more people get injured and die, or be forced into acting recklessly all because the Captain had orders to obey. All because the majority of everyone at NASA were pricks who were self-entitled and didn't think about the lives of others. At that point, I knew I was channeling Dad and all of his aggressions, fears, and doubts. I knew I was going a little overboard. But even as I tried to separate Dad's feelings and suspicions from my own, I knew deep down that there was something wrong here.

I could feel all the eyes on me, even as I forced myself to focus on the floor underneath my feet. The silence was thick and heavy, and I was about to just get up and leave.

And then Ian cut through the silence and asked, "Please just tell them?" He said it so softly, I had to look up to make sure I wasn't hearing things.

But Ian was no longer looking at me. His dark eyes moved between Harper and Jules. They knew something. All three of them knew something.

"What is it?" Aleksy asked. For once, his voice was low and hushed with worry, without an ounce of his usual humor shining through.

Besides talking to Darrien about the confusing events and the dispute we had had about when to journey down to this godforsaken planet, I hadn't talked to anyone else about my hesitations—well, no one aside from Dad. As I looked at Aleksy, whose questioning eyes pierced into Harper's, I loosed a breath at the realization that perhaps I wasn't overreacting, and maybe the others felt the same sense of wrongness that I had even before we boarded the shuttle, despite the fact that they hadn't spoken up about it as I had in our meeting with the

Captain. Though Aleksy shot daggers at Harper, it was Jules who began.

"Fine," Jules said. She wrapped the blanket she had been cocooned in tighter around her shoulders. She sat forward on the couch and leaned on her knees with a tired expression.

"Julianna!" Harper spat. "You know what the Captain said," she warned with a sharp tongue full of venom.

Without a beat, Jules brushed her off. "I know what Wayne said, and I don't care. Everyone on Earth is dying. Daphne makes very valid points. Harper, don't you want us to make it long enough to find a new planet for your daughters to grow old on? Give them a chance to have families and live without the fear of dying from the Fester?"

Harper's lips tightened into a firm line. She didn't say another word. Instead, she slumped down to sit on the floor and crossed her arms.

With a long sigh, Jules looked back at us. Everyone was close together, even Lata and Darrien inched in as close as they could without crossing into people's personal bubbles. Todd had even taken his beetle eyes off of the outside footage in order to gape down at Jules in nothing short of exasperation.

"We weren't supposed to come to this planet," Jules said slowly. "Well, not originally." Harper groaned a little and rubbed at her temples. "But—"

"No. I'm speaking," Jules said flatly as she held up a palm to Harper. "Just let me finish."

To my surprise, Harper didn't fight back; she just went back to rubbing her head with her long fingers, her graying hair shielding her face from us as she looked down.

"We were actually set to be in hyper-sleep for another few days," Jules went on. "But, NASA saw this stellar system as we approached our initial destination, and they made the decision to wake the captain early and stop the ship. We were originally meant to go in the direction of the Pink Planet."

My stomach folded in on itself. The Pink Planet, or Aine, by its given name, was where my mother and her crew had been exploring before all signals with them had been abruptly cut off. From my understanding, NASA and the other space stations still didn't know shit about the planet. However, we *did* know that it was more than likely as close in the atmosphere to Earth as they had found thus far. We only knew that much because of the numerous drones that were sent to take samples from the planet in the past few decades.

In the years following my mother not coming back from space and several drones not returning, people began regarding the Pink Planet as the universal equivalent of the Bermuda Triangle. There was a reason that no rescue efforts had gone to find my mother and her crew—or, if there had been and we never knew about it, then they hadn't made it back. Out of the two hundred and something drones that attempted to make it back from the planet, only six had come back. Of those six, no footage nor any pictures had come back with them; just long loops of empty camera feed and photographs of black nothingness. Because of one lucky drone that returned, scientists confirmed that the atmospheric sample taken *should* have made the planet completely compatible with that of humans. That was back when I was a child. Another drone came back with a sample of sand, barely the amount of a teaspoon. One other came back with a rock. The other three drones came back empty-handed. The meager samples gave NASA and scientists around the world close to nothing to go on.

"We were seriously going to go to Aine?" Saba cocked her head as she asked, a fire in her eyes coming to life that I hadn't seen before.

"Not the Pink Planet necessarily. But, yes. We were headed in that... direction."

Lata laughed coarsely. "So, has NASA been trying to kill us off this whole time, then? Just for shits and giggles? I thought we were out here to try and save the human race."

Jules shook her head. Her eyes became glossier than usual, and then a tear rolled down her angular face. "You don't understand. Please, just let me explain," she huffed, almost as though she was out of breath. We waited for her to collect her thoughts in silence, even though we were all seething with fury and unanswered questions. Finally, she sighed and looked up at us. "Earth isn't the only planet that has been taken over by the Fester."

My brow furrowed with confusion. Harper was rocking back and forth a little on the ground as she shook her head, and Jules looked like she'd rather jump off of a bridge than continue with the conversation. My eyes met Ian's—and there was a disappointment and sadness lingering in his. Even if I wanted to deny Jules's words, how could I? They had to be true.

"So, essentially, we were rushed down here?" I asked. "Because NASA spotted this random stellar system while we were still asleep and—?"

Before I could finish my sentence, a loud crash sounded, and the shuttle shook.

"Shit!" Harper screamed as she jumped up to her feet.

Immediately, Harper was back in front of the hologram. It was hard to see from where I sat on the couch, but there was something visible moving near the nose of the shuttle. The blood in my veins that had been heated a moment earlier turned ice cold with fear. Jules got up from where she was perched, ditching the blanket that she had around her.

"What in de hell—?" Aleksy stuttered as he stood.

The door to the bedroom we had left Raymond's body in snapped open, the door slamming against the common room wall with a loud bang. Before I knew it, I was practically crawling away from my spot on the sofa, over to the others.

Two juvenile sand-worm-centipede *monsters* crawled on the walls, and with hungry, snapping teeth came right for us.

12

EXTRACELLULAR EXPLOSION

Before coming face to face with literal aliens, I thought I'd seen some scary shit in my life—not just the death of loved ones, but stampedes of animals that could kill me upon impact, hissing cockroaches the size of rodents, and having a newborn baby in my arms and having no clue how I would take care of him properly.

Colossal centipede monsters with long, spindly legs and razor-sharp teeth that were salivating with hunger right after hatching—well, that had to be it. The scariest moment of my life, and probably the scariest for those in the room with me, too.

I had left the others behind in my haste to escape the one coming at me and was now cowering by the door that led to the flight deck and seating area. I thought of going back to help but thought better of it. Aleksy had thrown one of the chairs from the kitchen at one of the creatures, which made it roll around helplessly on the floor. The thing struggled to get the right side up on its hard shell before righting itself and going straight for him.

"*Pierdolić!*" Aleksy boomed as he dodged out of the way with a second to spare. Lata ran for him as Darrien sped up and walked over to me as best he could in his state. Somehow, the creatures weren't interested in him, despite his injuries. I wondered if they could smell his wounds and decided he was spoiled meat.

It dawned on me that my knife was still in the bed where I'd originally tried to sleep the night before. As if reading my mind, Darrien headed away from me, over to the kitchen, and sloppily pulled out drawers until he found one that held knives and other cooking utensils—he slid a butcher knife over to Lata and Aleksy across the small kitchen island. Before he reached me, he shoved another butcher knife into Ian's hand and a smaller cutting knife into Jules's. He saved the last two knives for us—both small butcher knives. But they were better than nothing.

Ian and Jules were throwing anything they could at the second arthropod, including blankets and cushions from the sofas. It snapped its glistening jowls at Ian and the sound that erupted from his chest as he threw a cushion at the thing was guttural and animalistic, like nothing I'd ever heard from animals back on Earth.

Harper stood near her hologram in total shock, right beside Todd. To my surprise, Todd had figured out that she wasn't moving, and tugged on her arm in an attempt to get her to hustle.

"Saba!" Todd yelled at her urgently from where she stood, unmoving.

Saba looked at him, then cursed under her breath and sprinted over to them before the three came over to stand beside me and Darrien.

Aleksy had done a good job of dodging the monster that sought his flesh, but it was becoming more intelligent and fluid as they fought—it became quicker in its movements and smarter about how it dodged Aleksy's blows. He barked something at Lata, then pushed her in our direction, too. Lata half stumbled, but regained her footing and ran to us. Ian had successfully gotten a blanket on his monster, but it was already gnawing its way through the fabric.

"Daph! Help me!" Darrien said, tugging on my sleeve.

I had been too busy gaping at the pandemonium—staring in awe just like Harper had been rooted to the floor due to her shock—to notice what was going on right beside me.

"Fuck," I muttered.

He was struggling to open the door, and I could have had it open already, but my brain ceased to work as I stared at it. What had Ian done when he let me in the first time? Darrien hadn't been there to see.

There wasn't a hand scanner or a thumb scanner like back on the *Hippogriff*. That's right. It was the damn code. Hastily, I entered in the code of 2123, right in the nick of time. The door slid open right as Ian and the alien he was fighting tumbled over the couch, right beside our feet.

As the door fully opened, a new wave of panic washed over me. Would I be able to close the door fast enough for us to be safe if one of the monsters decided to come after us?

Darrien came in quickly behind me, and the shuttle rocked —and not from the newly born monsters in the next room. I shivered and tried my best not to mull over whatever else was outside attacking the ship. Harper moved to close the door, but I snatched her hand away.

"We have to keep it open until the last possible second. We have to keep our eyes on the others, or they might not make it," I said breathlessly.

Harper took her hand from mine with a scowl as I stood in the doorway.

As I watched the chaos before me, I prayed Dad was okay flying the shuttle. Despite all of my anxieties about his coming to get us, I *really* hoped that he would get his ass here soon. My heart panged as though something heavy had been thrown right in the center of it as I thought of Jaxon back on the main ship without Dad or myself there with him.

Todd, Lata, and Darrien hovered behind me, watching the events take place, while Harper retreated to one of the seats and slumped down.

"I'm going to help Aleksy and the others," Darrien said.

"Darrien–no! You're not strong enough," I said.

Lata nodded. "Agreed. You need to stay here."

Darrien tucked a few strands of stray hair that had come out of my braid behind my ear, then pecked me on the cheek.

"I have to. I'll be back."

With that, Darrien ducked around where I was barricading the others from the doorway, and shot off into the emergency quarters with a small stumble. He gained his footing fairly quickly, to my surprise. In horror, I watched as he went straight into battle, fighting alongside Ian and jabbing at the damn alien with a fucking steak knife.

"I need to find a weapon that's better than a steak knife," I said to no one in particular. "I don't know where the laser guns that Jules and Ian used are. I need to go find one. Harper? Are there any on this part of the shuttle?"

Harper stared at the chaos in the other room, eyes completely glazed over, hair wild, and complexion pale.

"Lata? Todd? Keep an eye on the door," I instructed.

"Of course," Todd said, taking my place.

Lata was focused on her husband in the other room, but she nodded to me and squeezed my shoulder. With Darrien's help, Ian and Darrien made it halfway across the room. A deep purple liquid, which I assumed was the monster's blood, trailed behind it. I noticed that several of its long limbs had been cut off, or were dangling by a thread, hanging on by mere bits of tissue. Those legs that had been amputated still inched across the room, following the duo like an evil monster lurking in the background of a slasher movie. I swallowed down the bile that quickly rose in the back of my throat.

Though the head of the other monster had completely bitten through the table which Aleksy had tried to use as a barrier, Jules had managed to wrap several blankets around the creature to keep its legs in check and had her full body weight on the thing as Aleksy's large boot clamped down on the area just beneath its teeth. I turned to leave just as I saw him wield his knife down, straight into its mouth.

I crouched in front of where Harper was seated and snapped my fingers in front of her face to grab her attention. Slowly, she turned her stoic face to mine.

"Harper. Guns. Where can I find one?"

She blinked at me, totally out of it. I never thought that tough old Harper would be the one to shut down amidst chaos, but there she was.

"Harper! Please," I pleaded.

Harper lifted a hand and pointed to the flight deck door. I nodded and rushed over. The flight deck door had a similar system to the other door, but the opening was much smaller. I thanked my lucky stars that it opened with no problem after I entered the same code. In no time, I was inside the flight deck, skimming over every nook and cranny, searching for *something* that I could use to assist my friends.

The flight deck itself was cramped, but I had a hunch that they had things hidden away, either underneath the two large chairs, underneath all the buttons and controls that meant nothing to me, or somewhere else, perhaps within the walls. I sat down in one of the chairs and felt around the sides of the seat and underneath it. I tried my best to calm my rapid heart-beat, but the adrenaline vibrated through my entire body, and I couldn't help but note every passing second as a terminal countdown.

When I found nothing while sitting, I moved to crouch as much as possible to get a look underneath the control panel. The cramped foot space underneath the panel wasn't helpful, giving me hardly any leverage to move around. Running my fingers lightly underneath the panel, I felt nothing but smooth metal and a few switches. I dropped lower into the foot space and arched my head in order to look underneath the seat. All I could see were shadows, so I stuck out my arm and felt around blindly. Nothing.

I moved to the other seat and did the same. Just as I was about to give up and start searching for hidden compartments within the walls, my index finger touched something cool; I leaned in further and felt sharp corners. It had to be a box. After some straining and repositioning my body, I pulled out a slender metal box that was close to two feet in length. I had no idea how it had fit underneath the seat, but I couldn't care less. My heart thudded against my ribs like a time bomb as I silently begged for the contents to be something useful.

Of course, as I went to open the box, it was locked. I snatched the box up, stumbled, and then went back to where the others were as fast as I could.

Saba was in one of the seats beside Harper. Todd and Lata still stood behind the open door, waiting for the others.

"Harper!" I said breathlessly as I kneeled down on my knees in front of her. "Harper, do you have the keys? Is this a gun?"

She didn't answer. Saba shook her shoulder. Screaming ensued from nearby, and I knew I needed the box to open more than anything.

"Harper!" I screamed. I got back on my feet and shook her with all of my might. Now was *not* the time to have a mental breakdown. She could do that all she wanted to later. Right now, it was kill or be lunch. I slapped her as hard as I could across the face. Twice. She looked up at me with eyes that were stunned and angry, and I couldn't find any compassion within me to care that I'd just struck her.

"Open the fucking box, Harper! Or give me the goddamn keys!" I barked.

Our roles were reversed now. I was in charge and she was petrified. I felt bad for the red marks that seeped into her cheeks, but I would have felt worse if people—these people who were now like a weird family to me—died.

Without a word, Harper dug a hand underneath her sweatshirt collar and brought out a necklace. On the chain were several keys. She took the necklace off, found the smallest of the keys, and handed it to me. I could feel her angry stare on me as I unlocked the box. Whatever. She could bitch at me later.

The box clicked open, and within was the best thing possible. It was a laser gun similar to the ones the others had used yesterday, but it was bigger, and from what I knew about weapons, which wasn't much, I figured that meant it would do more damage. I had shot old-fashioned guns several times when Magda and Dad took me to the local ranges so that I could learn self-defense growing up. Though guns were very hard to get ahold of, the dome had several in lock boxes hidden all around the conservatory, because you never knew what would happen. Terrorists had attacked several Mother Earth buildings in the past, and sometimes animals could get loose or become ill, which made them rabid. We had never had to use the guns at the sanctuary, but I was overjoyed that Dad and Madga had thought to teach me.

That had been over a decade ago, and I certainly hadn't practiced with laser guns, or anything as large as the one that I now held in my hands, but I knew I could figure it out. I had to.

Todd peeked at me over his shoulder and motioned to the gun. "Do you want me to?"

He was still in no condition to do anything—especially not something like barging into battle against weird aliens. And Harper, though much better trained than me, wasn't either. I shook my head. Before I could consider the outcome of my actions, I ran past Lata and Todd and into the other room.

"Be careful!" Lata cried after me.

The alien that Aleksy and Jules had been fighting charged as soon as it saw me, despite being thoroughly injured and leaking more and more blood with every movement it made. Aleksy and Jules froze in their tracks.

"Run, assholes!" I screamed.

Luckily, they did that without trying to help me. What were they going to do? Throw more pillows and blankets at it?

I knew that the safety had been on when I took the gun out of the box. Fortunately, I had been clear-headed enough in my haste to disengage it as soon as I left the seating area. Now, it was as simple as pulling the trigger. I hoped.

The alien was only a few feet from me. Its teeth snapped and its blood from the amputated limbs and stab wounds flew around it like spatter paint as it scurried my way. It stood up on its back legs, which made the thing tall enough to tower over me. It bared its teeth, spraying silvery saliva all over me. *Mother fucker.*

"Bye-bye, ugly asshole!" I yelled as I squeezed the trigger.

A beam of blinding green light shot out from the gun and cut through the horrible creature as though it was made of paper mache. The beam shot through its mouth and split its jaw in half, and purplish guts flew everywhere—all over my body and face, onto the walls, the floor, and everything in between.

I didn't know if the blood was toxic like I assumed its fangs might be, so I ripped off my sweatshirt and wiped my face roughly before turning to the other monster, thankful that I had on my bulky sports bra underneath my sweater. Ian was stabbing it while Darrien continued stomping. No matter how many times Ian stabbed it or Darrien beat down on it, the thing continued to writhe and hiss and chomp.

"Out of the way!" I screamed. Ian was so caught up in trying to kill it, that it took him a moment to stop. As soon as he did, he and Darrien hesitantly backed off toward the exit.

For a small moment, I watched in amusement as the creature tried to get up off the ground. It was weak from the stab wounds, and the blankets that had been around it were shredded, but the motherfucker refused to give up. Right before it got up, I pulled the trigger and watched in delight as it exploded into millions of tiny pieces. I was actually laughing as I wiped myself of its blood and guts yet again, this time with one of the pillows that hadn't been used in the fight.

Ian had joined the others, but Darrien stood a few feet from me.

"Well, that was fun," I muttered as I put the safety back on the gun.

I decided that this was my gun now, and no one else could have it. We worked quite well together. Darrien was wiping blood off of his face with his shirt.

"Darrien," I said. I went to him and hugged him tightly. I dangled the gun from one hand. A knot formed in my throat at the thought of what could have happened to him. "Are you okay?"

I pulled back and he stared down at me. "Yes," was all he said.

"Can you do me a favor?"

"Anything." He beamed at me and a small hint of a smile tipped one corner of his mouth upward.

"I think it's best we get everything we need from here," I motioned to the common area and bedrooms, "and stay in the flight deck area. Raymond's body is still in the bedroom, and I don't know if more of those... things will hatch."

Darrien's head shot in the direction of the smaller bedroom. He swallowed roughly.

"Keep that door closed," I said. "And then get everything we need. Do you know where Ian's gun is? And Jules's?"

"I think they're both in the other bedroom," he said. "What else do we need?"

I looked down at my bare skin and the drying blood that decorated my torso. "Any clothes you can find, towels from the bathroom, and if you could wet some, that would be great." I sighed. "Anything else you think we need. I'll grab water and some food from the kitchen."

Aleksy came back into the room then. "I will help. We need our med kits, too," he said as he clamped a hand on Darrien's shoulder. He turned to the others who were crowded in the doorway, watching.

"If anyone needs to take a shit, now is de time," Aleksy said with a chuckle that told me he was trying his hardest to find humor after all that had just occurred. He pointed to the single bathroom closest to the door. "Use dat one."

"Good idea," I said.

"Darrien, I will accompany you," Aleksy said. He had his butcher knife in his giant hand and handed it to Darrien. "May I borrow your gun, Daphne?"

I peered down hesitantly at my gun but handed it over. They needed to be armed in case more of those awful creatures came about. Or worse, whatever continued to rock the shuttle.

"I promise do give it back," Aleksy winked. "You are better with it den I would be, I am sure."

With that, Aleksy motioned for him and Darrien to gather supplies. I stepped over chunks of giant centipede-worm-alien innards, broken chairs, shoes, and other debris. I gathered a couple of giant jugs of emergency water from the bottom of the small kitchen cabinet, several protein and granola bars, and a thing of nuts, and then I went back to the others.

Lata helped me set down the supplies. She handed me a thing of water that she had with her as I sat down next to Ian with a long sigh.

Ian leaned into me. "Thank you for saving our asses."

A humorless chuckle left my lips. "Happy to be of service."

13

ROCK THE SHUTTLE

"**H**ow will we know when William lands?" Darrien asked Jules.

We all sat in the seats beside the flight deck. Some, like Ian and Jules, sat on the floor with their backs up against the seats. None of us looked good. Jules's face, which was usually rich and light brown, was paler than mine. Aleksy, like me, was covered in dried alien blood on various parts of his body. We had all wiped off our faces and necks with the wet towels Darrien and Aleksy brought back with them, but the dark purple stains still remained. Aleksy had kept his word and given me back the laser gun when he came back. I gripped it like a lifeline in my lap. They had only found one of the other guns, and Aleksy kept it by his side.

If I looked how I felt, I probably looked like a giant dumpster that had been crushed into the ground. Darrien appeared to be feeling better than he had yesterday, and for that, I was grateful. But the rest of us? Well, we looked like we'd gone into battle and barely survived. I guess that wasn't too far off from the truth.

Jules cracked a couple of knuckles and said, "There will be

a loud sound from the flight deck that will alert us when he lands."

"Is there no way to touch base with him?" I asked.

Jules shook her head and gave me a sympathetic look. "Sorry. I wish there was."

"How did you all reach the Captain, then?" Lata asked for me. She and Aleksy were sitting next to me and Darrien. Lata hadn't let go of Aleksy's hand since he made it safely into the room. Her head leaned on his meaty shoulder, and he stroked her wrist with his thumb.

"There's a way to call the Mothership from the flight deck. That's how I contacted Carnell earlier and asked him when William was coming," Ian said.

"Couldn't we contact Carnell and ask if *he* knows how long it will be before he lands?" Saba asked. Her attitude had heightened and replaced her grief for Raymond. For the time being, anyway.

Ian glanced over to Jules and she shrugged. "We can. It shouldn't be long, though. I take the Captain not contacting us as a good thing," Jules said.

No one had brought up the conversation we'd been in the middle of before the centipede monsters rudely interrupted us. I had thousands of questions stewing in my mind about the whole thing—how was it possible that our planet wasn't the only one dying? A universal plague seemed impossible. How far would we have to dig into the vast universe to find a place far enough away that we felt safe? Wouldn't the Fester find our new planet eventually? The thoughts sped around in my mind on a loop, like one of those rides that spins faster and faster, then so fast you think you might fall out of the seat and onto the hard ground beneath you. Or puke.

The shuttle jostled again, making those of us who were seated shift to the left, and those on the ground tumbling. It did that ever so often; just a slight rocking back and forth that made us tilt. It never became normal, no matter how often it happened. Instead, each time we went rocking, I couldn't help but wonder when the shuttle door would pop off or worse.

But this time, something was different. As we were tilted sideways, I realized after a moment that we didn't move back down to where the shuttle should have been. The seats Darrien and I were in were more airborne than they should have been, and Ian and Jules slid across the floor all the way to the emergency quarter's entrance as whatever creature was outside pushed harder against the shuttle. I grabbed for Darrien's hand.

"Fuck, fuck, *fuck!*" Jules screamed. "I am so sick of this planet!"

The shuttle shifted again to the point where, Darrien, Lata, Aleksy, and I had to jump down and join everyone else because otherwise, we would dangle in our seats. I wished that the gravity wasn't controlled inside of the shuttle—that way we could move around a little easier. But no.

"We need to put on our suits," Ian gasped as the shuttle shook.

I stared at him dumbly. "Most of our suits are damaged. And in the other part of the shuttle."

Ian crawled to the space right in front of the flight deck door and reached up to the floor, which was now eerily above us. It was disorienting and dizzying to watch my surroundings. Nothing looked right. Nothing *was* right.

Ian felt around the carpeted floors with his fingertips. "It should be..." he trailed off.

"Try going to the left just a little," Jules suggested. "And up. I think."

I had no idea what he was doing. The rocking of the

shuttle made it hard to concentrate on anything other than what would happen to us next.

Something large—larger than what had been hitting us—whacked into the shuttle, which sent Ian back down to his ass with a harsh thump.

I knew better than to ask Harper, who was huddled in the corner closest to the exit ramp, so I directed my question to Todd, "What was the thing you and Harper were looking at earlier on the video feed?"

Todd pinched the bridge of his narrow nose and sighed. "Well, it's hard to say." He glanced at Harper. The mischievous light that usually occupied his eyes was totally gone. "Harper got a better look at it. But...from the one small look I got, it almost resembled a... tentacle."

"A tentacle?" Lata and I asked in unison.

"Yes."

"A tentacle. A tentacle that came from the sand?" I asked, bewildered.

Todd nodded and directed his attention to Ian and Jules, who were both trying to find something on the floor above us after the shuttle stopped moving.

"What—that doesn't make any sense," I murmured, mostly to myself.

I thought of every cephalopod I had ever worked with, which truthfully wasn't a lot compared to that of marine biologists. Octopuses, squids, cuttlefish—the ancient and strange nautilus with its unexpected beak and ninety tentacles—and every single one of those organisms lived in the ocean. Perhaps the alien didn't have *actual* tentacles. Maybe it just seemed that way. Or maybe it did have tentacles and had the ability to live within the water and sand. Either way, it wasn't a comforting piece of information.

"Aha!" Ian cheered, bringing me back to reality.

"Good job, man," Jules praised.

Ian's fingers pressed into a hidden compartment. How many hidden things were in the shuttle? I might have said it was overkill had we been in a different situation. He pressed harder, and then a hoard of spacesuits and helmets fell out of the floor and knocked him down onto his ass again.

"Oh, my God!" Jules cried. "Are you okay?"

Ian sat up after his fall into one of the seats. He rubbed his forehead but smiled proudly. "Yes. I may have a small goose egg, but at least we have the suits."

He sighed contentedly and leaned his head back. He grinned at me and I gave him a thumbs-up and a wink. Jules sorted through the suits and helmets that had fallen all around us.

"Usually, these would have been organized by my suit and helmet size," she sighed. "But we'll figure it out."

"I'll help you," Saba volunteered. "The sooner we get those suits back on, the better, I would think."

I nodded in agreement. In the commotion, my braided hair had come almost completely undone. As Jules, Saba, and Ian organized the suits and helmets, I combed through my locks with my fingertips and tied my hair up in a tight bun at the base of my skull in preparation for the helmet. When I was done, Darrien had a half grin spread across his face as he gazed at me. I raised an eyebrow.

"I like the bun," Darrien said softly. "I like it best when it's down, but the bun is..." he trailed off, eyes roaming over the bun, my neck, and lower. "Well, I like it." Then, his lips inched toward the shell of my ear. "Remind me to thank you for saving us. Later. When we're alone."

Liquid heat seeped in between my thighs, but I composed myself with an eye roll. "Shouldn't you be more concerned about getting a space suit on? Or whatever monsters await us on the outside of this shuttle?"

He hummed. "No. It's much less stressful to look at and compliment you. And think of all the ways I'll be giving you my thanks later," he purred into my ear.

A blush heated my cheeks as Saba handed me a suit. "Is this your size?" she asked me, cutting Darrien and I off from our conversation. I read the printed size on the inside collar. It was.

"Perfect. Thank you, Saba."

Saba and Jules handed out the new spacesuits to the rest of us, and they weren't nearly as flashy as the ones we'd worn originally. I only hoped that they worked as well as the others did. The backup suits were all a simple, iron black. Yet, they all still had the Todd Darcy emblem on the right side of the chest, just as the sweaters and other suits had. Of course, they did. Even in space, his team back on our home planet had wasted no time in utilizing their marketing skills.

Ian gave us our helmets as the shuttle shook once more. The helmet was bulkier than the others we had worn the day prior but looked like it worked the same. I wondered if these suits and helmets were the set they had made before creating the other, prettier ones.

"Well. No use in being shy with each other now," Jules said as she stripped off her sweater. Underneath, I noticed she was even more well-endowed than I was, which was saying something. She wore a similar, unflattering sports bra like mine. We all stared at her as she took off her pants, too, until she shot us all glares and motioned for us to get changed along with her.

"You're all pervs," Jules muttered as she pulled on the legs of her suit.

I couldn't help but grin. Lata started cackling, and the rest of us followed suit. Jules rolled her eyes, but laughed, too. Even

Harper seemed to come out of her haze a little as a small smile perked up on her lips.

We were all kind of perverts, looking at each other as we all changed, but it was all in good fun. Somehow, doing something so natural as changing became a distraction from the current situation we were in. Lata whistled as I took off my sweater, and Jules wriggled her eyebrows. Darrien had a look on his face similar to the one he had in the shower last night as he savored my body, and I tried not to focus on how that made my chest warm.

Harper stripped, and showed off a complete six-pack, which made my jaw drop.

"God damn, Harper," Ian grinned.

Harper, finally coming back to the land of the living, replied, "Turn away, Ian. I'm old enough to be your mother."

We all roared at that, and despite Ian's dark complexion, I knew by his shy eyes and pursed lips that he was likely blushing. Hard.

Aleksy stripped and revealed a full chest of tattoos that I couldn't quite make out. I did notice that he and Lata had matching tattoos of text tattooed in thick calligraphy on their ribs. Lata was toned, but not very muscular. I was once again a bit jealous of the beautiful bralette she was able to wear. Before they had even gotten all the way undressed, Aleksy planted a sloppy kiss on Lata's full lips.

"Get a room, you two," Darrien muttered. He had remained sitting as the rest of us got ready. I was going to help him as soon as my suit was on. I may have gotten dressed a *little* slower than usual because I was enjoying the way his eyes slid over every part of my body with each tiny movement I made. That gaze was currently on my ass as I slid the suit up over it.

Aleksy chuckled and leaned over to pat Darrien on the head. "You are one to talk, Dr. Park."

Aleksy winked at Darrien and then at me. Lata snickered a bit as she zipped up the rest of her suit, then worked to put her hair up.

Once my suit was on, I crouched in front of Darrien, which was awkward with the seats in the position they were in.

"Can you lift your arms?" I asked.

"I think so."

"Be careful," Lata warned as Jules helped her with her helmet. "I don't want to have to pack any more of those wounds."

Darrien smiled as he carefully lifted his arms above his head. Aleksy helped me with the other side of his sweater as we gently pulled it up and over his head. Before I realized what I was doing, I scanned his chest, making sure there were no weird marks. No egg sacs. I exhaled roughly when I realized it was his regular chest, back to its healthy golden complexion.

His fingertips caressed the underside of my chin. "I'm okay, Daph."

I forced a deep inhale as I nodded. "Let's get you standing. We need to... get your pants down."

Before Aleksy could make a vulgar joke, I shot a glare at him. Aleksy's bright eyes crinkled in amusement, but he held his hands up in surrender. Again, he assisted me in helping get Darrien's clothing off, and then we worked on either side of Darrien to shimmy his suit up. I was thankful for the help. Once his suit was on and zipped, Darrien sat back down slowly.

"Thank you," he said to both of us. "I can't wait to be able to do that by myself again."

I didn't blame him. I would have hated having to get help with getting dressed, going to the bathroom—or for anything, really. It reminded me of when I had felt so helpless those first few days after waking from hyper-sleep and having to rely on

Lata for almost everything. Especially when I was so used to doing most things without assistance.

"It won't be long until you're able to move easier," Lata commented, though we could barely hear her through her helmet.

Harper came over to me and helped me with my helmet while Ian helped Saba with hers and Jules secured Darrien's.

"Thank you," Harper told me. She looked more coherent now. More like her usual self—the light had come back in her eyes where they had looked vacant only minutes ago. "Thank you for taking over and for—well, thank you for stepping up to the plate and saving us."

She tugged on the helmet, connecting it to my suit.

"You would have done the same for me," I said.

Once all of our helmets and suits were on, Ian dispersed the spare sets of boots, which were less clunky than the others. They reminded me of rain boots and for some godforsaken reason, they were the color of orange highlighters.

"I don't know if we will have exact sizes," Ian said as he examined the inside of the shoes.

The shuttle rocked again, but this time, whatever lingered outside of the shuttle crashed into us like a wrecking ball, and we were completely upside down. We all fell in jumbled unison, and I crashed into something hard and sharp on my right hip. Lata fell on top of me, worsening the impact, and Aleksy fell not far away from her with a grunt. A pained sound came from Darrien, and after blinking several times, I realized he had fallen on his chest, right where his wound was.

"Fuck!" I hissed. I hauled Darrien up with all my might so that he was sitting up again, despite the screaming pain in my hip.

"We have to get the hell off this planet," Harper muttered.

The boots were everywhere. Aleksy and Ian gathered them

and tried to match them together by size. Ian handed me my gun, which had dropped to the other side of the small room with the impact. With a huff, I sat back against the wall and laid the gun across my legs. Then, I squinted through my helmet and examined my hip.

A small piece of metal stuck out right in the tender area underneath my hip bone. I had no idea where the metal had come from, but it was the size of a pencil, and it hurt like a bitch. I hissed through my teeth as I pressed my fingers around the area where I'd been impaled. When I brought my fingers back up to my line of sight, they were bloody. In my fresh suit, too.

"Great."

I was about to ask Lata for help when a piercing alarm sounded from the flight deck. *Dad.*

Soon enough, my pain disappeared and my nerves went haywire. If the alarm was sounding, that had to mean he had landed. Suddenly, the piece of metal sticking from my body didn't concern me all that much.

"I've got it!" Jules yelled before disappearing into the flight deck. She practically had to climb to the door and fall into the flight deck, but she managed to do so with grace.

"Alright, fuck sizing these shoes. Do your best to find some that aren't too large, otherwise, the suit won't lock into them. A shoe size one or two sizes too big should still work. We have to prepare to get the hell off of this shuttle," Ian said, confident with his orders. Much more confident than the young man who was full of hesitancy and nerves before flying this same shuttle less than twenty-four hours ago.

Now, I had trouble bending, too. I looked at Lata before speaking, remembering how the mic system worked. "Lata?"

She shot her head at me after picking up a pair of shoes closest to her. I pointed with a gloved hand to the metal shard.

"Oh. Well, that's not good," she observed.

No shit. "Yeah. I didn't think so."

The alarm stopped, and I took a shaky inhale. Lata pressed on either side of the piece of metal with delicate fingers.

"We're going to have to pull it out and tend to it once we are on the other shuttle," Lata said. She patted my knee. "It doesn't look too bad, and I know the suit will stitch back up. I'm sorry I can't do anything more right now. I–I don't even know where my kit flew off to." She gave me a sympathetic smile.

"It's okay," I reassured her. "You're sure the suit will still hold?"

She nodded. "It can take it from what Todd and Carnell told me and Aleksy before we left."

"What happened?" Darrien interjected, looking over at us with saucers for eyes. He noticed where Lata's hands were placed, and though the helmet shaded his features, I could tell he was worried by the way his lips turned down. "Are you okay?"

"Yeah. I just need someone to get me some boots, please?" I asked.

"You and I both," Darrien scoffed. "We're doing great, aren't we?"

I snorted. "Yeah, we're awesome. Neither one of us can bend, and we've both been impaled."

Our being impaled wasn't funny, but we laughed anyway. Todd handed Darrien a large and smaller pair of shoes. He glanced at the shard in my hip and turned away, growing pale at the sight. Still, he managed to help me get the boots on, and he even got them in my size. Once I was good to go, and Lata had her boots on as well, she glanced down at the shard and gave me a questionable look.

"How bad does it hurt?"

A drawn-out sigh left my lips as I repositioned myself. Of course, as soon as I was back in a proper position, the shuttle started jostling around once more. Lata sighed in frustration. Finally, Jules came back, carefully making her way out of the flight deck.

"William is here! And everything is okay. He did great," she reassured me. "He couldn't land too close to us, unfortunately. It'll be about a half-mile's walk."

Despite the pain in my hip and the nonstop anxiety and adrenaline that consumed me each time the shuttle rocked or flipped, I managed a weak smile. Dad made it. He was safe. Soon, I could wrap my arms around him.

"But what about everything that's... out there?" Saba questioned nervously.

Harper tapped her knee. "I don't know. We can check the outside cam before we let down the ramp and see if we can actually see something worth noting. Otherwise... Aleksy has a gun. As does Daphne."

After I had obliterated the two aliens in the other room, no one said anything about me or my gun. Harper didn't ask for it, and neither did Jules or Ian. I had given Harper the knife that Ian had retrieved from the bunk bed I'd shared with Darrien last night so that she would have something, but I wasn't letting go of my gun. Jules had a similar knife, as did most of the others—or they had a butcher or steak knife from the kitchen. The knives wouldn't be great if things were attacking us on all sides, but they were better than being empty-handed. Or at least that's what I told myself to serve as some sort of comfort.

"Let's take a look at the camera feed, see what's out there if possible... and then we will have to run, or hop, or whatever works for us out there—like *hell*," Jules said. "As soon as William sees us within a few yards, he will let down the ramp."

The shuttle was still once more. Jules put on her boots, as did Saba. Finally, all of us had on our suits, gloves, boots, and helmets.

"Does he have a weapon, too?" I asked tightly through gritted teeth.

Jules nodded. "Same one as you."

We all breathed for a moment while the shuttle stood still. There was no way to prepare for what was to come. We just had to do it. Leave this shuttle, escape the monsters, and fly away to safety. I was looking forward to yelling at the Captain when—when, not *if*—we got back.

As Jules stood up and crawled to the door of the ramp to prepare to open it, whatever creature roamed within the sand outside hit us with its biggest blow yet—we went spinning again, but this time, the shuttle rolled and rolled several times before it stopped. Red emergency lights flickered on, disorienting my vision, and an earsplitting alarm blared at us.

Jules, Ian, and Harper rushed around us and turned on the oxygen in our helmets. The hiss sounded in mine, and I knew I was good to go. There was no reason to wait around any longer.

"Fuck the camera feed," Harper sighed. "We have to go. Now."

I hated that I agreed with her, but she was right. At any minute, whatever it was that was crashing into us would be inside, and we couldn't let that happen. Still, I couldn't help thinking that escaping was easier said than done.

14

JAWS

The good news was that the shard of metal that had been in my hip dislodged itself at some point when we all went flying to various sides of the shuttle as it flipped and rolled. One moment, I was in one of the chairs, the next, I crashed harshly into the ceiling, and then the seats again. Finally, the shuttle halted and stopped upright, leaving all of us to fall on the floor or in the chairs.

The bad news was that when I came crashing down to the ground, my back landed on something equally sharp as the shard, if not sharper. My hand was wrapped around my gun so tightly, my knuckles strained and blanched. I strained but forced myself to sit up.

Bright red emergency lights flickered in between bright white lights, blinding my vision and leaving me overstimulated and in a heightened state of panic. The piercing alarm didn't cease and came not only from the flight deck but from the room we were in. It was worse than any fire alarm I'd ever heard, and no one could hear each other speak in the mics of our helmets because of it.

But we all knew what the lights and alarm meant. The shuttle was officially damaged by presumably the large, tentacle-ridden creature looming outside in the sand, and we had to flee immediately.

Darrien landed closer to the ramp door, and right on his poor chest. He crouched down and rubbed at his aching wounds. He caught me looking, and gave me a thumbs up, even though I knew that landing where he did had to have hurt like a bitch. Especially since Ian had landed on top of him, too. Ian patted Darrien's back in a silent apology as we all stood.

Jules and Harper made their way to wherever they had landed over to Darrien and Ian and began preparing the door and ramp for our escape as someone poked my arm.

Aleksy waved at me and then pointed at my back. It was hard to think with the piercing alarm going off, and that had been a great distraction for my pain. I twisted my neck, trying to see what had impaled me this time, but couldn't see. Aleksy held up a finger and forced my arms at my side. I took in a breath and exhaled roughly as he quickly yanked out the object from my back. Despite everything at the moment, I felt very thankful that whatever it was hadn't hit a nerve or something worse.

Aleksy waved a steak knife in front of my eyes, and I felt my jaw loosen and my jaw drop. He grinned and shrugged, then wiped the blood off of the utensil and handed it to Lata, who was waiting along with everyone else near the ramp door.

I stood behind everyone else and paused to feel around where I'd been impaled in my hip. The material had repaired itself, but even so, my fingers came back with a slight tint of blood. The pain was sharp when I moved, as was the other wound in my back, but I could move.

I could run. I could fight and run.

The knot in my throat grew as each second passed with us waiting for the door to open and the ramp to lead us out to battle. I expected more jostling or more rolling, but the shuttle remained steady and upright. Somehow, that was more unnerving. I wanted to ask what direction Dad and the rescue shuttle were in, but I couldn't. I wanted to ask if we could see where the monster was on Harper's camera feed, now more paranoid than ever, but knew there was no time to wait. It was hard to have so many questions on the tip of my tongue while the fear of the unknown was heavily draped over my shoulders like a weighted blanket.

Harper held up her little camera feed—the one that connected to the hologram and reminded me of an old-fashioned baby monitor. She waved until we all looked up at her hand. Thank God she decided it was worth looking at. She pointed for us to go to the left. Thank goodness we at least had a general direction.

My heart sped up, my throat closed and swelled uncomfortably, and my fingers tingled as she held up three fingers. *Two.* Jules had the door open, and the ramp began to lower. *One.*

Like the adults that we are, everyone tried to exit the shuttle at once in pure panic. You would think we would have been more aware of rushing at one another, but no. I was last, so I had to watch in amusement and horror as Harper pushed Ian, Ian pushed Saba, and so on and so forth. Finally, they figured it all out. Aleksy pushed past everyone, Lata holding the one hand that didn't hold the other gun. Lata had the steak knife that had previously been in my body strapped to her belt. She held out her hand to Harper. Harper took Jules's hand, and then Jules took Ian's, and then Ian tried to take Darrien's hand as well. Darrien shook his head and pointed for me. My heart skipped, in awe that he wanted to wait for me given the situation. I was at the end, after all, with Todd right in front of me. I hastily grabbed Todd's hand and then Darrien's. If I was anyone else, I'd have preferred to be in the middle. Ian shrugged and took Saba's hand instead. Darrien squeezed my hand twice, reminding me of the descent down to this God-awful planet. Had that only been yesterday?

Taking Darrien's hand was like coming home or releasing a huge breath of air after being underwater. I didn't like the space that had been forced between us, and that thought felt foreign and scary, but I squeezed his hand harder, pushing it away for later. For when we weren't about to run for our lives.

The chained line we created began moving, and soon enough, I was stumbling behind Darrien down the ramp, tugging Todd behind me, where we made our way back onto the sand. As our boots hit the ground, some of the others released their hands from others. I thought it would have been smarter for all of us to stay together, but what did I know? At least everyone remained close together.

I refused to let go of Darrien's hand. Or Todd's.

We ran the best that we could in the sand and in the awkward gravity of the planet. A person would run, then glide a few feet before their boots hit the ground again, leaving a small shower of sand in their wake. My gun was at my side, latched onto my belt, safety off, and ready to go.

I looked behind us at the shuttle we had left behind. It was shocking that the alarm hadn't gone off earlier—the entire outside of the shuttle was dented, scratched at, and maybe even bitten by the centipede creatures. It was hard to tell. Either way, it looked like a crushed soda can that had been run over by a semi-truck.

What was more unnerving was the fact that we didn't see anything but sand in front of us. As we ran in the direction that Harper had instructed, Aleksy at the head of the pack, gun at the ready, we all nervously glanced around, expecting those damned centipedes to emerge from underneath our feet. Or whatever larger creature had destroyed the shuttle. Or something worse.

The cut in my back sent a shooting pain up and down my body. I winced but kept running and gliding with Darrien and Todd, keeping up with the group, reminding me of pack hunters in the wild. My hip throbbed each time we landed, making it hard to keep up with the pace.

I decided to look ahead in the distance for the other shuttle. For Dad.

To my surprise, things remained calm. After a couple of minutes, Aleksy whooped into the mics and said, "I see Will! I see the shuttle!"

We picked up our pace as much as possible. Finally, despite everyone being in front of me, Darrien, Todd, and I finally saw it. In the distance was a shuttle almost identical to the one behind us. It shined in the sun, making it hard to look at it for long. But I did. I stared at it and watched as the shuttle got larger the closer we got.

Dad. My father. My safe haven.

My face was wet. Tears had slid down my cheeks, though I hadn't felt them come. I blinked hard, not wanting the salty tears to blur my vision even more.

Darrien looked at me. "Are you okay?"

I nodded. "You?"

He huffed. "I'll be better once you and I are in that shuttle."

I noticed how he hadn't mentioned anyone else in the crew, though I knew he cared about them, too. Still, it made my stomach flutter just a little.

"Me, too," I said.

We were mid-glide when a giant arm emerged slowly from the glittering sand below. It did resemble a tentacle, but there were no suction cups on the underside of it. It was sleek and

B. G. THOMAS

smooth, but massive enough to instill fear despite its lack of teeth or suction cups, or—anything else pointy. The arm was the exact color of the sand; the perfect camouflage, just like the alien centipede-worms. It rose right underneath where Saba and Ian ran—right in front of Darrien and me. Darrien shoved us out of the way, to the side, which was easier to do with the minimal gravity. I yanked Todd along with us. We were still gliding above the arm, but the push that Darrien had given us led us farther out, in front of Saba and Ian.

They stood on the tentacle and rose with the thing as it lifted high up into the air. A giant whooshing sounded, and it was then that the size of the thing registered in my mind. Just one arm had to be close in length to a humpback whale, if not larger. The end of its arm was yards and yards out to our left, and then wherever the arm began was far off to our right—and presumably, whatever it was attached to. I gulped down the anxiety thick at the back of my throat.

Aleksy and Lata were close to the shuttle—close to Dad. But Aleksy heard everyone's cries for help within our helmets and came bounding back, gun in hand.

I scolded myself for not being quicker to draw the gun and aim at the arm. I dropped Todd's hand and grabbed it, taking it from my belt in a clumsy, fast manner. The thing hit Saba and Ian and sent them flying up into the air, before doing it again. Almost like the thing was playing with them.

Right as I took aim, a sharp scream sounded from in front of us. It sounded like Jules, but it was hard to tell. The *mother-fucking* centipede-worms. They emerged quietly from the sand and approached on either side of our group. A couple of them crawled on the arm of the other alien, headed straight for Saba and Ian with glistening jowls.

"Not those fuckers again," Darrien swore.

"Tell me about it," I huffed.

We continued to run out of the way of the titanic arm as well as the centipede monsters. I successfully shot the fanged creatures that tried to attack Saba and Ian, but before I could shoot the arm, I whipped around just in time to see one of the smaller aliens about to fling itself onto Darrien's back. For good measure, I shot that one twice. And then again.

Even through the helmet, Darrien's eyes were wide as he gazed at me in awe.

"Behind you!" Todd yelled from where he ran behind me.

Several more of the aliens came for me, and I blew them up, one shot after the other. For not having shot anything in years, I was a little impressed by my aim, especially in the midst of the pandemonium. They exploded in that purple goo that was their blood. Unfortunately, some got on my helmet. I wiped at the screen with the sleeve of my suit to better my sight, then scanned our surroundings.

Harper hadn't frozen up this time around, and I was grateful. She decapitated one of the centipede creatures as it tried to lunge for her ankle. Aleksy had shot several of them, like I had, and was roaring like a warrior in battle. His suit was also properly drenched in purple slime. He was far away from where Darrien, Todd, and I ran, but assisted Harper in killing a few more of the pesky things before finally running closer to meet Lata.

Lata had stayed closer to the other shuttle, seemingly okay, but alert and knife at the ready. Jules had reached where Lata stood.

Ian wasn't far behind them, having escaped the tentacle, though Saba was still trying to escape. Ian stabbed one of the creatures with one of the larger knives we'd gotten from the kitchen. After he killed it, he glanced back at Saba and hesitated.

"Go!" I screamed at him.

"Fuck," he muttered to everyone.

Aleksy reached where we ran and we all stopped now that there were fewer centipede aliens attacking. We observed the arm that still threw Saba into the air like its plaything.

"What is it doing?" Aleksy barked.

"Get me down!" Saba shrieked.

"You shoot on that end," I nodded toward the end of the thing's arm. "And I'll shoot at the other side. Yeah?" I asked Aleksy.

"Got it."

We both took aim and shot in unison as Darrien and Todd scanned our surroundings for more of the terrifying creatures. I had the gnawing feeling at the pit of my stomach that more of the pesky centipede-worms would come after us soon enough.

Adrenaline pumped through me more and more as each second ticked by. Our lasers didn't weaken the beast after the first few rounds. Finally, I decided to keep my finger on the trigger—attempting to cut straight through. Aleksy noticed what I was doing, and with a dark chuckle, joined in my quest.

"Are we okay?" I asked Darrien.

"So far so good," Darrien said on the mic.

I half expected another arm to come and take the rest of us. Or, perhaps something else would sneak its way up from the depths of the sand and grab our feet, pulling us under. The string of bad thoughts was unending as I continued firing into the monster.

Layers started to peel away from the mass. The top layer bubbled and gave way, revealing the same kind of purplish blood as the centipedes, along with a deep green ooze that I didn't want to think about. Underneath that layer was muscle, and then underneath that was something like an endoskeleton. The laser went through the bones, and finally, with a loud crack that we could hear through our helmets, the arm cut off on my end. Not long after, it split and broke off on Aleksy's side, too.

Aleksy and I cheered as Saba came back down to the sand, gasping and clutching her chest.

The monstrous, carved-up appendage dropped to the sand, unmoving. The blood and guts and various layers slopped over its sides and into the sand below our feet.

"I think now would probably be a good time to run as fast as we can," Darrien urged.

"I second that!" Todd said.

They didn't have to tell us twice. Though it was fascinating to look at, and I would have loved to take a closer look had our lives not literally been in danger, it was time to *go*.

Darrien grabbed my hand again, pulling me close to him, and towards the shuttle. This time, we lead the new group forward with Aleksy and Saba running behind us.

The sand was still and absolutely daunting. The planet's sun was higher in the sky than it had been yesterday, and the orange orb made the sand shine so brightly that it was hard to look at, so I focused on the shuttle in the distance instead. My lungs were on fire despite the oxygen in my helmet and despite the break from running that we had when we glided above the ground. The wounds in my body throbbed and begged for me to sit still. I knew that if I was in pain and struggling, Darrien was feeling it in a more severe way—as was Todd, whose legs made him stumble ever so often. They both should have been resting after all they'd gone through yesterday, not running for their lives.

After what felt like an eternity of attempting to breathe and willing my legs to push on, the shuttle along with the rest of the crew got closer and closer, to the point where I saw the ramp door begin to open.

Dad.

Lata, Ian, and Jules got close enough to the shuttle to board, with Harper not far behind them. As each second went by, I moved my body harder, forcing and willing it to go as fast as humanly possible. Darrien kept up, sensing my urgency.

A quick glance behind my shoulder showed me that Aleksy was on our heels, with Saba not far behind him. I wished they'd held hands to keep together too.

The ramp lowered down more, with half of it jutting out to the sky. Right as Darrien and I came to an abrupt halt behind Jules and Harper, it lowered completely, and there he stood.

Dad was in one of the newer spacesuits, one of the navy ones. He had on the nicer helmet, too, and he leaned in the doorway so casually, it was almost as though his having to fly down and rescue us was no biggie after not being in space for over three decades. He waved.

"I have a feeling you all are ready to get the hell out of here?" Dad chuckled gruffly.

The sound of his voice almost broke me apart. My chest ached and my chin wobbled with the strain of the tears I held back.

He looked at me and said into the mic, "Hey, kid."

I laughed, but it sounded like a weak cry. "Hey, Dad."

"Come aboard, folks!" Dad said as he moved out of the way.

Aleksy had caught up with Lata, and they trudged up the ramp and into the shuttle with Harper, Jules, and Ian following. Darrien took a step on the ramp and I followed suit, ready to sit down, ready to give Dad a hug, ready to be back on the Mothership.

And then Saba screamed.

I didn't want to look, but I forced my neck to move to look behind us.

The creature whose arm we had amputated was very, *very* angry. It was no longer just a stray arm playing with us. Now, it craved vengeance.

A mass of bulbous skin that was the creature's head had come up from the sand. It reminded me of a blob-fish, especially with how its colossal, chubby mouth was turned down at the corners in a permanent, disapproving frown. The other arms poked out in the distance, but the one closest to its mouth held Saba by the very end, where the arm came to a point. Todd hung on to the arm, further down, and was attempting to crawl up to Saba. The skin must have been slimy, or smooth because Todd kept slipping and cursing.

"Holy fucking hell," Dad said slowly.

"Get on the ship, Darrien!" I said, letting go of his grip.

He stumbled a bit as I moved forward, closer to the giant alien. "No!"

"Do it!" I commanded.

I didn't turn to him to make sure he did what I asked—I couldn't risk it. All I could do was hope that he listened. I didn't know how to get Saba out of the situation she was in. I think she knew that, too, as she looked down at me, where I pointed the gun up once more, aiming for the monstrosity in front of us. Dad came beside me on the ramp with his gun at the ready, too. I wanted to scream at him to also go back inside, but I knew it would do no good. He wouldn't listen.

"Todd!" I belted. "Get on the shuttle!"

"No! Saba—I can't leave—"

I choked back a sob that was lodged in the back of my throat. "If you don't get in the fucking shuttle, I'm going to shoot you. I swear to God, Todd, I'll do it. Get on the shuttle. Now!"

Todd looked up hopelessly at Saba. The alien was studying her with four eyes that resembled the beady eyes of a spider. A chill tiptoed down my spine, and my body grew cold from the inside out.

With a shake of his head, Todd kicked off of the monster, and back onto the sand. Saba thrashed and tried to break free. Todd was hesitant as he made his way toward us. He couldn't take his eyes off Saba.

I didn't blame him. If I had been in his position, I don't know if I would have been able to retreat, either. Dad all but shoved Todd up the ramp and into the shuttle as I took aim and fired at the beast. Dad turned around and joined me. I went straight for its eyes, and Dad aimed for its mouth. Both of us were careful not to hit Saba.

And then, a smaller alien of the same species jumped out from underneath the sand that now mocked us. It was just as ugly and became uglier as it opened its down-turned mouth to reveal rows upon rows of razor-sharp teeth larger and pointier than any I'd ever seen on any shark. The smaller alien lunged, and despite the laser that I pointed at its face, ripped Saba in half. Screams and gasps echoed around in my helmet—some of which were my own and Dad's. The larger alien looked at us; met our gaze with those giant, black eyes, and then revealed its own teeth—even pointier—almost like it was grinning at us, then chomped down and consumed the second half of Saba's body.

Saba's blood-curdling screams rang in my ears, as did the gruesome sound of gargling as her head was crushed. Within seconds, the screams and gargling stopped.

The creatures eyed me and Dad as we sprinted up the ramp into the safe haven of the shuttle.

15

FLY THE NEST

One of the alien's arms struck at my ankle as I hobbled up the ramp behind Dad, adrenaline pulsing and heart pounding in my ears as I lunged toward the doorway. The thing wrapped its smooth, slimy appendage around my boot—enough for me to wince in pain as I kicked at it like a wild boar trying to outrun a leopard.

The creature let go of me right as we entered the threshold because Dad shot at it several times in the head. The most abhorrent sound erupted from the creature, like a high-pitched scream of pain mixed with gravel and sand, and its roar shook the ground below us. I knew it would haunt my nightmares for years to come—if I have years left.

I crashed into my Dad so hard that we stumbled back into the shuttle and landed on the floor. Our helmets knocked together painfully, leaving my temples throbbing, and my gun hit Dad underneath his jaw. After regaining my footing, I manage to get off of Dad with the help of Aleksy and Ian.

The most horrible sound of both monsters screaming out filled my helmet, and as the ramp door is forced shut thanks to Harper and Jules, I'm tempted to rip the helmet off. It's hard to breathe, and that sound, that God awful sound—

Todd rocks his body back and forth on the ground, and shrieks as loud as he can each time Darrien attempts to touch him. Todd couldn't have done anything, but my heart swells in heartache for him and the guilt he must already bear. Dad and I did our best to save her, we really did. Still, my own guilt spreads through my chest and weighs heavy on my shoulders as I blink back warm tears. I know that nothing I say or do for Todd right now can help.

Matthew's face flashes in my mind as I think of the husband and wife who both met their end on planet Virginia; the freckles that coated his cheeks, the untamable, brown mop of hair, and the shy smile, and my heart aches even more. I squeeze my eyelids shut, forcing him out.

I love you.

I will always love you.

But I can't think of you right now.

I can't fall apart.

At least now, Raymond and Saba are together, not having to live on without the other. That's the only thing that gets me to regain my composure.

Dad sits up beside me, rubbing underneath his jaw, and I lean into him.

"I'm so sorry I hit you," I said. The laser gun lay across my lap. His own gun is still in hand. "Are you okay? Oh, God, I'm so happy to see you," I breathe shakily.

Dad wraps his large arms around me and squeezes the living daylights out of me. I welcome the tightness. His arms are home, and the crook of his neck underneath my head, even with the helmet, is the safest space I've ever known. I exhale, and the tears slide down my face despite my best efforts. My lungs swell while he rubs at my back in a slow, soothing motion.

"I'm okay, kid. Nothing I can't handle."

He lets go of me right as the shuttle rocks in a similar way to our last one.

"We need to get the fuck out of here," I whispered.

There are no windows to know what was happening outside, and Harper didn't even mention if Dad had access to his own camera feed on this shuttle or not.

"Buckle up, folks!" Harper belted before disappearing into the flight deck with Jules on her heels. "Jules will be my co-pilot."

I moved to sit in the seat closest to the ramp. Dad joined me on the seat beside me. Aleksy and Ian hauled Todd, who now clawed at his helmet and moaned, up to one of the seats across from us. No amount of reassurance from us is helping him. In fact, his emotions and guilt ate him up entirely. Miserable sobs erupted from his chest as Ian buckled him in.

"Let's sedate him," Lata said over the noise. She peered over at Dad. "Did you bring a med kit?"

Dad got up and crouched in front of one of the seats that were situated in the middle, and came out with a black med kit the size of a shoe box.

"I don't know if there will be a sedative, but it's worth a shot," Dad said. He opened the box, and he and Lata rummaged through it in a hurry. The lights in the small passenger area had begun to go dark, with the same faint red lights coming to life. Ian worked his way around the small space, securing us all in. The engine was warming up, and it would only be a matter of minutes before we took off.

"Everyone, keep your helmets on!" Jules advised through the mic. "At least until we are back on the Mothership and quarantined."

Jesus. I hadn't even thought about the fact we would have to be separated from the others on the main ship. The last thing I wanted to do was be forced into quarantine once we returned. More tears leaked from my eyes. All I wanted to do was hold my son in my arms.

"A-ha!" Lata held a small vial in her gloved hand and a syringe in the other. Todd fought against the tight straps securing him into the seat, despite Aleksy's strong hold on him, and Ian's cooing. They were really trying their best.

Darrien exhaled loudly next to me, unaware that his mic was on, as he looked at Todd thrashing around. He sat down next to me, taking Dad's original seat, and I helped him get buckled up. I hoped Dad wouldn't mind him taking his place.

Lata went over to Todd in a haste and found the space in his arm to inject the sedative. It was a damn good thing that the materials of the suits could be punctured easily.

Dad locked up the med kit and then took it with him on his way back to me. He stored the box underneath him and watched Lata give Todd the shot before settling into the seat beside Darrien.

"I know, Todd, I know," Lata said, patting his knee. She capped the syringe and handed it to Aleksy, who stored it in his boot for later due to the lack of a disposal bin. Ian took a seat next to Todd and buckled up. It didn't take long for Todd's eyes to flutter, and for his head to lull to the side, with his arms and legs limp.

We all let out a communal sigh of relief to see his body rest. Before sitting down, Aleksy made sure Lata got secured in her seat across from me, Darrien, and Dad, then he strapped in himself.

The shuttle rocked harder, and the dreadful noises from the two large aliens outside sounded, even through my helmet and the whirring of the shuttle's engines.

"L minus sixty seconds," Harper's voice sounded.

"Is Todd okay?" Jules asked right after.

"Sedated," Aleksy answered for us. "Thankfully."

"Good," Jules murmured with a sad sigh. "Turning off the communal mic system. Prepared to play music unless there are any objections?"

When no one objected, the mics were turned off and the same soothing music as yesterday—how that had just been yesterday was surreal to me—filled my helmet. The low instrumental music played softly, and I found that despite the horror we had just endured, my shoulders relaxed ever so slightly.

I was also glad that no one could hear the incredibly loud sigh I let out as I leaned my head back in my seat and closed my eyes. Dad reached over Darrien's lap and gave my hand a quick squeeze.

"L minus twenty seconds," Harper said.

The creatures knocked into us again. I anxiously opened my eyes to make sure that the emergency lights didn't jump to life. What if the aliens damaged something? What if we crashed?

My helmet alerted me that my heart rate was far too high.

"Fuck you," I told the helmet out loud. "I *know.*"

I closed my eyes to prepare my body for the jolting sensation that would come with liftoff. My body flinched forward as the image of Saba being torn in two and eaten came to life in my mind. I blinked hard and focused on my boots.

Darrien laid a large hand on my thigh. I looked at him in the dark, and though he couldn't tell me anything, his helmet was leaning in my direction. His fingers rubbed my thigh, just above my knee, in small, tight circles, as if to tell me things would be okay. I didn't know if it would be okay. No one did. But somehow, his touch made me feel the smallest glimmer of hope.

"Three, two..." the engine roared louder as Harper counted down. "One."

I would never get used to the sensation of flying in a space shuttle, I concluded. As we hovered into the air and prepared to go outlandishly fast, my stomach dipped and twisted, and a thick knot formed in the back of my throat. This was the same reason I was never a fan of flying in planes or riding on roller coasters. The sensation was too similar to that of my panic attacks, and I had had enough of those already, thank you. Nausea rolled through me before the ship lifted off completely. I grabbed at Darrien's wrist which rested on my thigh and squeezed.

He took my hand in his, interlacing our fingers, and let me squeeze at his hand with all of my might as the ship took off, away from planet Virginia—away from the awful centipede worms that killed Raymond, away from the disgusting sand aliens that tore Saba in two, away from the flower that stabbed Darrien, and away from the monsters that lingered in the water.

I wanted to puke, sob, throw shit, and sleep for a whole week straight. Instead, I did my very best not to think of Raymond's bloated dead body, or the ligaments that tore away from Saba's body and the bones that snapped as she was ripped in two—I tried very hard. I tried to think of my sweet Jaxon; his smile, that crazy hair, the way I'd hug him after quarantine. I thought of how Dad made it here safely and saved all of our asses. My father and my boy were *safe*. And though I calmed down a bit, every time I tried to focus on something else, flashes of the dead, including Matthew and Magda, reminded me of the situation we were in.

Concentrating on Darrien's touch didn't help, nor did the fact that Dad was right beside us, occasionally reaching over and patting my hand. I loved that they were beside me. I was fortunate that they made it.

As someone who was familiar with and well-versed in grief, I felt it within others deeply. We were lucky that we didn't come out worse. We were lucky to be on our way back to the *Hippogriff*. Lucky. It didn't feel like we were lucky, though. For some reason, it felt like the beginning of something worse.

16

THE MOTHERSHIP

We made it.

I had been convinced that the shuttle would give out thanks to the blob-fish aliens crashing into it so much before we left, but a little after an hour of flight, Harper landed us smoothly into the landing bay attached to the *Hippogriff.* The shuttle slowly moved within the large Mothership before coming to a complete stop.

Todd was still knocked out, thank goodness. We all assisted one another in taking off our helmets, then we unbuckled and stood together in total silence. It was hard to feel truly safe after what we'd all gone through.

Jules and Harper exited the flight deck, helmets also off. Once the door that opened up into the vast universe closed behind us and the air in the room was neutralized, Ian and Dad opened the ramp door. Just like that, we were back standing in the same room from where we disembarked only yesterday.

Captain Carnell stood in the middle of the room. Comet was in his arms, even though Carnell was wearing a bulky hazmat suit the color of a ripe pumpkin. The helmet he wore was similar to the ones we had just taken off but slimmer. It was more clear and I could see the hard lines on his dark face. His brow was furrowed, even as he attempted a smile.

Despite everything, I wanted answers. Needed them. My mind had put the supposed planetary plague that Jules informed us about on hold as soon as we all were forced into survival mode on planet Virginia. Now, I wanted to corner Carnell and ask him what the hell was going on. I wanted the truth and not just the watered-down version. All of us deserved the truth. No more lies.

But before I could march up to him and give him a piece of my mind, he said, "Welcome back, crew." His eyes looked from me to Darrien, then to Todd, who was carried by Ian and Aleksy, and the others. His eyes looked pained. "I see we've lost a couple of members?"

Harper sighed and nodded.

"Okay," was all Carnell said. He shook his head.

Comet hopped down from the Captain's grip and pranced over to me. He sniffed at my boots, then peered up at me as though he smelled something putrid. Then, the feline pawed at my shin. I crouched down and picked him up. The kitty nuzzled into me and gave me his belly. I couldn't help the tiny smile that pulled on one side of my mouth. If Carnell brought his feline companion here with him, he must not have been worried about us possibly passing something on to Comet. I was glad for the kitty's comfort.

"Shit. Is Aster okay?" Darrien asked. "I left her in my room—"

Carnell nodded. "Yes. She's currently with Emma, Austin, and Jaxon, watching a movie in the common room."

Darrien's shoulders eased back.

"Unfortunately, the protocol states that you all must go into quarantine," Carnell said in a monotone voice. "You all must go to the dorms at the end of the rooms, and be separated for seven days. Even you, William—sorry," Carnell said with a sigh. "For now, we're going to stay right where we are in space. Once the quarantine ends, we will regroup." He sighed again, but this time it was deeper. "I assume no samples were brought back?"

"Fuck the samples," Jules grumbled at him. I was shocked to see her so pissed off at him. "Nothing good can come from that planet."

Harper looked at her friend and nodded her agreement.

"Well, we may explore the other planets in this sola—"

"Over my dead body," I said coolly. I walked up to the Captain, his cat still bundled and curled up in my arms. "We may be going into quarantine, Wayne…" I used his first name because I was pissed and wanted to shove him into something hard. "But I am personally going to want to have a long talk with you whenever I'm out." I glanced behind me at the others, drained and fuming, standing with their arms crossed. "I have a feeling I'm not the only one, either."

Carnell looked at the others and gulped. I liked the Captain. Hell, I could even consider us becoming friends one day. But whatever he had done alongside NASA—whatever they had been keeping from us, the ones who agreed to go on this mission in the first place—well, I wasn't pleased. Quite the opposite.

Unfortunately, I knew that now wasn't the time to berate Carnell with questions and demands.

The rest of what was left of our group stayed behind me and Carnell. They remained quiet. Comet purred against my chest and I rubbed at his chin.

I wasn't a mean person, but my temper did get the best of me at times. A trait that I'd gotten from my father. I forced a deep breath, eased the tightness in my shoulders, and unclenched my jaw.

"Seven days. And then I—" I turned to the others and motioned with my free hand, "*we*—will want the truth, Carnell. Don't you think we deserve that much?" I asked. I couldn't help but think that the people behind me weren't just coworkers or crew members to me. We had survived together. In a little over twenty-four hours, we had become much more.

Carnell's deep brown eyes met mine, and he nodded. "You do. You all do. And I'll give it to you. After quarantine. After you all rest." He looked at the rest of us, and then back to me. My eyes were hot with tears of frustration. Carnell patted me on the shoulder as Dad came up to stand next to me. "Do you want to take Comet into quarantine with you?"

I looked down at the giant mainecoon curled up in my arm. My back ached with just the weight of the cat in my arms, but his warmth and purrs eased my nerves. I nodded, and Carnell smiled the smallest smile. "He's all yours."

17

QUARANTINE

B eing quarantined has been the loneliest I've ever felt in my life, and it's only been two days.

The quarantine dormitories, or "suites," as my Bots have called them a couple of times, are at the very end of the hallway where the single traveler rooms are located. Only a thick wall and steel doors separate them from the other side of the ship, just in case something especially awful takes place. After seeing what happened to Raymond's body, the precautions seemed necessary to me, despite how miserable I was.

The bed that Comet and I shared (and I mean that, because he knows how to take up a large portion of the bed) is the same kind of fluffy mattress as the one back in my regular room, similarly made up with soft sheets and several blankets. When Carnell had said we'd have to go into quarantine, I'd pictured a single cot in a stark white room, perhaps a toilet and sink, a stiff top sheet, and a single pillow. I was pleasantly surprised that we at least got to spend our days of solitude in comfort. And that there was a large screen projector on the wall across from the bed. I spent a lot of time watching my favorite comfort movies to pass the time.

On the first night, I'd been so exhausted that I don't even

remember showering before Comet and I crawled into bed together. But, I must have washed up, because when I woke up only an hour later with a scream lodged in the back of my throat and the picture of Saba's torn-up body brushing the back of my eyelids, I'd smelled of fresh soap, and my hair was damp in its braid. After that, I'd stayed up watching comedy movies with Comet, barely registering anything that was on the screen, but making myself stay awake to escape the horrible memories.

The Bots took care of me and the rest of us in quarantine. As soon as we had finished our discussion with Carnell, several Bots swarmed the room where we had exited the shuttle and tended to each one of us precisely and carefully. They set us up tiny booths in seconds and doted on all of our varying medical needs. After that, we were stripped down and assessed in each of our private booths. My Bot took off my clothing with a speed I didn't know was possible, and then as if my wounds were nothing, the machine cleaned my wounds and had me stitched up in no time. I was forced to take an antibiotic, and then I was sprayed down with a decontamination spray that the little Bot spurted from one of its four appendages. The spray had stung my skin and smelled of chemicals and fake citrus. As the scent wafted up to my nose, it took a lot of willpower not to heave. My stomach was barren and the nausea within was strong. I knew I needed nourishment, but eating sounded like the very last thing I wanted to do.

Once rinsed off and dry, we were all dressed in plush robes, forced to put on masks similar to the one Carnell had on, and marched down to the quarantine suites, each of us following the Bots assigned to us. Well, except for Todd, who was transported via a stretcher that hovered above the ground, along with his own Bot.

None of us spoke. None of us waved or said goodbye or see

you later to our crew mates. We were all too exhausted to do so–shells of the human beings we were when we first boarded the shuttle down to planet Virginia. Dad gave me a wink before entering his room. Darrien gave me a tired look and a half smile before he entered his own. After we were all ushered into our respective rooms, we were given a smoothie to drink that tasted like kale and vitamins and instructed to drink the whole thing. After that, my memory became foggy, and I wondered if perhaps there had been a sedative or anti-anxiety within the smoothie. If so, I was upset it hadn't knocked me out fully and taken the night terrors away.

On the second night, and during each cat nap I had attempted throughout the "day," the same thing happened. Nightmares flooded my mind, making the events worse than what really happened in some scenarios, or just replaying the same treacherous thing over and over again until I jolted awake.

I'd suffered from the same kind of nightmares as a child when Mom didn't come back from space. Then again, when Matthew didn't come back from Africa. Once more when Magda died. And now. They were not foreign to me, but they were not something I would ever get used to, either.

Every time I woke with my pulse racing, heart throbbing, sheets sweaty and twisted around my legs, I didn't call out for Magda or Matthew when I became lucid, as I tried to come to. I didn't even call out for Dad. Instead, I'd called out for Darrien.

Darrien and I hadn't spoken. We were able to do so via the video calls on the ship, and we conveniently had everything we'd need tech-wise in our rooms, but I didn't want to bother him. I was too exhausted still to even think about talking or what had happened between us. I had called Jaxon as soon as I thought I could muster a sentence and a smile, and seeing my boy's beautiful face did help lift my spirits for a little while. But it would have helped me so much more if I'd been able to hug him, run my fingers through his untamed hair, and smell his scent.

Five more days.

I thought that Carnell would bring one of the Bots to retrieve Comet from me after the first night, but he stuck to his word about letting me borrow his feline friend. Instead, whenever I was brought food, a small dish of wet food and dry food and a bottle of water to refill Comet's small water bowl came with my meals. I was still angry as hell with the Captain, but as each hour passed in my lonesome, and the more I thought over the events of what took place, what Jules had said about the plague, and everything else that happened down on planet Virginia—well, I was still upset...hurt, more like it—but it all came down to wanting answers more than anything. Honesty. A team without honesty isn't really a team. Not to me. I wanted to trust the Captain and the other astronauts. I knew that I would never completely trust NASA after everything that had happened with my mother's disappearance and after the downfall that happened in Virginia. But, I knew I was still able to trust those on the *Hippogriff*, and if we were truly going to find a solution to the plague on our home planet, we needed trust. Lies would lead to miscommunication, or worse. More death.

A planetary plague didn't seem like something we could overcome. It was apparent that NASA was scared out of their minds, and for good reason. Did that mean most of the planets were affected or had we simply found more than a few? Was it more than ten? Fifty? Was it hundreds?

Every time I paced around the room and thought of all of the *what-ifs* that came to mind, I could feel myself spiraling. Still, I did it. I couldn't help mulling it all over. Because there wasn't much more to do or think about. If there really was this massive planetary, no, *universal* plague, then what the fuck were we even trying for? It was hard to see the big picture as I stood alone in my room, in the middle of space. Survival made sense. Temporary survival with the same outcome as staying on Earth did not. Wouldn't the human race be more at peace if we stayed on our own planet, and let nature take its natural course?

But no. My scientist brain knew that could never be so. Humans are animals. Animals fight for survival. They fight or they flee. In this case, I guess we were in the midst of both. The instinct was embedded in our DNA and was only natural.

Truthfully, I should have felt more fortunate. Instead of being on Earth, watching the land and the animals and those around me waste away, I was safe on the *Hippogriff* with my family, and so far, I physically felt fine after our haunting trip to planet Virginia. With my friends. Instead of fighting for food or water, I was provided for up here. Guilt spread through me once more as I pictured Darryl and everyone else back on Earth at the wildlife conservatory. My animals. Didn't they deserve a shot at living, too?

The questions that kept me awake at night were much too philosophical in nature for me to answer; especially when I didn't have all of the information. But thinking was much safer than falling asleep and reliving Darrien getting stabbed in the chest, or the centipede-worms coming after me or growing in size to the point where they were almost as large as the blob-fish aliens, teeth glistening with drool and blood, beady eyes hungry, jowls snapping at me, or Dad, or Jaxon.

My Bot had offered me sleeping pills. I didn't take them. Not because I didn't want to sleep, because I desperately did. But the thought of closing my eyes and not knowing what my subconscious would come up with from my memories left me paralyzed in fear.

On the third night, as I listened to Comet purr on *his* pillow next to me, I stared up at the ceiling. Tears pooled at the corners of my eyes because I knew sleep was inevitable at that point, and when I woke with sweat beading my brow, with that same scream in the back of my throat, I'd still be alone, with only my furry companion for comfort.

The few hours of peaceful sleep that I'd gotten while nuzzled into Darrien's body on the shuttle was the best sleep I'd had in years. It may have been the best sleep I'd had since before Jaxon was born. I'd never been a good sleeper, even when Matthew lay beside me in our old bed, breathing softly with one arm above his head, and the other on his chest. Darrien, though. It was like curling up to him eased every bone in my body. It was no easy feat, and he'd accomplished it without trying.

I didn't know what that meant. A part of me had always wondered if I had just settled for Matthew. I loved him with my whole heart, I really did. But, I'd be lying if I said there wasn't a part of our relationship that had been lacking, even from the start. Matthew's sense of humor didn't match mine. He had often not understood when I tried to be playful with him in an attempt to flirt. He was sweet, serious, and, as Dad put it when I brought him home the first time—plain.

And though he *was* plain, he had been great to me. He had given me our sweet boy, and for that, I would love him forever.

As I spent those last few days in quarantine, overthinking and avoiding sleep, I also came to the point where I finally allowed myself to register what had happened with Darrien. The smiles and the hand-holding. The way his body felt underneath mine. Our conversations. How he looked at me. How, if he hadn't been injured and we had been in that shower together, I would have done *so* much more.

Unlike hooking up with Todd, where I didn't have the craving to do it all again, being with Darrien had left me wanting *more*. And not just sex, or fooling around, or kissing. I wanted more of *him*. I wanted to know about his parents. I wanted to know about his career and his schooling and his childhood memories. I wanted to know about the small scar on the inside of his forearm that I'd noticed in the shuttle bathroom, and how he got it. I wanted to know his favorite movies and shows, and if he liked to read for leisure, and if so, what genres he loved.

I wanted to know it all.

Instead of that fact paralyzing me with fear—fear of getting in too deep and losing yet another person—it sparked something else inside of me. Something that I think resembled excitement.

On the sixth night, I took the sleeping pill that my little bot offered me after I ate my dinner, which had been a delicious stew and side salad, probably courtesy of the Captain. After I ate, I took a long, hot shower, because the bathroom was just that; a stand-up shower, toilet, and sink. No bathtub, unfortunately. After I exited the shower and brushed my teeth, I wrapped myself up in a long t-shirt, got under the covers, and took the pill alongside my other medications and vitamins. I nuzzled into Comet's fur after he jumped on the bed and laid down beside me, and finally fell into a dark abyss that included no nightmares.

18

PLANET AINE

I had come to several decisions during the week-long quarantine.

One, it was okay for me to take sleeping pills occasionally. I had taken one on the sixth and seventh nights, and they gave me no dreams and no night terrors. Just blissful rest, which my body desperately needed. The much-needed rest had allowed my wounds to heal almost completely. Physically, I was in decent shape. Mentally, well—I was getting there. I knew from experience that trauma never truly went away. It could come up at unexpected times, and it would linger, and that was okay.

Two, I wasn't mad at Captain Carnell. He had left Comet with me all week and even video-called me once to check in, though he made it clear that we wouldn't be talking about anything of importance until I was rested and out of quarantine. He had said in our call that he would give me, and everyone else, answers. We would talk openly and freely once we were all out. He knew that I would hold him to that promise, and I knew he would keep it. So, I wasn't mad. But I was *very* ready to talk and get answers after stewing in my own thoughts for a week.

And three. I liked Darrien, and I wanted to pursue him in a

serious manner. Every time I thought of Darrien, my heart rate picked up. I wondered if his heart did the same thing when he thought about me. I wondered how his wounds were. I hoped that what had happened between us on planet Virginia wasn't just because we were there. I prayed he didn't have regrets about any of it. I certainly didn't. Yet, I didn't know Darrien all that well, still, even though I felt like I'd known him for months. There was no way for me to predict what would happen with us. All I could do was remain cautiously optimistic.

At eight in the morning on the eighth day, my Bot came to my door and opened it. This time, the little robot left the door open for me to exit.

It had given me some clothes the night before, which I slipped on after washing up when I woke an hour beforehand. Black leggings and a simple gray sweater along with black flats that the Bot retrieved from my normal living quarters. I had done my hair in a French braid, and that was about it. No makeup was at my disposal. At least I had a small thing of deodorant to put on.

Comet jumped up into my arms from where he lounged on the bed. I think he was just as ready to leave the room as me.

I walked outside of the door and exhaled the nervous sigh in my lungs. No one else was in the hallway.

As if the little, navy blue Bot with bulbous eyes could read my mind, it stated, "The others are being retrieved. Everyone is to gather in the common room."

"Thank you, Blue." During my week in quarantine, I'd asked the little Bot, which looked kind of like a little owl, what its name was. It told me they never had a "regular" name, just a model number, so I told the Bot that I would call them Blue if they were okay with it. Blue loved the idea.

"Do you need anything, Ms. Daphne?" Blue asked as I walked and they glided towards the exit doors.

I shook my head. "No, Blue. Thank you. I'll see you soon?"

Blue twirled around in the air and looked at me with their big, round eyes. "Of course."

A smile crept up to my lips. "Good. See you soon, Blue. Keep the other Bots in line." I winked. Blue gave me their version of a little laugh, which sounded like a high-pitched purr, and then opened the exit doors for me before gliding away.

I didn't encounter anyone else on my way to the common area. I wondered if I'd been one of the first to be released. Once on the shuttle to the common area, Comet jumped off of my lap and rolled around on the floor, begging me for tummy rubs until we arrived. Obviously, I gave him what he wanted. That cat had me wrapped tightly around his little toe beans, and he knew it.

We entered the common area, Comet in front of me with his tail flicking side to side, and I noticed that no one was there. I didn't let disappointment creep up. I knew the others would come shortly. I made my way to the CoffeeMaster, despite feeling wide awake and alert already. My nerves buzzed so loudly in my body, I swore I could hear them. Still, coffee gave me something to do and sip on as I waited. I selected a latte and waited.

Comet yelped and mewed at my ankles as I sipped my latte and leaned against the counter.

"What do you want?" I asked.

"Wet food."

I looked up, and there was Captain Carnell, casually dressed in jeans and a red t-shirt that accented his broad, muscular chest. He chuckled, then dug for something in one of the cabinets. He came back with a small, packaged thing of wet food in his large hand.

"This stuff is like his crack," Carnell rolled his eyes as he opened the wet food and placed it down in front of his cat. Comet immediately ran to the food and began lapping it up like I hadn't fed him and even given him treats from my own food over the last week. "I hope I don't run out of it. I brought enough to feed ten cats for a decade."

Carnell stayed down, now in a crouch, and caressed his cat.

"I missed my buddy. Was he good company?" He asked, peering up at me from his position on the ground.

I nodded. I didn't know what to say now that I was out of quarantine. Last night, I had a whole list of questions for Carnell. Now, my mind was utterly blank. I took a sip from my scalding mug of coffee and pretended the liquid didn't burn my tongue.

"We'll talk when everyone arrives. Want to sit on the couches?" Carnell motioned to the couches in front of the giant television. I nodded. "The Bots are going to bring up some fruit and pastries in a bit. I accidentally slept in. I'd planned on making breakfast, but I'd been up late watching the video messages from NASA and..." he trailed off and shrugged. "Anyway, I stayed up too late."

"I'm sure no one will be upset about fruit and pastries."

We sat down on the comfy couches, and I rested my mug on my knee. Comet jumped up on the couch, already done with his meal, and began to make biscuits on Carnell's leg.

"He's such a whore," Carnell muttered.

I couldn't help but snort at that. "Yeah. And he knows how to take up a pillow."

"Back at home, on Earth, I mean, he has his own king-sized pillow in each room of my condo," Carnell admitted. "Along with his own kitty condo in the living area."

I grinned. "You really are a sap deep down, aren't you?"

Carnell coughed a laugh but nodded, right as the doors opened, and Jaxon ran in with Emma and baby Austin behind him.

"Mama!" he screeched.

I quickly put my mug on the coffee table before he launched onto me and spilled the contents all over us. Just in time, too, because as soon as I set it down, my baby boy was in my arms. I squeezed him as tightly as I could and kissed him all over.

"*Mom!*" Jax groaned.

I didn't care about his cries for escape; not even a little. Tears pricked at my eyes, but I blinked them away. I picked him all the way up and put him in my lap, and held him. Jax stopped fighting and let me. I smelled his hair, looked into his bright eyes that matched mine, and brushed his nose against mine. There had been several moments down on Virginia where I had been convinced I'd never see my baby boy again. And here he was, with his golden hair, his light skin covered with the occasional freckle, his long lashes, and his father's smile.

After a couple of moments of hugging him and asking him how he was while I was gone, I let him go from my grip. For a young kid, he tolerated my affections pretty damn well, and I didn't want to push it or make him uncomfortable. Seeing him took a giant weight off of my chest, though. Emma and Austin sat next to me on the couch. I reached for my coffee and took a swig now that it was a more manageable temperature.

"Thank you so much, Emma," I said on an exhale. I reached out for Austin, and he gripped one of my fingers in his little land. "Thank you for being here and taking care of my little man."

Emma blushed but smiled at me. She squeezed my arm in the silent *you're welcome* that only moms know.

The doors opened again, and Jules, Harper, and Ian came through. I took Austin from Emma's lap as Jules ran to her partner. Jules picked Emma up—which was quite impressive given Emma's height—and twirled her around. They kissed deeply and held onto each other. Emma cupped Jules's face in her hands. I looked away from them but smiled nonetheless. Austin cooed in my lap, then reached for Jules.

I stood up and brought her son over. Jules had tears streaming down her face, coming together at the bottom of her chin and sliding down her neck as she took her son in her arms and proceeded to smother him in the same way I'd done with Jaxon.

Ian poked me on the shoulder. "Hey," he said.

"Ian," I breathed. I wrapped my arms around him, and he squeezed me firmly. I had to reach as far as I could on my tiptoes to reach his height, but it was well worth it.

"Ian!" Jax screamed excitedly. Ian pulled back from me with a boyish grin tugging at his lips, then bent down and picked Jaxon up.

"Hey, buddy! Did you play some good games while I was gone?" Ian asked.

They proceeded to talk about games I didn't understand, and a deep, maternal emotion leaked down my chest like melted honey. I was so thankful for Ian. And Emma, and Jules, and Harper, and even the Captain. Harper sat next to Carnell and he squeezed her hand, though she gave him a playful glare.

Aleksy and Lata were the next to come. They walked hand in hand, and Lata rushed up to me instantly. She talked a mile a minute and pressed me on whether or not my wounds were healing properly or not. After a kiss on my cheek from Lata and then Aleksy, they took the two seats on the loveseat that sat underneath the television set.

The doors opened once more, and Dad and Darrien came in. I knew better than to expect Todd to be with them, but to my surprise, he walked behind both of them, and he was dressed and clean. He didn't smile, and he didn't look at any of us. His head drooped, and his gaze fell to the floor as he followed Dad and Darrien. Darrien said something quietly to Todd, and then Todd came to the couches and took a seat as far away from all of us as possible. Dad came over and gave me a tight hug.

"Baba!" Jaxon squealed in instant excitement.

"Hey there, kid," Dad smiled down at his grandson. "Miss me?"

Jaxon's answer was to wrap his lanky arms around Dad's long legs. Dad ruffled his hair and looked at me with a couple of unmistakable tears in his light eyes, his complexion growing redder and redder with emotion.

We all sat down after exchanging more embraces. Dad and Jaxon sat on either side of me, with Ian sitting on the other side of Jaxon, naturally. On the other couch, Jules and Emma sat with Austin in Jules's lap. Harper and Todd sat next to them. The Captain had gotten up during the reunion to grab several chairs from the conference room for himself and Darrien.

Darrien.

Darrien came back after a couple of moments and sat next to the Captain. He carried a couple of steaming mugs and sat one on the coffee table in front of Todd. After he sat down, he cupped the other mug in his dominant hand. He took one sip of coffee, and after his lips retreated from the rim of his cup, that's when our eyes locked for the first time since he had smiled at me before we all entered quarantine.

An instant bolt of electricity shot down the length of my

body as my eyes met his deep ocher ones. He was more handsome than ever in a simple, iron black v-neck paired with dark wash jeans. Like me, he looked and seemed much more rested than the last time we'd been together; his plump bottom lip had returned to its usual rosy brown, his golden skin was less pale and more vibrant, and the dark circles that appeared after he had been stabbed had vanished completely.

It was hard not to stare at him and think of those lips on mine, or how talented and tasty his tongue had been inside of my mouth. My gaze dropped to the hand that was gripping his mug, and tingles ran from my nipples down to my very center as I recalled the touch of his hands, his fingers hungrily exploring my body in the cave and in the shower.

Hell. Captain Carnell was talking, and I'd completely spaced out like a hormonally charged teenager. My eyes jumped from Darrien's hand back to his face in horror, as I realized I'd been openly ogling him instead of listening to what was being said.

As though he could read my mind, Darrien brought the hot mug back up to his beautiful lips and hid a smirk within his cup as he took another swig. I grabbed my own mug and took a sip in hopes that it would hide the deep blush I could feel on my cheeks. Instead, I almost choked on the drink and made a fool of myself, which only made my face heat more.

I decided it was best *not* to look at him for the remainder of our little meeting. At all.

Dad gave me a weird look and arched a brow in a silent question. *Not now, Dad. Please.*

At least it didn't seem like I'd tuned out anything crucial, for the Captain stretched his arms over his head in a sigh before he started, "Well, it's good to see you all."

He paused as several Bots swarmed in through the doors

with various platters of fresh fruit that I assumed had been grown in the lab, alongside some very appetizing danishes.

Carnell waited for the Bots to finish laying out their spread before continuing on. I looked for my Bot, Blue, but they weren't within the group. The robots flitted around and laid out the various platters, gave us all napkins, and then dispersed reusable plates around our circle before taking their leave.

"Please, help yourselves," Captain Carnell said. His voice strained, but he made a point of taking some fruit and a cheese danish before leaning back in his chair. Comet tried to jump in his lap, but he wouldn't allow it while he was eating. Because I'm a sucker, Comet came up to me, and I let the feline hop in my lap. Captain Carnell shook his head but laughed. Dad gave me a similar reaction but dished enough fruit and danishes for the both of us to share on his plate. I popped a strawberry in my mouth and chewed as I waited.

Once everyone was situated, the Captain finished his danish, then peered at all of us long and hard. We all looked back, except for Todd, who still looked at his toes. He hadn't touched the tea that Darrien had gotten him, nor did he make himself a plate of food. It was apparent that the guilt from not being able to save Saba was still eating him.

"Well, I guess I'll cut right to the chase, then," Carnell said with a huff. I almost wondered if Jaxon should have been there for the talk, but I also knew that whatever was said in this room, I'd have to tell my son eventually, or he would beat me to it, as usual, and figure it all out himself. He was remarkably good at doing that. "We had our suspicions before we left Earth that our home planet wasn't the only one suffering." Carnell swallowed. "And when I say *we,* I mean the NASA higher-ups. I wasn't told about their concerns until I was woken from hyper-sleep before the rest of you." He motioned at us with his arm.

Jaxon ate his fruit in silence while he leaned on my arm. A sense of contentedness overcame my bones, despite the conversation at hand. I rested my cheek on top of his head.

"So, essentially what happened was that I was woken up from my hyper-sleep several days before the rest of you because NASA had decided while we were all asleep that they wanted to explore a nearby stellar system that they had never seen before, instead of going in the direction of Aine, or the Pink Planet as most of you know it." Carnell paused and gathered his thoughts as he placed his now empty plate on the table and crossed an ankle over a long, muscular leg. "Before we left Earth, NASA told me that they thought the Fester had only affected Earth as well as a handful of other planets." He smiled grimly and held his hands up. "And before the scientists come for me, I promise I am telling you everything I know. They didn't give me an exact number of the planets affected, just a loose explanation, such is their way."

I realized that my mouth was hanging, and snapped it shut. My attention was fully on Carnell now.

"They did tell me that Mars is affected and that the people who chose to reside there so long ago, who cut off all contact with us, are more than likely dead. They believe that the pestilence struck Mars before Earth. Jupiter has met the same fate. Other than those planets, NASA and several of the other space stations noticed that a planet here and there—again, their words, not mine—which were discovered after combing through their drones' footage, are also plagued. Obviously, none of those planets have life on them, or at least not in the same way as Earth, but it's still devastating.

"When NASA woke me up, they told me all of this, albeit cautiously, despite all of my questions. Then they ordered me to keep it all confidential so that you all would cooperate and not lose sight of our end goal."

I scoffed out loud before I could help it. Lata rolled her eyes so hard that I thought her eyeballs might pop from their sockets. Dad muttered a displeased, "Of course, they did," under his breath.

"I know, I know," the Captain continued. "Truthfully, even despite the Fester and all, I was worried about what would happen if I disobeyed NASA. It's been ingrained in me since the beginning of my career with them. I'm sorry that I didn't have the guts to disobey them and do what was best for our crew. Truly. I am so, so sorry. For everything my decision put you all through." Carnell sighed. Comet leaped down from my lap and went back to sit with his father. Carnell lazily scratched at Comet's chin with his fingertips as he went on. "Obviously, after the hell that occurred on planet Virginia, I decided to hell with their orders. What are they going to do at this point? Fire me?"

Harper and Jules snickered and exchanged a pleased look.

"After NASA explained everything initially, they went on to let me know that many more planets than they originally thought had been taken over by the Fester. They took the data from our trip and analyzed it while we were all asleep, and only stopped the ship when we were far away from any possible plagued planets—or, so they say. Again, not in my control." He sighed. "I was ordered to wake you all after some initial tests were sent down to planet Virginia. Truthfully, all they did was take a sand sample and send it back up here, and from there, everything was sloppy."

As the Captain spoke, I thanked my gut for telling me that everything had been off from the start. Sometimes, it felt like I was crazy for having such strong feelings about things before they happened. Perhaps if we hadn't been forced into rushing, we wouldn't have had to go through hell and back on Virginia.

Perhaps Raymond and Saba would still be sitting with us—

Raymond listening pensively on the couch, and Saba sitting next to Ray, her head cocked to the side in that permanent quizzical look she always had plastered across her face.

"So, I owe everyone an apology for that. We should have done more research before going down. We should have been able to take more time. If this had been any other mission, I never would have allowed *any* of you to go down there when we knew so little." Carnell's eyes held mine. "All I know is that things must be really bad, both on Earth and on the other planets, for NASA to be so terrified that they go against the protocols and rules they set in the first place."

I nodded. Yeah, that made sense.

"It wasn't worth our lives," Ian said quietly.

Silence coated the room around us. I wanted to say something, but for once, I was at a loss. Ian was right. But, Carnell had spent his whole career taking orders from NASA. What was he going to do, even though he didn't agree with them? I can't say I wouldn't have done the same had I been walking in his shoes.

"I know," Carnell said. He looked at Todd and scratched the back of his neck nervously. "I know."

"I mean, really, what would dey do if we'd all died out dere?" Aleksy growled from his spot on the loveseat. "It's not like Earth is overflowing with healthy, qualified personnel."

Carnell nodded and stroked Comet. "Truthfully? I have no idea what NASA would have done. I am thankful I didn't have to find out, despite the recklessness and neglect they put on you all."

"What about the other ships?" I asked. "Have they found anything?"

A beat passed before Carnell shook his head once more. "One ship had to retreat back to Earth after running through the Oort Cloud at too high a speed." At my confused expression, along with several others, he explained, "The Oort Cloud is a part of the universe with a *lot* of comets and icy objects."

"Oh." Well, that would do it, I supposed. "And the others?" I asked.

I could feel Darrien's gaze on my face as I spoke. It took everything in me not to look at him, and to instead keep my eyes glued to Carnell's face.

"I haven't heard much. I do know that a few of the other ships are still in a state of hyper-sleep, and are traveling farther out than we did."

Now that the gears in my head were turning, I couldn't help but blurt out another question. "Why were we originally headed for Aine, Carnell? Everyone knows that it's—" I wanted to say *a death trap* but caught myself before the words could slip out. I wasn't going to say something like that in front of Jaxon. "Everyone knows that the Pink Planet tends to lead to more casualties or disappearances. We don't know enough about that stellar system."

"I'll admit that Aine and the surrounding planets have a bad reputation, but we know more about those planets than we've led the people on Earth to believe. Before the Fester overtook the Earth, a drone from the European Space Agency actually came back with several legitimate samples and data. They were able to conclude that the atmosphere on Aine is similar, if not better, for humans than our own atmosphere back home." My jaw dropped, and I couldn't help but look to see how Darrien reacted. His face was serious—brows knitted together and beautiful lips turned down—as he stared at and took in every word coming from Carnell's mouth. "The drone also came back with footage from the daylight hours on Aine. I believe it managed to record and bring back close to six hours of video."

"And?" Dad asked when no one else did.

"And, from what I've heard, it looks like a very real option for us. I haven't seen what the drone brought back. I've only heard from what my colleagues have told me over at the ESA," Carnell said. "But, I don't think NASA is wrong to send us there and scope it out. We have a team that is incredibly resourceful. You all proved that out there on planet Virginia."

"Is that where NASA plans to send us?" I asked. My voice broke, and I cursed myself for it, but thoughts of my mother and her missing crew flooded my mind, leaving me twitchy.

Carnell nodded with pursed lips.

"If some of the other ships are still in hyper-sleep, that must mean that this...universal plague has spread a far distance. Right?" Darrien's voice caught me off guard. His arms were crossed across his broad chest, and I noticed his fingers dug into his ribcage on either side. He was upset, and rightfully so. "And, what about the handful of ships that have never returned from Aine or its stellar system? What about the drones that never came back, or came back damaged?"

Carnell chewed on his bottom lip before replying. "Yes. The plague has spread a far distance, but not every planet within a stellar system is affected."

Before Carnell could answer Darrien's second question, Lata cut in. "So, how will we even know if the plague won't come after us, even if we *do* find a new planet?" Her tone was dark, and her brown-eyed stare was icy.

The Captain rubbed at his eyes before he looked at her and Aleksy. "I don't know. I'm sorry, but I don't. Neither does NASA. I wish I had more answers." He sighed and rolled his shoulders. Then, he turned back to Darrien. "As for the Pink Planet, well, yes. Some weird things have happened around there. But as of right now, NASA believes it's our best shot. Unless we happen to bump into another random stellar system with some healthy planets, it's the only course of action that makes sense for us moving forward."

"Why should we trust NASA?" Dad said with a voice that was full of humor and underlying grief. "They didn't even tell you their suspicions *before* sending you and an untrained crew out here. They forced you to change your original plan, forced you to rush the majority of us down to another planet that ended up being a death trap, and seem to be feeding you information little by little. Why trust them?"

Carnell stared at Dad with heavy eyes for a long moment. "Do you have a better plan, William?"

Dad rubbed the palms of his hands over his face. "I guess I don't."

I patted Dad on his knee.

Jaxon looked up at me with millions of questions behind his young eyes, and I knew I'd have a lot to explain to him in private later on.

"So, we go to the Pink Planet," Jules said. It wasn't a question, but a statement.

Carnell nodded. "Unless anyone else has a better idea?"

I cursed at myself for not having any other idea that made any sense to voice to the group. I'm sure that Dad was doing the same thing. My stomach lurched abruptly with the thought of flying in the direction of Aine—but there wasn't anything else we could do.

"How far is Aine from where we are now?" Ian asked. He leaned forward, elbows resting on his knees, deeply immersed in every word the Captain spoke.

"We had to go a little out of our way to stop here. Unfortunately, we will all have to go back into hyper-sleep, and from there, it should be a two-and-a-half or three-week travel time."

Are you fucking kidding me? Hyper-sleep? Again? I'd rather chop off one of my toes unmedicated than do that again. There was nothing I wanted less—except to be back down on planet Virginia.

"I know you're all probably thrilled to hear that, but the travel time will be cut down significantly, and the side effects of the sleep shouldn't be as harsh this time around," Carnell informed us. I could practically feel the fury rolling off my father's shoulders. Aleksy's face had turned pale at the mention of going back into the pods. He'd had it the worst out of the lot, and I didn't blame him for feeling scared. My breath had caught at the mention of the deep sleep that made me sick only weeks ago.

"When?" Harper chimed.

"Two days."

19

JUST BEFORE THE MORNING

After our meeting ended, we all made our way back to our respective quarters to take in all of the information and to prepare to go back into the pods in the next couple of days, which meant drinking more of the awful pre-hyper-sleep drinks. Except for this time, we had to drink more of them in a shorter period of time.

Dad came back to me and Jaxon's suite, and as expected, Jaxon began to ask us a hundred questions a minute as soon as we made it through the threshold. Though I wanted nothing more than to be with my Dad and my son, and despite the sleep that I had gotten during the last couple nights of quarantine, a deep level of exhaustion washed over me. Still, I stayed awake with my family until it was at least appropriate to take a nap.

To my surprise, I napped easily, and it took me no time at all to fall asleep. Dad had also gone to take a nap in his personal room, so I snoozed while Jaxon played one of his games in the living area. I was so groggy in the evening that I'd had Jaxon and Dad bring me back a plate of what had been prepared for dinner.

All of my rest during the day made the nighttime almost

unbearable. Fear rolled through me each time I thought of going into the pods, and then intensified when I imagined whatever awaited us in the future. It wasn't very calming to find out that Captain Carnell was left in the dark to an extent, too. I had to talk myself out of several panic attacks in the midst of a couple of hours, and no amount of deep breathing or distractions helped. I had even tried cleaning the bathroom and small kitchenette area, but of course, both were kept spotlessly clean by the Bots.

I wanted to go back to the dome. I wanted to swim with the penguins in the Galapagos Habitat while the tortoises judged me from their spots on the bank. Instead of being in the pods, or in the nice bed in my room on the *Hippogriff*, I craved my lumpy and well-used mattress back at the house where, Dad, Jax, and I shared a modest space and a lot of land.

At two thirteen in the morning, I gave up on sleep, cleaning, and everything else that might have occupied my time. A bath might have been a good idea, but I didn't want one. I could have gone to the common area for a glass—or a bottle—of something to drink away my worries, but that didn't sound great, either. Getting drunk might have made whatever sleep I found restless and full of night terrors, and I couldn't bear any more of them.

Before I knew it, I was closing the door to our rooms quietly behind me, and I was in the eerily quiet, scarcely lit hallway. I knew that Jaxon would be more than okay on his own for a little while. Ever since he was a two-year-old, and finally began to sleep through the nights, once he passed out for the evening, he was out like a light until morning, unless he was sick. I wouldn't be able to be gone for too long, though.

I found myself outside of Darrien's room at two forty-three in the morning.

After the meeting, we hadn't spoken. Darrien had cast me a

look that I couldn't read and then assisted Todd back to his quarters. I'd concluded that Todd must have been on some sort of sedative or anti-anxiety still because his eyes were vacant and dark, and he seemed to have trouble moving around.

I hadn't even made the conscious decision to come to Darrien's room in the middle of the night, but there I was. I wore nothing sexy, and my hair wasn't brushed. Instead, I wore a simple tank top and a pair of fuzzy, light pink sleep shorts. I wasn't even wearing a bra, and the panties underneath my shorts were simple and beige. As I stood outside of his door, I raked my fingers through my hair in an attempt to make myself look somewhat presentable to wake Darrien from his slumber and to—do what? Have a nice chat in the middle of the night for no reason other than *I* couldn't sleep?

With a sigh and shake of my head, I turned to walk back to my room. I'd been acting selfishly. There was no reason that I couldn't wait and talk to Darrien at a more decent hour.

I'd made it a couple of steps when the door opened.

"Daph?" Darrien's husky voice sounded.

I whirled around, and there he was. His hair was tousled in a way that told me he had been in bed, but his eyes were wide awake like mine, lacking the haze of sleep. His lips parted as if to say something, and then came together again in a soft smile. He wore no shirt, just a pair of charcoal gray sweatpants which rested right below the sharp accent of his V.

The area in the center of his chest where he'd been stabbed a little over a week ago was healing at a rapid pace thanks to Lata and the power of modern medicine. All that remained from the hole in his chest was a raised patch of reddish-pink flesh. It was hard to look at his shoulder from where he stood right in front of me in the hall, but I knew it was probably in even better shape.

"I—I'm sorry," I stuttered. For some reason, tears filled my eyes. I felt stupid and embarrassed.

He closed the distance between us until he was right in front of me. His tall frame towered over me, and wordlessly, he swept his hands up to my face and caught the tears that started to fall with his fingertips.

"What's wrong, Daph?" Darrien whispered.

"I—"

How did I begin to answer that question? He had been stabbed right in front of me. Saba was dead. Raymond was dead. We had all been forced into quarantine, and I'd missed him but didn't want to reach out because of my own stupid anxieties. Every word that came from Carnell's mouth in our meeting frightened me to my very core. The nightmares I'd had after we first got back haunted me each second I was awake. Dad and I would have to go to the last place we'd ever imagined —and confront a lot of baggage and pain from decades ago. I'd had to explain what a planetary plague was to my five-year-old earlier, and then I'd had to tell him the specifics and the unknowns, all of which were hard to grasp. Everything I'd ever known or thought I'd known had come crashing down. Everything was wrong.

I didn't want to live inside of my head anymore. Not after a week of it.

"I'm sorry I couldn't speak earlier," he murmured. He wiped away another tear that escaped, brushing it away with a knuckle. "Todd needed me. He's zonked out of his mind, but I felt like, I don't know, someone needed to try and help him get through that meeting."

"No, no, it's okay, I'm fine..."

And then, he hugged me, and I came undone. He wrapped his muscular arms around me and lifted me up and into his chest. I buried my head into the familiar crook of his neck and shoulder and cried as I clasped my heavy arms around him. Without another word, Darrien picked me up completely. I wrapped my legs around his strong torso as he walked the two of us back into the safety of his living quarters.

"Shh, shh," he murmured in my ear as he stroked my knotted hair. After a moment, he sat down. My ankles touched something soft, but I paid little attention. I gripped him as though he might disappear if I loosened my grasp; like he was an apparition instead of right in front of me. He didn't complain as I sobbed, as I dug my chin into his shoulder and wet his skin with my salty tears. We stayed like that until my tears finally ran out, and I started to breathe regularly again. Darrien just let me be, right there in the safety of his lap.

Suddenly, I felt ridiculous and embarrassed, coming to his door in the early hours of the morning, throwing a fit, and making him comfort me. I pulled my knees into my chest.

I moved from the soft, warm space of his neck, and looked up at him. "I'm sorry. I should go—"

His lips brushed mine delicately, and when he pulled his head from mine after only a couple of seconds, my lips felt like they were on fire, and all feelings of shame washed away.

Darrien's eyes, dark in the dim light of the room, bore into mine. "Don't be sorry. For anything."

After that, I slowly leaned into him and kissed him back, just as softly as he'd kissed me, but for much longer. I lingered over his lips, our breathing staggered and heavy in the dark. Darrien ran his fingers through my hair gently, then he cupped my chin in one hand as his other held the back of my neck. He pulled me to him in a rush, almost like he couldn't bear the space that had been left between us any longer.

His warm tongue trailed my bottom lip, and the moan that escaped me made his body tighten underneath mine. Yet, he remained soft in every movement. His hands trailed down my neck and back, all the way down to my hips, where he grasped onto me and pulled me in closer, closer, as close together as we could possibly be while simply kissing.

"Daphne," he broke away. For a moment, the possibility that he hadn't wanted to kiss me turned my blood stone-cold. "I don't want to rush you, or do anything you don't—"

I didn't let him finish that sentence. My answer showed him how very much I did want this. How much I needed *him*. I allowed myself the luxury of exploring his jawline with my tongue as my fingers curled into his hair. I nibbled at the soft spot underneath his earlobe, then worked my mouth up and flicked the lobe with the tip of my tongue, all while one of my hands trailed down his chest delicately, making sure to take in every taut muscle underneath my fingertips while avoiding the area where he'd been stabbed. His chest was smooth, with barely any hair, and the sleek skin underneath my roaming hand made my back arch in anticipation.

My lips collided with his once more, and this time, there was nothing gentle about the way our mouths moved against each other. We were both overtaken with an insatiable hunger, and my body relaxed in relief knowing that he wanted me as much as I wanted him. A low and breathy moan sounded from his chest, and the heat that had already pooled in between my legs intensified to an unbearable level. Darrien laid me back on the pillows, and only then did I realize we were on his bed and not the couch.

Darrien looked down at me from where he was perched on the bed, hovering over me. My legs were still loosely wrapped around his hips. His gaze swept from my own and down, down to my breasts, where my nipples were clearly visible and pointed through the thin material of my tank top, and then further down, to the strip of my skin that was barren in between where my shirt ended and my shorts began. His warm hands caressed my thighs on either side of him, and he rubbed up and down, up and down, until his hands reached my waist once more and stayed there.

"I missed you," he said gently.

I could have cried all over again at the words, but didn't. "I missed you," I breathed.

"I wanted to call you—during the quarantine," Darrien specified. "But—well. I didn't want to bother you, and I needed time to process everything that happened. I figured you felt the same–but then, after our meeting with Carnell, I was worried you thought I was giving you the cold shoulder."

For scientists, it turned out that neither one of us was the brightest when it came to relationships.

A small chuckle came from my mouth. "I thought the very same thing."

We stayed silent for a little while, just looking at each other. Finally, right when I was about to break the silence, he beat me to it. "Seven days was a very long time to think about how I wanted to leave off from where we'd stopped in the showers." Darrien's voice was deep and gravelly as he said the words, and every nerve ending in my body became alert at his words. Anticipation rolled through my veins, and my breath hitched in my throat. He chuckled and dug his fingertips into my hips, which elicited a tiny squeak from me. "And this time, there will be no pesky Aleksy or anyone else to stop me from doing *exactly* what I want to do to you."

A visible shiver made its way throughout the length of my body.

"But, only if you are okay with it, Dr. Blaine." Darrien smiled a crooked smile and every bad thought and worry that had lingered in my mind vanished and was replaced with excited thoughts that were very, *very* bad.

"Please proceed, Dr. Park," I said in a voice that felt much too low and sultry to be my own.

He was on me in an instant, lips hovering just over my own, hot breath caressing them. "I don't think you know how badly I was hoping you would say that."

He crashed into me in a flash. Darrien's hard chest pressed against my breasts as he kissed me with a need that was unrestrained. As he nipped at my bottom lip, I felt my toes curl and my pulse pick up. Liquid heat rolled through me as his tongue swept over the part of me where he'd bitten, and a low moan escaped my lips while I ran my hands up and down the length of his back, exploring every inch of his bare skin.

He moved from my mouth down to my neck. The caress of his swollen lips on the tender stretch of flesh just underneath my jawline had me fumbling with the drawstring of his sweats, eager and full of unrelenting need.

Darrien pulled back, but only for a second to wag a finger at me. "No, Daph. Not yet." I'd never loved hearing my nickname coming from someone's mouth so much. He bent down and kissed me again, consuming all of me, and I took in the familiar scent of him as he did so, basking in the sunlight I craved back on Earth, and reaching back toward his pants with no self-control left. "Don't make me tie those beautiful hands of yours up," Darrien said roughly. A smirk grew on his lips, and his eyes danced in mischief before he dipped his head down once more and resumed his position on my neck.

My hands wanted to be in his pants, touching and stroking every inch of him. I was tempted to do so just to find out if he really would bind my hands together, but as his lips moved lower down, I decided that I'd test him on that another night. The anticipation and my eagerness to find out his next move was more important than my other fantasies. For now.

Darrien lifted me up from where I was on the pillows just

enough to rip the tank top up and over my head, and just like that, every inch of my chest was on display for his eyes only. Even in the dim light of his bedroom, our eyes had adjusted enough for him to see each one of my curves, and I wasn't the least bit self-conscious.

With a very satisfied chuckle, he laid me back down, leaned down, and gazed up at me as he flicked the hard bud of my nipple with his tongue before clamping down on my breast with his teeth with urgency and longing. He sucked, and I felt it in more places than one. My thighs clenched together underneath him, and he groaned in pleasure as he continued his work, now on my other breast.

I moaned loudly and dug my fingertips into his hair, happy that I didn't have to contain myself now that we weren't in a public bathroom on board a shuttle with our crew-mates. Instead, the walls surrounding us were thick and soundproof— we could make as much noise as we wanted to for as long as we needed.

Darrien lifted his head with heavy-lidded eyes. He smirked up at me and said, "You taste fucking immaculate."

The lowest part of my abs clenched and rolled with liquid heat. He moved up, and I could see his hard length through his sweatpants, begging to come out. He caught me staring, and I bit my lip, not embarrassed, no—quite the opposite. I was completely entranced by Darrien Park, and I wanted him to know just how much.

Darrien's long fingers moved underneath the waistband of my tiny shorts. He moved them down my legs hungrily. I lifted my legs to assist him, and he moved the shorts down my legs, all the way down, and then threw them somewhere to the side of the room, all while keeping his eyes locked on my torso. As he took me in, naked aside from my panties, and licked his lips. He moved his middle and ring fingers on his right hand around my navel in soft circles, moving lower at an achingly slow pace until his fingers were on top of my panties. Soon, he was low enough, and he knew exactly where to press, and how much pressure was needed to make my back arch. Even through my underwear, the pressure of his fingers on my clit was enough for me to groan out in pleasure.

When I straightened myself out again, I glanced down and found his head in between my thighs. He toyed with the hem of my panties, then ran that exquisite tongue of his right above it. I was practically whimpering with need as my hips moved against him and raised ever so slightly from where I was laid out on the bed.

"So very impatient, Dr. Blaine," Darrien purred.

His words made me even *more* impatient.

"God, Darrien," I whispered. One of my hands stayed locked in the waves of his hair. I planted my free hand atop one of my breasts as he slowly started removing my panties with his teeth.

Holy mother of—

I lost track of his head and gripped the comforter as he worked his way down until my panties were gone, and then without a moment of hesitation, he was back in between my thighs. He found my hand gripping the bed and forced it up, intertwining my fingers with his. He removed my other hand from my breast and moved my arm down until he was holding both of my hands and wrists down with his strength, not allowing me to move a single inch as that talented tongue ever so slowly, teasingly, pressed roughly into the bundle of nerves on my clit.

"*Darrien*," I moaned.

"Do you want me to stop?" he asked against the apex of my thighs.

"No. *More*," I demanded. My orders made him stop. I could feel him grin against one of my thighs.

"More?" he taunted.

"Darrien, I swear if you don't give me—"

"You swear, what? What are you going to do if I stop? If I just keep you here, held down? What would you do to make me slip my tongue into your wet center? Would you beg for me, Daphne?" he all but purred.

His eyes were heated and playful as they looked up at mine.

"Well, I guess I'd have to tell you every single thing I plan to do to you when I finally get out of your grasp," I shot back.

He licked me slowly again, then swirled his tongue on top of those sensitive nerves, making my thighs quiver.

"I *so* look forward to listening to all of your fantasies later on." Another slow, tortuous lick. "But for now, I'm much too hungry, so I suppose you're in luck…" he whispered.

Goosebumps rose over every centimeter of my flesh, and then, his tongue picked up the pace. Lightning struck from my clit and traveled down the length of my legs, and up my torso. My hips bucked. Not being able to touch him as he performed his wickedly wonderful strokes made my desire climb more and more, close to the peak where I'd come undone.

Darrien let go of one of my hands, only to then use it to thrust a long finger inside of me. I ground against his finger and his tongue, which hadn't stopped the pace, not once since he last spoke. In fact, he picked up the pace. My body tightened and curled within itself, tensing up with the undeniable release forming inside, just as he moved a second finger inside.

"So very wet," he growled, taking a break. "So *very* ready for me, aren't you, Daph?"

My answer was a low, rumbling moan, and an impatient lifting of my hips up and down.

"Please," I gasped.

I didn't have to ask him twice. Darrien resumed his position and worked me with his tongue and fingers, fucking me and taking his time. Just as I was about to come all over his lips and his fingers, he pulled back to look at me with a knowing, mischievous grin.

"Oh, my God," I shuddered. "*Please.* I am fucking begging you!"

"Mmm. Just a while longer," Darrien said slowly as he looked down at the fingers taunting my opening. "I enjoy the taste of you far too much to stop now."

If his words could have given me my release, they would have. My eyes fluttered closed and I squirmed at the feel of his tongue back inside of me. He grazed my clitoris with his teeth, and that was my end. The lightning inside bolted throughout my body, and I came hard, gasping and panting and screaming his name. Through heavy-lidded eyes, I peered down at him while he continued to touch and kiss me everywhere, cherishing the waves of my come down on his tongue.

Breathing hard, I tried hard to move my one free arm to touch him. He leaned back enough so that I couldn't reach his pants, but allowed my fingertips to graze the hard set of abs that were on display right above the waistband of his sweatpants.

"You are really, *really*," I struggled to find the words, "demanding in bed. You know that?" I asked.

He inched his body closer to mine so that I could finally pull at his drawstring.

"Yes," he murmured. "But I had a feeling you were in the mood to jump my bones without much of a first act." He grinned, lips glistening. "And I needed to taste you and feel you release all over me before we did anything else. Because it's all I've been able to think about since I first met you."

Fucking hell. This man.

"Have you been a naughty boy, Dr. Park? Have you been fantasizing about me with your first wrapped around your cock right here in the confines of your room?"

Never in my life had I talked dirty to a man I was in bed with. Sure, I'd had plenty of dirty thoughts, but I was always too embarrassed to say them out loud. I was shocked to find how comfortable I was saying the words to Darrien.

He grinned wickedly and nodded. "Every single day. Sometimes more than once. But I don't always dream of eating you out. Sometimes, you're bent over. Other times, I have you tied up to this bed."

Heat flooded my cheeks and neck. I bit down on my bottom lip, with the mixed feeling of flattery and lust. After a moment of teasing him through his pants, I asked, "What if I want to feel you in *my* mouth?"

Darrien chuckled and ran his free hand through his messy curls. I was still unable to move further to fully grasp him. It was infuriating, because watching his muscles tense with each movement he made above me had me hot and bothered all over again.

"Daph, if you so much as kiss my cock, I will come undone in an instant. And personally, I'm dying to be inside of you instead."

Oh. Well, I wasn't about to complain about that. At all. "So long as you promise I get to put you in my mouth next time," I said with a feline grin of my own.

"Oh, I'll be daydreaming about that until it happens. Trust me..." He gulped as he stared down at my naked body, completely splayed out for him to take. "I'm very curious to find out just how gorgeous you will look with my cock hitting the very back of your throat."

Darrien and his *words.* I trembled underneath him. He

moved away from me and hopped off the bed. I rubbed my legs together, feeling the slickness between them, and stayed exactly where I was as he undid the tie of his drawstring, and smoothly glided his sweatpants down his long, muscular legs. I sucked in a breath at the strong hamstrings that accentuated his legs, at the beautiful curves of his hips as he kicked off the sweatpants and then pulled his black boxer briefs off.

And I certainly didn't breathe as *all* of him was finally revealed to me.

Darrien tossed the pants and briefs over to a chair, and he stood there, eating me up with his ochre eyes, naked and sure of himself. His confidence was so sexy, I didn't know if it was comparable to any other sexual experience I'd ever had. Even with Todd. Everywhere his lips had been on my body was set back on fire as he took me in. I was sure that my face and neck were tomato red in the fierce flush that took over my skin and left me tingling.

He grasped one large hand around his shaft and moved it up and down as he stared at me. A smile that was all pleasure and fulfillment grew on his lips, and it took all of my control not to beg him to crawl on top of me—to push that beautiful cock inside of me, and fill up every last inch of my aching center.

"You are stunning, Daphne Blake," Darrien whispered.

Every time he complimented me, I fought the urge to squirm. I stared at him, and then my eyes roamed down his body eagerly to where he fisted himself slowly in front of me.

"So stunning, I'm not sure how long I will last inside of you."

I chuckled huskily and reminded him, "We can always go for a second round."

With that, he crawled onto the bed and stalked toward me

like a mountain lion stalking its next meal. His eyes were sparkling in the dim light, and his skin was hot to the touch.

Back on Earth, every married woman and man who had already had one child was forced by law to choose a sustainable kind of birth control to keep our population control in check. I had had an IUD implanted a year after Jaxon was born, and it was still good to go for several more years. Single men and women usually took similar precautions, by law. So I wasn't the least bit concerned about accidentally conceiving when Darrien's tip teased my entrance.

Before we resumed, though, he kissed me. Tender and feather-light. I tasted myself on his lips but didn't mind. He kissed me and kissed me, and I could have easily just done that for the rest of the night, but we had both waited long enough. Having his lips on mine and his tongue caressing the inside of my mouth was a high I'd never experienced, and I never wanted it to end.

His lips trailed against my cheekbones, and then met my ear. He swept some of my unruly locks behind my ear, then grazed my cheek and said, "I'm going to fuck you now, Daphne. Is that what you want?"

"Yes," I moaned, hardly able to stand the feel of him so close to me in between my legs.

"Fuck yes," he moaned back.

Darrien trailed kisses up and down my neck as his cockhead moved through the seam of my entrance, and then with a small thrust, he worked himself inside. I whimpered in need and tried to force myself down on him. My core was aching with the need to feel all of him. He smiled into me as I met him for a deep kiss, cupping either side of his face in between my hands. His teeth nipped at my upper and then my bottom lip, then his tongue slid inside of mine, a small brush as our tongues tangled together and he slowly, agonizingly, made his way inside of me. All of me.

I screamed out, and that shocked him, but once he noticed I was screaming in absolute pleasure, he grinned devilishly, showing off his dimples. He moved inside of me slowly at first, and then picked up the pace until we went from making love, into straight-up fucking.

And I wanted to be there in that moment with him *forever*.

Darrien had me wet and ready, and the feel of him inside of me wasn't uncomfortable in the slightest, despite his being *very* well-endowed. With each deep thrust, every time he hit the sweet spot rooted inside, I shouted out his name. My hungry eyes looked down to where we were joined, at how thick and long he was, and I bit my lip so hard that I felt the sharp tang of blood in my mouth.

"If you keep doing that, I'm going to come immediately," Darrien roared from above me, gripping the pillow underneath my head for leverage.

"Can't help it," I gulped. "You're setting my body on fire. Please, Darrien, fuck me. Hard."

"Christ."

With that, Darrien brought his arms underneath me and heaved me up and onto him so that we were sitting just as we had in the shower back on the shuttle. And, oh, *my*, this felt so much better. My head fell back as he lifted my hips up, teasing me with the tip of his thick cock.

Darrien bit one of my collarbones, then nuzzled his head into the crook of my neck. "I don't think you understand how fucking fantastic you feel—how tight you are." He released my hips, and I slid down onto his rock-hard length.

It was hard to think with the rolls of pleasure vibrating throughout my body, yet I managed to speak. "I should seduce you on dangerous planets much more often," I teased. My voice was barely audible, but his neck popped up and he cocked his head to the side in a playful way.

"I think *I* am the one who did the seducing, Daphne. You're the one who gave in."

"Hmm...I don't think s—"

I wasn't able to finish my sentence. Darrien flipped me over onto my stomach in one fluid motion that knocked out whatever breath was still in my lungs.

"I think I ought to prove to you how badly I wanted to take you in the shower on that shuttle, just to shut that pretty mouth of yours up for a while," he threatened.

He turned my head to the side and saw that I was smiling wickedly in delight. The thrill he was pouring into me was something I'd never thought was possible. Sex with Todd had been hot and steamy, but having sex with Darrien was like rolling around and spreading a forest fire. Untamed, wild, and spontaneous in the best way. I suddenly understood how some people could be addicted to sex.

Darrien gripped the back of my head and some of my hair, then pulled my head back to meet his own in a starved kiss. He thrust into me, deep and fast, then as fast as he could fuck me. I arched back on all fours for him, displaying my body in a way I'd never done before without any second thoughts. His large hands gripped my hips, using them to steady his thrusts.

I called out for him over and over, and then he took away one of his hands to find that sensitive bundle on my clit yet again. He swirled and pressed against my clit without stopping his movements inside of me. It didn't take very long until he cussed and groaned behind me, and came inside of me, right as the tight curling within me released and exploded.

Darrien shook on top of me, but he braced himself on his arms so as not to crush me with his weight. I laid all the way face down on my stomach, hair splayed over the part of my face that I had turned to the side, and Darrien laid down next to me, with half of his body still on mine, his face meeting mine with a worn out, sexy smile. He moved both of us so that we were in a more comfortable position, laying side by side. One of my legs hooked over his, and then he fisted a blanket nearby that was wadded up on top of the bed and threw it on top of us.

Darrien couldn't stop smiling, and neither could I as we lay there and looked at each other. Our breaths were ragged and unsteady for a long while, and our sweat meshed together as our hot bodies stayed tangled together as we came down from the euphoria.

Sex had never been like that before. Not for me, at least. It had been decent with Matthew, and okay with a couple of men I'd slept with before that, but it was never *hot*. A close second to having sex with Darrien had been with Todd, but that still wasn't on this level. Every touch of Darrien against my body had made me come to life. His fingers and his mouth and his— well, he was talented in ways I never knew were possible.

Darrien moved my hair from my face and kissed the tip of my nose. "Are you okay? Was that okay?" His brows scrunched together a bit, and I realized he was legitimately concerned that I hadn't enjoyed myself.

I couldn't help my high-pitched giggle as I grabbed his face in mine. "That was much, much more than okay, Darrien. I'd even dare to say that it was fucking mind-blowing."

His face relaxed and he kissed me in a much more intimate way than he'd done before. He breathed into me, and I did the same, smelling the earth and the pines on his swollen lips.

"By the way," Darrien said, voice still low and full of lust, "I want to highlight the fact that even though I'm a bit bossy in the sack, I do, in fact, like you. A lot."

My heart thundered against my ribs right after it had just managed to calm down.

My cheeks ached with a broad smile. I couldn't stop grinning. "I like you, too. And, I *really* like how you boss me around, for what it's worth." We both laughed and curled inward, toward each other. "But, next time, I get to do some bossing of my own," I ordered against his cheek.

Darrien groaned. "Don't say that kind of thing, or I'll be ready to do exactly that in a matter of minutes."

My hands made their way through his black locks of hair, explored the curve of his chest and abs, and wandered all the way down to where I could cup his ass as I teased and taunted him without abandon. His eyes closed and a contented smirk rose on his lips.

My fingers grazed the patch of skin on his chest that was still healing. "Does it hurt?" I asked.

Darrien shook his head. "Thanks to Lata and your blood, I'm feeling just fine. Better than fine." He brought my fingertips to his lips and kissed them.

"Good." I paused. "Wait—where is Aster?" I panicked.

Darrien laughed and pointed to the living area. "She's in there, on the couch. You didn't notice when we came in, but she definitely tried to come in here with us, which is why the door is closed. Aster can be a little pervy." He winked.

"Oh, God." I rubbed my hands down my face, grinning. "Poor Aster."

A long time went by with us laying together underneath the blanket. We didn't speak, though our hands explored one another in a specific kind of intimacy where we both acquainted ourselves with every nook and cranny on each other's body. After what felt like a good half an hour, I finally turned and sat up with a groan. I looked behind my shoulder at him—his bulging muscles, light golden skin, sharp and glowing light brown eyes, with hair that *definitely* counted as messy post-sex hair. His lips were glistening, and patches along his neck and chest where I had nipped and sucked and kissed were lovely deep red and pink reminders of what had occurred between us.

"I need to go," I whispered. He leaned up in bed, too. "Not because I want to," I assured him, "but because I need to get back to my room. To Jaxon."

Darrien's hand ran up and down my bare back. He burrowed into my shoulder and kissed along my collarbone.

"Want to take a shower first?" he whispered.

Well, there was no way I could possibly say no to that.

B ack on Earth, close to three years have come and gone
since the *Hippogriff* and the nine other spaceships in
search of a viable planet disembarked from Earth's orbit.

Outside, what once were trees are now rotted trunks and
branches. The small skeletons of what used to be vibrant leaves
litter the ground and rest on dirt and mud. Long gone is the
grass that children used to frolic through, where couples had
picnics, and where people of all ages gathered around to play
frisbee on days when the sun shone high up in the sky.

All is silent on the outside. Occasionally, a small breeze will
lift up the leave's skeletons and rustle the leftover feathers of
decayed birds. There are no more flowers, only dirt where color
used to flourish in front garden beds and around community
buildings.

Weathered corpses lay in the streets, in front and back
yards, in abandoned vehicles; they lay in looted shops and
grocery stores, long forgotten. No one is left to remember them
or the lives they once held on this desolate planet.

Inside, the people who are left are few and far between. It is
impossible to know exactly how many human beings are left,
aside from what the government knows to be true. Eighty-

seven people reside at the M.E.I.'s Dome in Texas. In the twelve NASA headquarters left after the Old Glory States separated from the United States of America, six hundred and forty-two people are left. The majority of military and government personnel throughout the world has dwindled, with one hundred and thirty-three government officials left in the U.S. and 74,376 troops left, collectively.

The Fester does not have many more lives to take, and so long as people remain inside, the humans left on planet Earth are safe—but as each day ticks by, resources decrease. Medical insulin is rare, and those with Type 1 Diabetes are in serious danger of experiencing ketoacidosis. A small portion of the general population who were in the air before seeking shelter after the Fester came about have suffered from late-onset symptoms such as internal bleeding, blindness, deafness, tinnitus, and in severe cases, pustules. People with female sex organs who give birth will occasionally have Fester Prone Infants. These infants suffer from the Fester despite being exposed to the outside atmosphere, and in turn, live no more than seventy-two hours.

These are the things that Senator John Barry mulls over in his mind at his daily briefing with his cohort at the Johnson Space Center in what is left of Houston, Texas. Since the Fester began, the Senator has lost countless members of his center. Since everyone was contained inside the space center, he feels fortunate to have only lost three in three years.

Senator Barry grips a scalding hot cup of Joe in between his shaky, wrinkled palms and stares at the astronomical map projected on the large screen in his overused conference room. His assistant, Sandy, pours a packet of coffee creamer into his mug and stirs it with a spoon, then sits back down to the Senator's left with a steel rod back, poised and ready to take notes.

The rest of his cohort stare at the map, too. All fourteen of them. The map switches between locations of the remaining eight spaceships that journey the vast universe in search of a new planet.

The *Pegasus,* which has had seven casualties, is headed back to Earth. The *Phoenix,* which got a late start after the other ships lifted off, is set to explore an intriguing stellar system many light years away—where the most promising planet only has four hours of starlight each day. The *Harpy* is set to explore the same stellar system that those aboard the *Hippogriff* refused to venture toward, and the *Elemental* will soon arrive at a smaller stellar system close by. The *Sphinx* and the *Nephele* have come together to venture down to a large stellar system farthest away of all, composed of eleven planets and eighteen moons, with a star at either end. The *Dragon* will soon be meeting up with the *Hippogriff* several light years outside of Lugh Stellar System which holds the infamous Pink Planet and seven others. The Senator grins to himself. It isn't often that he gives one team orders to interrupt another team, and he knows that Captain Carnell and those aboard the *Hippogriff* are in for a rude awakening once they wake from hyper-sleep—little does Captain Carnell or the others know that the Senator has been watching. Listening to their every murmured sentence. Carnell's crew has begun to revolt, and Senator Barry has no intention of letting them do so.

The Senator places his coffee in front of him atop the large round conference table. "Status of the *Hippogriff?*"

One of his officials switches the screen over to where the *Hippogriff* is racing across the stars. "Right on schedule, Sir."

"ETA?" The Senator questions.

The official jots down a few numbers on his notepad and does a calculation on his watch. "They are set to slow down outside of Lugh and wake from hyper-sleep in four days, twenty-nine minutes, Sir."

The Senator rubs his hands together. "Excellent."

B. G. constantly has several fictitious storylines playing out in her head—especially when she's trying to go to sleep. She aims to write diverse characters and storylines, with emphasis on those in the LGBTQ+ community and those who struggle with their mental health as she does. B. G. can often be found chasing after her toddler or one of her various pets whilst in desperate need of (more) coffee (or wine, depending on the time of day). For B. G.'s Male/Male romance, check out *April Renegade* by B. G. Wolfe.

www.ingramcontent.com/pod-product-compliance
Lightning Source LLC
Chambersburg PA
CBHW022037240626
47154CB00007B/2453